THE
GRAND
PROMISE

ISBN 978-1-7370408-5-9
Library of Congress Control Number 2022931006

EMPTY BOWL
14172 Madrona Drive
Anacortes, WA 98223
www.emptybowl.org
emptybowl1976@gmail.com

Printed at Gray Dog Press, Spokane, WA.
Cover illustration by Thomas Cunningham
Cover and book design by Lauren Grosskopf

"*The Grand Promise* is more than a gripping debut from a writer of grand promise. Anderson has given us a poignant exploration of the costs and benefits of progress that is at once hopeful and redemptive. A great addition to the northwest canon."

— Jonathan Evison, author of *West of Here* and *Small World*

"Rebekah Anderson's wonderful debut novel *The Grand Promise* is a roiling, remarkably ambitious saga exploring the lives of a complex array of characters forever altered by the construction of the largest dam in North America—the Grand Coulee on the Columbia River. Deeply researched, the book evokes with remarkable specificity these ordinary and extraordinary people living in rural Washington in the late 1930s, as they're pushed and pulled by this outrageously ambitious project, their lives swept up and overturned by the forces of history."

— Peter Mountford, author of *A Young Man's Guide to Late Capitalism* and *The Dismal Science*

"One of the dominant stories of the American west during the first half of the 20th century was the story of water. Rebekah Anderson's riveting debut, *The Grand Promise*, perfectly captures the crackling energy of that time, delivering the gravity and complexity of the building of the Grand Coulee dam, telling a story both intimate and epic, and revealing the beating heart of those who benefitted and were harmed by the project. Informative yet compelling, educational but deeply moving, this fantastic novel represents the best of what historical fiction can do."

— Alan Heathcock, author of *VOLT* and *40*

"Rebekah Anderson imagines the repercussions of building the Grand Coulee Dam for riverside communities riven by prejudice, need and hope. To make it through The Great Depression, her characters destroy, scavenge and rebuild to salvage their homes and self-images. A most American story of survival and self advancement in the name of questionable progress, *The Grand Promise* posits questions about prosperity whose answers are playing out in real time. Amidst shanty towns of a Pacific Northwest more akin to modern times than most people want to believe, each generation raises the stakes for the next."

— Kristen Millares Young, author of *Subduction* and *Good Mother*

"In her engrossing debut novel, *The Grand Promise*, Rebekah Anderson deftly weaves an intimate family story of conflict and redemption into a sweeping historical narrative bringing to life one of the most important stories of the 20th Century American West—the construction of the Grand Coulee Dam."

— Shawn Vestal, author of *Daredevils* and *Godforsaken Idaho*

"In these harsh times of extreme political tribalism, it takes true courage to tell a story without proselytizing for one side or the other—to let the story do its job by simply unfolding without the interjection of moral judgment. And that's exactly what this fine new novel by Rebekah Anderson does. Lets the reader make up his or her own mind about what it means to 'progress;' what it means to 'preserve,' what virtue has to do with accruing power and wealth. But what I admire most about *The Grand Promise* is that in the end, what we have here is an epic love poem to the Northwest and all those who inhabit it."

— Finn Wilcox, author of *Too Late to Turn Back Now*

"Rebekah Anderson's novel, *The Grand Promise*, presents a compelling picture of the personal human disruptions brought on in the 1930s during the construction of the Grand Coulee Dam. Communities and the people who lived in them had their lives and their livelihoods changed as dam construction required thousands of workers and as the rising reservoir behind the dam slowly drowned long established settlements and ways of life. Anderson pictures the drama of those changes on a personal level through the interwoven lives of a few men and women who the reader comes to know in depth. The work is an excellent read for anyone interested in that era, Grand Coulee, The New Deal, or Washington State history."

— Paul Pitzer, author of *Grand Coulee: Harnessing a Dream*

"*The Grand Promise* is a gorgeously written account of a part of America that literature often overlooks. With rich descriptions and complex characters, Rebekah Anderson offers a much-needed view of Columbia River towns during the Great Depression. In the tradition of classical working-class writers such as Sinclair and Steinbeck, but with a fresh contemporary voice and an eye toward inclusivity, Anderson fairly and carefully portrays the stories of workers and the Native Americans whose lifestyles—and dignity—are threatened by poverty, progress, and imminent domain. This powerful debut is certain to be a welcomed addition to regional fiction."

— DeMisty D. Bellinger, author of *Peculiar Heritage* and *New to Liberty*

"In *The Grand Promise*, Rebekah Anderson deftly reveals the individual and community conflicts a grand infrastructure project forces onto a close-knit rural community, and the ways in which progress cuts a divide between those bent on preserving history and those eager to write the future."

— Jane Hodges, author of *Rent Vs. Own*

For my mom, Sandy, for inspiring this story

And to E.L Doctorow,
whose mentorship meant so much

THE GRAND PROMISE

BY
REBEKAH ANDERSON

EMPTY BOWL
ANACORTES, WA

PART 1
FERRY
CROSSING

October 1935
Washington State Route 25

Under the shelter of the ponderosas on the riverbank, two white trucks hugged the road heading north. The waters of the Columbia River churned in the bottom of the canyon below, its massive current roaring over rocks and fallen trees. Bold emblems were painted on the doors of the new Dodge panel trucks.

The river's shores were still bloated with the runoff from the summer snowmelt, even though the weather had long cooled into autumn. Brown and red fallen leaves mottled the banks that careened up at a steep incline to the road above. In the distance, patches of bare trees, gnarled and black against a silver sky, broke the deep evergreen line of ponderosas.

The trucks stopped and four men got out. They pulled equipment out of the truck beds and carted it gingerly down the steep trail toward the water, each team several feet apart. One man set up a tripod and looked through it, while the other scaled the bank. The man with the tripod called out, his voice fractured by the rushing river, the other man jotting notes in a notebook.

The men moved a few feet down closer to the shore, called and jotted again, and pounded a marker into the ground. They climbed back up the trail with their equipment, piling into the trucks, and drove upriver to where they looked like tiny toys. They started their procedure over again.

The men packed up their equipment and carted it back to the trucks over and over. Soon their taillights were all that was visible as they headed up the highway, flashing a red mirage across the wet roadway.

CHAPTER 1
Christmas Eve 1935

Carter Price panted down the highway from his wife's house in the dark, the bruises on his face pulsing with his heartbeat, the rifle blast during their argument still ringing in his ears. He'd really messed it up with Mae this time.

The cold air stung his lungs, and he was nearly out of breath from running through the snow. Too bad he tossed his whiskey bottle during his fight with her new fellow. A swig of that would help against the cold and bring a bright clarity to his mind.

Carter knew she would call the sheriff, was always looking for an excuse to do that. The first place the sheriff would come looking for him was his father's house. Everyone in town knew he was staying there since she'd kicked him out.

The fishing tackle bag he'd retrieved from his former garage bounced against his hip as he jogged, and he slowed to a brisk walk, his brain racing, the whiskey wearing off as he thought of what to do next.

He pushed up the sleeves of his father's coat, hanging heavy and oversized on him. His father would be angry with him for taking his coat from the house, but Carter couldn't go back there, not now.

As Carter walked through the night, the events of the last several weeks swirled in his mind, all their lives upturned in a matter of days.

By the time he slowed down to catch his breath, he was close to his cousin Lloyd's dairy farm in Daisy. If Carter was this far, he'd made it almost twenty miles from Kettle Rapids during the night. It would be close to four in the morning by now.

Outside Lloyd's house, he could see the Christmas tree through the living room window, presents for the kids underneath, backlit in the amber of the kerosene lamp against the morning's soft purple.

He knocked on the door, trying to think what he would say to his cousin about why he was there at this hour, but it was Lloyd's wife, Marie, who answered, her face expectant and then perplexed.

"Carter?" she said, her voice puzzled. She looked at his tackle bag and oversize coat, then beyond as though expecting a caravan behind him. But there was nothing. No family. No car. No gifts. And then she registered the bruises on his face and hands.

He tried to make his voice cheerful, but "Merry Christmas" came out like an apology. She steered him to the kitchen table and said, "Sit," with the commanding matter-of-factness mothers have, and then went to get his cousin Lloyd.

Lloyd walked into the kitchen, his hair sticking up, beard heavy, wearing an undershirt and pajama bottoms. He sat down at the table with Carter.

"Looks like you had a night," Lloyd said, looking over the bruises on Carter's face.

"You could say that."

November 1935

Weeks earlier, the town was abuzz with speculation about what would be announced at the town hall meeting to propose an irrigation dam downriver. How to solve the region's water problems had been hotly debated for more than a decade, and it seemed something was finally about to happen. Sightings of Starks Company vehicles in the area raised suspicions even more. Everyone from Kettle Rapids would be at the meeting.

Ozzie Price wound the coil that spooled his steel ferry cables, working as quickly as he could in the cold morning, the smell of frost and river water strong on the air. He wasn't as quick at this as he was when he was young. He'd never been a svelte man, but middle age had cursed him with a growing girth and slower pace. He was, however, known for being an amateur singer, with a booming voice that carried across the river when he needed it to.

The metal strands of his cables groaned and scraped against each other. He stood on the dock, facing out over the vast expanse of the Columbia while he worked, his landing not far north of the confluence with the Colville River.

Winter had come on early, beating even Thanksgiving. The snow melt from the mountains refroze, the river lower than usual. Ice crusted along the sand next to his small wooden pier, and Ozzie's fingers ached. He squeezed his hands, pumping blood back through his blue fingers. Wet and cold was the worst way to work, but he'd owned this business so many years now, he should be used to it. Yet it always found a way to surprise him.

"Ready?" His teenage daughter, Ona, walked up to the loading dock, her blond curls poking out from under her winter hat. As she got older, she looked more and more like her late mother. He wished he found that comforting, but it made him miss his wife that much more.

"Was there anyone waiting outside the gate?" he asked, pulling off his work gloves and tossing them in the tackle box where he kept his tools handy.

"Everyone's headed to the town hall meeting like we are," she said. "Don't worry, you're not going to lose any business today by closing early."

"Is your brother in the car?" He snapped the padlock on his tackle box and stood up to face her.

"No," she said, stuffing her hands deep into the pockets of her wool skirt.

"What do you mean? Where is he?"

They walked down the drive toward the gate, where the car was parked.

"He said to go without him."

"Without him? How'd you get here?"

"I drove myself."

His old Ford was there, safe and sound, the hood warm.

"Why can't you kids do what I tell you?" he asked, opening the driver's door.

She climbed in next to him, the car creaking from age.

"We're not kids anymore."

"You are until I say you're not."

She snorted. "Carter's definitely not. Twenty-eight is ancient, if you ask me."

Ozzie turned the car around and eased it onto the highway. His son certainly wasn't acting like a man of nearly thirty. He couldn't understand why his son had given up so easily. Carter had been fired from his job—the final straw with his wife—and come home needing work and a place to live. Not even trying to set things right. He wasn't like that before. He worked hard, saved money.

Ozzie even helped him build his house, and yet Carter handed it all over to her the minute she shamed him with threatening a divorce. Ozzie didn't raise his kids this way. He raised them to be people of action, to fight for what they cared about.

"He knew how important this was to me," he said to Ona.

Ona didn't say anything, but Ozzie knew what she was thinking. He was vocal in the community about his stance on the irrigation projects. He did all the things he was supposed to, like write letters to elected officials and the local papers; he supported the local grassroots pumping plan, rather than the gravity plan that mostly benefited big power interests in Spokane. It was his civic duty, and yet his daughter seemed to find this endlessly embarrassing.

He glanced away from the road at her, hurt by her indifference. "Well, at least you'll be there," he said.

"I want to know what they say too," she said. "You know how Carter can be; you're not used to it anymore."

"It's been months."

"I know, but he's different now."

"I wish he'd do what he says he's going to do, that's all."

They sat in silence the rest of the drive, with tall, dark sentries of evergreen trees lining their path. They encountered a few cars on the highway, passing some empty houses Ozzie hadn't noticed before were no longer occupied. He could remember the relative vibrancy of this town when he was a young man. Decades ago, the Homesteading Act brought people here from all over the world, including himself. Free land to anyone who dared. They'd survived, until recently.

Now things were different. People who moved here since then couldn't afford their mortgages, but they couldn't sell either because there was no one around to buy. Or they had no income to afford basic necessities. They closed up their homes and tried to rebuild someplace new. Now the town stood cold and quiet, a few old Christmas garlands hanging on lampposts of downtown.

His own financial situation was precarious, though he didn't dare tell either of his children. The crash of 1929 hurt everyone, and in small towns like Kettle Rapids, when work dried up, no one had money for the ferry crossing. Recent road projects kept some men employed, as did the construction of the bridge across the Columbia. While he appreciated the jobs these projects created short-term, they cut into his profits now that anyone could drive across without taking a ferry.

Carter followed the snowy road from his father's house that led to town, his lithe frame shrouded in wool to keep him warm, his skin tan even in winter, a trait he inherited from his mother along with her light hair. Ozzie would know by now that Carter hadn't joined his sister to ride together to the town hall meeting that morning. He knew his father would be furious with him for telling her to go without him, but he wanted a moment of peace before the entire town watched as he saw his wife for the first time since he moved out of their house.

He hadn't been to a public event since news of his firing from the mines after a near accident made its way through town, prompting Mae to make them the first couple that he knew of in their community to ever discuss divorce, a distinction he did not want. They had problems in the past, their relationship always tempestuous, but she'd never gone this far before. He needed time to prepare himself for how he would be received in town, how she might react, without the constant din of his father's critical banter.

At the main highway, cars turned past Carter on their way into town, and he watched anxiously from between his hat brim and his collar for Mae in their old car—he'd let her have that too. It wasn't easy asking his father for work or living at home again.

He was independent before, made his own way, and now everyone, including his father, saw him as a failure.

He crossed the highway and skirted the main road into town, cutting down a side road muddied with melting frost that led him through the back neighborhoods of Kettle Rapids. A few of the homes on the street were boarded up, their owners having left them behind.

Half the businesses in town were gone now too, and many of the storefronts he passed on his way to the town hall were empty. The sidewalks and streets were quiet, and Carter figured most people were already at the meeting by now.

He remembered how busy this intersection was when he was a young boy, shoppers and horse-drawn buggies and wagons far outnumbering any automobiles in the street. Shopping with his mother once, he lost a marble through the wood planks of the sidewalk. She told him to leave it, but he begged until she let him crawl through the dirt to get it back. He finally found it, muddy and bright, like a shining eyeball in the dirt. He looked up through the slats, searching for her, wanting to show her, his hair and face coated in cobwebs and muck, but he couldn't find her.

Instead he saw from this new vantage point the whirlpool of the undersides of women's skirts, amazed he'd never tried to look up them before. Swirls of white ruffles like the petals of a carnation. As he watched, mesmerized, he could see only layer upon layer of white ruffles that never revealed anything but more layers of ruffles underneath.

Carter crossed through town to the shoreline where the Kettle River dumped into the Columbia, riverbanks littered with big boulders pushed there under the skirts of an immense glacier. Or so said some geologist he read about who believed all the coulees and riverbeds and valleys like this one that branched off the Columbia were part of a major glacial carve that stretched for hundreds of miles south into Oregon and California.

In the river, water swirled in tiny whirlpools. Carter could smell the familiar mineral scent of the water, and the whirlpools burbled over the low din of rushing water. His father and sister were probably in the town hall already, but he sat on his favorite boulder where he had come to sit and fish all his life, not ready to face everyone yet.

A lamprey clung to the rock by its sucker mouth, pulling itself up the rapids until it could find another fish to cling to. He remembered watching men in canoes try to shoot the falls, and the salmon season when the local tribal leaders put out baskets to catch the massive fish as they returned to their spawning ground. He was awed by the tribal ceremony, by how big the salmon were and how many they pulled from the river for food each year.

Carter's breath plumed vapor clouds in the cold. This river had been part of his life, his family's livelihood since his father claimed the land. He picked up a cold stone and worried it in his palm. His father couldn't bring himself to see anything but his own point of view. Instead, he stampeded through life without any reflection, so how could he possibly understand Carter's regret and humiliation?

At the meeting, they were going to talk about the fate of the river; that much Carter knew. Since he was a kid, men had come up with ideas how to dam it, divert it, or otherwise control it. Ozzie wrote letters to senators, the governor, and the local newspapers protesting all those ideas. He couldn't understand why Carter didn't have the passion for the river and the town he once had. It was hard not to dwell on it when every eye, every building, every name bore some reminder of his failures and there was nothing he could do about it. It was hard to want to preserve a place with such memories. Hard to even walk its streets.

Carter tossed the rock into the water. There was no point in trying to skip it here. The river spun on the kettles from which the town took its name. They were formed by deep grooves in the glacial rock, wide enough for a man to sit inside up to his neck where the water coiled.

The divorce papers Mae gave him were still in the top dresser drawer in his old bedroom at his father's house, but he was too ashamed to sign them. Carter tried to clear his mind back to reality. It was so easy, so routine now to get caught up in his thoughts. He climbed off the boulder, his boots sinking in the loamy sand along the riverbank, the thin ice on the shore crackling underneath. Carter tugged his hat down over his ears as the wind shuddered through the evergreen trees around him. His boots left tracks in the muddy road as he made the short walk to the town hall.

Harold Burnes cranked the arm of the pencil sharpener anchored to his desk until he heard the smooth turn of the blades against wood and smelled lead and pulp dust. The newspaper offices of the *Colville Scintilla* were quiet this early. Harold was a judicious note taker, but his notes were harder to read later if his lead was dull.

The writers had a bank of typewriters to share, and he found the early morning his best chance to peck out his stories before the others arrived. He was usually the only reporter on the staff of three who would jump at the inconvenient assignments, and today was no exception. He was on his way to cover the town hall meeting in Kettle Rapids, organized by the Starks Company, along with the Bureau of Reclamation and Columbia Basin Commission, following the Starks Company's shocking win of the government contract to build a massive dam on the Columbia. The river certainly seemed to bring out the greed in some.

It was still dark outside as Harold saddled his horse, but a sliver of pink sun peeked over the Eastern horizon as he packed his leather-bound notebook and pencils into his hip bag. He fingered the business card of "M.J. Starks" that his editor gave him earlier in the week. Their newspaper had covered the opening of the bid for work on the huge dam. At the Spokane hearing a few months earlier, the Starks Company won the project with a jaw-dropping low ball that caught the attention of the entire state. Harold didn't know M.J. Starks, but he finagled himself a meeting with him before Starks was to speak at the town hall meeting in Kettle Rapids, a community with the good fortune to sit on the confluence of two rivers, the Kettle and the Columbia.

Harold was eager for his big story. He'd come up this far from his small-town home in Oregon to make a name for himself, and that was what he was going to do, come hell or high water. He had an investigative mind, and he was proud of that. And he had an astonishingly good memory for facts and figures.

His editor, John Raymond, was a skinny, manic man ten years his senior who wanted to cover every major story himself—including President Roosevelt's visit to the site following the bid—a trend that drove Harold mad with indignation. Raymond had been covering the Water and Power Company's plans to build a dam at the rapids for years, and when they learned the Starks Company would be paying the area a visit, Raymond nearly shouted in the newsroom: "Burnes! Counterpoint!"

Not that Harold was complaining. He was thrilled to have a chance to knock the wind out of Raymond's obsession with the debate over the local irrigation project. There were two competing plans: the pumping plan championed by local farmers to pump water out of the Colombia to use for irrigation, and the gravity plan, mostly supported by power interests from Spokane that did not want the competition for electricity sales and proposed using gravity to drain water from the nearby Pend Oreille River for irrigation instead.

Harold's editor might see his counterpoint as a secondary story, but Harold was determined to make the most of it, however he might need to. He hoped no one from the *Spokane Review* or *Wenatchee Journal* would be at the meeting. He was determined to file his pages before one of the bigger papers broke the story.

A wind kicked up off the Colville River and cut through his wool overcoat and suit jacket. Under his hunting hat, the shearling flaps warmed his ears. The road was quiet as he rode the two hours to the neighboring town.

When he rounded the corner onto Main Street in Kettle Rapids, he encountered a line of Colville tribal representatives on horseback wearing traditional attire of feather headdresses and bone breastplates. The horses were mostly pinto, splotched brown like cows, with one palomino appaloosa out front, her white speckled rump even with Harold's mare as he set pace with them.

M.J. Starks saw nothing but the trunks of pine trees sailing by as he rode in the backseat of his company's new sedan, a vague smell of exhaust and oil clinging to his driver. The trees seemed to pause when they were flush with his window and then whizzed behind them. The chains on the tires crunched snow on the gravel road.

On trips like this, he always traveled with security in case trouble flared up among the townspeople. Two of his security detail sat up front now, the driver and an armed bodyguard. He'd seen some bad scenes: mob brawls, spontaneous lynching, and labor riots that left people trampled. What he could never understand is why no one could see the long view on these situations, or why so few people looked for the personal opportunity like he did. There was always a way to land on the right side of any situation—if you wanted to.

He was on his way to the community meeting in Kettle Rapids, a tiny town on the banks of the massive Columbia River, where he and Frank Banks from the Bureau of Reclamation would brief the town on their plans to dam the river. He smiled remembering the outrage and surprise when Banks had announced that the Starks Company won the bid over the builders of the Hoover Dam in Nevada. Everyone assumed the other company would get the contract. The whole affair had a farcical nature that amused him, including a joke bid from someone pretending to be Mae West telling the engineers to come up and see her sometime and the thousands of people filling the streets for a parade and celebration, quickly forgetting the upset.

On the seat next to him in the car, Starks rested his hand on the soft wool of his homburg hat. His wife, Minerva, bought it for him from the Sears, Roebuck catalog the Christmas before she died. He missed her still. Now that their children were grown and had children of their own, there wasn't much he could do without her except work more and farther away. His mansion in Minneapolis sat empty but for the maids. He moved from one construction village to the next, living in tents and makeshift buildings that reminded him of his army days.

"What do you want me to do, sir?" The driver slowed down.

A few yards ahead, a family with small children walked on the edge of the road, its lines obscured by snowbanks piled alongside.

Starks looked out the back window at the security car behind them. The driver extended a hand out his window, signaling he saw the delay too.

"Go around them slowly and don't use the horn," Starks said. "They look harmless."

His driver eased into the oncoming lane. "Do you want to talk?"

Starks pondered this. They had no car or maybe no money for gasoline. Their clothes looked worn and mismatched. The children were young, not close to working age. The father held the smallest by the hand, which meant to Starks that he was not the kind of man to head out into the unknown in search of work if it meant leaving his family behind. They were not likely a family with influence in town, and there weren't any laborers among them.

"No," Starks said. "Keep moving. Don't startle them is all."

They passed quietly, and Starks raised a hand through the window in salute. The family stopped and stared as his small caravan passed, the children's eyes wide and dark between their scarves and knit caps.

Before the public meeting, Starks was to meet privately with the people from the local commission and Bureau of Reclamation representatives at the Grand Hotel, which from what he saw so far was no longer grand. He'd also agreed to speak with a reporter from a nearby newspaper if there was time. Dealing with the press was always a necessary part of the job, which he preferred to leave to his press secretary back home, but that wasn't always feasible in these far-flung construction locations.

Starks was the first one there. He always pitied the government liaisons. Their cheap suits, the long hours they toiled for barely more than a living wage. Today would be no different. They were indispensable, though, so he studied their kind carefully over the years, their pride in working for the good of humanity and sticking up to business interests while simultaneously contracting people like him. He made it his mission to understand why any one man chose this path from the others when there was money to be made and pleasure to be had. What was it about this man that made this work rewarding or absolving for him? What was he outrunning? What was he afraid of?

The chandelier in the hotel foyer was dusty, and a woman around Starks' age worked the front desk in the sleepy lobby. She escorted Starks and his detail to an equally shabby meeting room, its one saving grace a well-polished mahogany table that stretched down the center and took up nearly the whole room.

In Starks's early days, he tried to wine and dine the government men, but that backfired on him. They resented having only a taste and were often outright hostile in a circumstance where they felt out of place. A county clerk might scarf down a steak dinner and then complain to the waiter about a meal he wasn't even paying for. A man who appreciated the finer things in life didn't choose this line of work.

Cash worked with some, and he hired as many of those as he could. It was his own type of conversion, to show them what life could be like if one embraced wealth. Of course, this became impossible in recent years as work dried up, stocks crashed, and homes foreclosed. With the more pious among them, his best recourse was to feign that he was learning a new value from them, that they could persuade him to think less like an opportunist. This new lot he hadn't officially met yet outside some exuberant hand shaking at the parade in Spokane, but he was seasoned enough in this line of work to be ready for anything as he anticipated his meeting with them.

He didn't like to sit while he waited, so he and the security detail stood near the door with their hats and overcoats on, waiting for the other men to arrive. The thickest-necked of his team held Starks's leather file that contained the signed contract, permits, and plans for construction.

He wondered what this newspaper man would be like. The reporters were a different story. They had an impenetrable, righteous belief in their perception of the truth, but as far as Starks could tell, they made up that truth as they went along.

Starks breathed in deeply, the room's dank smell permeating his nose and lungs. These moments of calm before construction started were usually the last. Outside the window, a gust blew flakes of snow around in a swirl and then dropped them back to the ground.

Charlotte Powell strode into her orchard, her border collie tearing ahead of her into the apple trees, then running back to nip at her boots and tear off again. Despite the practicality of her attire when she was working, she still took the time to pin curl her bobbed hair each morning like she had since she was a girl, even though now her hair was almost completely grey.

The air smelled like snow and the sweet, pungent aroma of decaying fruit, and cold snuck into the folds of her wool coat. The hem of her overalls was crusted with mud and snow, but that would have to do since she had no time to change before the town hall meeting.

Cold weather was good for her stalwart apple trees, dormant in winter. Coming from Seattle, she'd known nothing about farming when her husband died suddenly of heart failure in his late forties, leaving her with a business to run. But widowed life hadn't been all that bad. After the initial shock of her husband's death, Charlotte fell into a routine of comfortable self-indulgence.

Both men in her life were next to each other in the Kettle Rapids cemetery on the banks of the Columbia River. They buried their son in the plot meant for her after he fell during a timber accident when he was only nineteen. It never occurred to them to prepare a burial spot for their boy, and it all happened so quickly, it seemed the right thing to bury him in her place. Now, her son and her husband lay side by side in the patch of green she'd picked out overlooking the river. When she missed them, which she still did after all these years, it was a lovely walk from the orchard into town, the dog trailing behind with his tongue lolling.

The dilapidated Lincoln limousine she used for carting apples to town was parked in a cleared patch of mud at the edge of the orchard. Her late husband bought it for a song at an auction when one of the hotels in Spokane closed its doors during the crash. She found it under a tarp next to the barn when she did the accounting of all their assets. What a strange feeling that was, to catalog all their belongings for the probate lawyer. Twice now, she'd packaged up the evidence of a life, someone she loved very much, and figured out what to do with it. Now that there was no one left to do the same for her, physical things didn't matter so much anymore.

Trinkets, heirlooms, all lost their meaning. Where would they go besides an antique shop or the dump? Physical items in Charlotte's world were reduced to their immediate purpose. Would it serve her in this life? Then it was useful. Would it not? Then it was garbage.

The Lincoln was definitely useful. It was old and its paint was faded, its seats torn, but it was perfect for loading with forty-pound crates of apples with room for her and the dog up front.

They had finished the harvest only a few months earlier, and the branches of her trees reached out bare, freshly pruned, gnarled and dark against the overcast sky. The cold months following the harvest made the fruit easier to store—no massive blocks of ice needed—but distribution was her primary pursuit. Surpluses were farmers' most recent problem around here these days.

After her husband died, she took to the business quickly, surprising herself and the staff of seasonal workers unaccustomed to working for a middle-aged woman. This was the good time of year, when the harvest was done, the pickers gone home, and she and a skeleton crew of warehouse fellas, grateful for the work, got the fruit to market.

It was the summertime that kept her up at night. The arid conditions of Eastern Washington were tough on the trees. They dried up and the bugs came out, right when the blossoms started their transition to fleshy miniatures. Irrigation was a hotly debated topic of late—one she'd not tracked much before she'd taken over operations, but now she was consumed with it from the time the snowmelt evaporated in June until the rains started again in October.

The men in town had been in a tizzy over who backed which of the two proposed irrigation plans, but the politics didn't interest her as much as the engineering dilemma.

Pumping, gravity, who cared. She wanted a solution that worked. Sooner would be nice. All the chest thumping only delayed matters. They were all apes, and always would be apes, if the dog-eared copies of the *Tarzan* series on her nightstand could be believed.

The door of the Lincoln creaked open in the cold, and the dog hopped into the passenger seat. If she was heading into town for this big brouhaha meeting, she may as well load up the Lincoln with some product to drop at the markets in town.

Harold Burnes cut past the Colvilles on horseback and ducked down Broadway toward the Grand Hotel. He was surprised when the Starks Company's press secretary agreed to give him a private interview with M.J. Starks. He'd never worked on a story like this before, and he expected roadblocks, lies, or even company goons shaking him down. Although that all remained to be seen, he supposed.

The Grand Hotel had seen better days, but Harold still felt out of his element in a place designed for the rich. He slid off his hunting cap and smoothed his hair in the huge gilt mirror across from the front desk. How the old woman who managed the desk could stand to stare at her reflection all day long was beyond him. Mirrors were only tolerable for necessary grooming. He hated looking at himself. He much preferred to have his attention focused on others.

Harold retrieved his pad and pencil and stuffed his hat and gloves into his bag and followed the clerk down a creaking hallway.

M.J. Starks was standing when Harold was shown into the opulent meeting room that smelled of cedar and candle wax. A warm flush of embarrassment lit Harold's cheeks at how under-dressed he was in riding clothes compared to these company men, their ties wedged perfectly under their vests, hankies poking neatly from suit pockets. M.J. Starks had an expensive overcoat thrown over his arm and held a grey homburg hat, its stiff brim curled around the edges in a tight coil with no feather, Harold observed.

"There's no feather in your hat," Harold said.

"Excuse me?"

"You don't…," but Harold stopped himself, feeling foolish.

Instead, he made a mental note that Mr. Starks wore a homburg hat of dark grey felt and a matching grosgrain band around its crown—with no feather. Starks also wore his grey mustache in the style of Teddy Roosevelt, trimmed and combed straight down. His suit jacket was double-breasted, with broad padded shoulders, giving him an imposing thickness that Harold thought might be a mistake for the occasion. Starks's spectator shoes, already showing a trace of mud from the town's unpaved walkways, were sure to get a chuckle from the working men in town.

"I don't have much time, son," Starks said, fingering his hat impatiently.

Some reporters went for the throat. That wasn't Harold's style. A defensive source is a guarded source. If they saw him as no threat at all, they nearly always revealed something useful.

"This is a vocal town, and I'll no doubt hear from many of them with their opinions and theories about what happens here today. Before all that, before they react, what's your personal take on this? I've read the statement from your press secretary. I know what the company line is. What do you, M.J. Starks, think of all this?"

Starks paused. "I've been through many projects like this one, son. Though it may seem difficult at first, the eventual outcomes are always worth it."

"It's easy to compare the differing rationales on both sides of this project, not to mention the competing view for a gravity dam, but what role do you think human nature plays in the success of a project like this one?" Harold asked, his pencil poised for notetaking.

"Our adaptability and response to uncertainty reveals our true character," Starks said. "A soldier on the battlefield is concerned only with survival, his mind is not on winning the war, but when his survival instincts also support the overall goal, everyone wins."

"You compare this project to a battlefield? Do you expect casualties?"

"Literal casualties? Of course not." Starks lifted his homburg to his brow. "With that, I really do need to go."

Harold scratched in his notebook: *What Starks Company projects failed?*

CHAPTER 2
November 1935

Ozzie and Ona crossed the sagging porch of the old town hall building and waited in the foyer out of the wind. A huge wood frame on the wall showed a drawing of the original grid plans for the city. Ozzie pondered it, rocking back and forth on his heels while he waited for his son, the dust in the air threatening to bring on a sneeze.

With boom times over, they rarely used the town hall meeting room for anything official anymore. These days the building was mostly used for cheap weddings and Christmas bazaars, and a worn-looking silver tinsel garland hung from one side of the doorframe.

Ozzie paced from the foyer to the porch as cars filled the parking lot, the wood floors creaking under his weight. He nodded to his neighbors and town folk as they jostled past him to the meeting room where the clerk lit the woodstove. Horses and buggies were hitched around the side of the building, and he could hear the squeak of leather and clatter of metal horseshoes on gravel as the animals shifted in their gear.

"He said he was coming."

Ona shrugged and rolled her eyes. "I'm going in where it's warm."

Ozzie went back to the porch and watched snow blow on the breeze.

Charlotte pulled the Lincoln into the gravel lot behind the town hall, wearing her driving goggles to keep the snow out of her eyes.

She left the dog to guard the car, and he gave her a wistful look as she shut the door. She clucked their secret signal to him, and he cocked his head, letting out a soft, slow whine as she walked away.

Oscar Price was pacing from the porch to the front lobby and back in his usual manic state. Oscar had proposed to her not five months before. It had come completely out of the blue. They knew each other, sure. She transported apples across the river on his ferry from time to time. He'd perched nervously on her sofa, turning his hat in his hands, his grey hair pasted down in a ring, then flapping out beneath where his hat had been. The sofa creaked awkwardly under his bulk.

It made sense why he would ask: they were both widowed, of the same age, and both business people. She didn't know what had prompted it then after so many years of them both being on their own. Charlotte suspected the orchard and its acreage was a large part of her appeal. She didn't mind that really. It was easier to turn down what came out like a business proposition than something romantic. It was a relief he hadn't bothered with any ceremony like a ring or getting down on his knee or god forbid, courting.

Charlotte walked slowly toward the town hall porch, hoping Oscar would clear out so she could go in and get a seat without embarrassing him. He paced, then barreled into the room. Who knew how long he'd been out there fuming and shuffling. She wouldn't have been able to deal with that kind of agitation in her calm world, despite whatever logical argument could be made for the benefit of having him as a partner.

The room was stifling hot from the woodstove in the corner, and Charlotte peeled off her coat and hat and found a seat. She still wore her good wool coat and cloche over her work clothes. May as well put them to use. The town was long over being scandalized by her overalls. She worked in an orchard. What was so hard to understand about that?

Large posters with drawings and maps had been placed in the front of the room. These men. What would they do? Was there any possible chance they might not muck this up?

Oscar caught Charlotte's eye with a red face and nodded sharply. She gave him her warmest smile. Poor Price. So unnecessarily wound up. He'd probably end up with a spastic colon.

His daughter was with him, looking bored. Ona was getting older now too. Probably ready to leave home in a few years. Charlotte liked Ona. Had hired her during the busy season to help with the harvest. Pretty thing. Too pretty for this town, but not pretty enough for the talkies, or anything like that. She wouldn't have any trouble finding a husband, if that was her mind, which it seemed like it would be. She wasn't a flirt per se like her brother's wife, but she was conscious of the men's attention at the orchard and had a deft subtlety to how she encouraged it. No hip-wagger, bosom thruster, this girl. Just shy smiles that drove them all wild.

Charlotte pulled a beat-up crossword book and pencil from her coat pocket and busied her mind while she waited to hear these men's latest nonsense.

Harold Burnes found a seat close to the front of the meeting room so he could hear well, but far enough back from the speaker's table that they would be less likely to see him writing notes. He wanted full candor.

On his way from the Grand Hotel to Town Hall, he encountered the Colville men on horseback again and stopped to ask them about the project, scribbling furiously in his notebook about their worry for the salmon runs and their traditional sites along the river.

By the time Harold arrived at the town hall, the room was nearly full. It was unlikely he would recognize anyone. Colville was a much bigger town than this one, and there was rarely a reason to come out to these outlying communities, except when the Wenatchee and Spokane papers covered their news sporadically.

To Harold this spelled opportunity. He would need to post his first article right away to make sure he beat anyone else to press. Then his full piece would appear in the following weekend edition. So he had a few days to expound.

Harold settled into his seat, ready to pounce on anything interesting that might spark debate, and better yet, convince Raymond to give him more meaty assignments.

Carter stood on the empty porch of the town hall building. Everyone was inside already like he'd hoped. The floorboards creaked under his boots as he crossed the foyer, and he stopped and took a deep breath. His heart pounded in his chest. He could still leave, turn back.

The doors to the meeting room were propped open a few inches, and he peered inside, not wanting to be seen. His father sat in the back row, turning his hat in his hands. Carter's sister, Ona sat next to Ozzie, scanning the room as though cataloging who was there. Carter didn't see Mae yet.

The crowd inside was waiting anxiously, stirring against one another in the combined heat of their bodies. He looked for a path to sneak in with little notice and stand in the back. The warm fire in the woodstove caused those in the front row to drape their coats across their laps, hang them from chair backs, or fold them in their arms. The windows fogged against the cold. Rows of folding chairs filled with men and women from town. Behind them, people stood in the back and lined the walls to listen.

Carter had not seen so many people he knew in the same room since his mother's funeral. His face turned hot imagining what they were thinking about him and Mae as he contemplated entering the room. It was a small community which extended out over homesteads of dozens of acres each. Faces from miles away were present. His cousin Lloyd was there from Daisy. Carter nodded to him and Lloyd waved to him. Lloyd's father, Milton, sat in the row in front of Ozzie and Ona. People Carter came up with through school were also seated there. Families he'd known from town. His grade school teacher was there even, a strand of hair stuck to the sweat on her forehead. She fanned herself with a piece of paper.

Behind him, he heard, *excuse me,* and there was Mae, wanting past him into the meeting room. She looked surprised to see him. They'd always had that kind of timing. It was part of why they fell in love. Right when he was wondering where she was, she'd walk into the room.

She was wearing a matching pale pink skirt and jacket with a puff of crimson silk spilling out the neck, something he'd not seen her in before. She looked thinner, her lightened hair perfectly waved, eyes green and bright in the firelight, her full lips dark with red lipstick. He felt the same electricity he always did when she was close, prickles in the small of his back and in the places that remembered her best.

"Mae…," he started, wanting to beg her to reconsider, aware of the eyes on them.

"Not now," she hissed, giving him a tight smile, her red lips a thin line. The heat from her body met his as she squeezed past him into the crowded hall. He watched her silently, his expression still.

Then his father saw him, and he was stuck. The two men nodded at each other in recognition. The place was packed with people standing any place they could find, and luckily, there was nowhere for Carter to sit by his father. He watched Mae press into the left side of the crowd near her own family, and Carter went the other way to avoid her. He found a spot against the back wall and waited with all the rest.

In the front of the hall, the old oak table that had been there for fifty years seemed uncomfortably empty, large posters placed against the wall begged explanation. Carter leaned against the wood paneling of the back wall, trying not to look at Mae. He could feel her location in a red flush on that side of his face. He stole a look at her. She caught his eye and looked quickly away, her face unyielding.

The room went silent as a group of strangers shuffled into the doorway, one man in a modest brown tweed suit holding the door open for the rest of them as he tried not to drop the dog-eared sheaf of papers under his arm. The air filled with murmurs as the men made their way to the front of the hall.

Two men took seats behind the oak table. By their clothes, one was clearly better paid than any of the others. The rest of their cadre pressed into the front of the crowd. The better-dressed man surveyed the room as he strode to the table.

Carter wasn't sure he cared what these men had to say. He looked at Mae, and she caught his gaze again, frowning. Carter felt a panic in his chest. The room felt suddenly overbearingly hot and crowded.

He focused his attention on the large oak table up front and noticed name placards on the table for the first time: Frank Banks from the Bureau of Reclamation and a man named M.J. Starks from the development company.

Before the men started speaking, Ozzie was on his feet: "What were your men doing surveying the shore by my ferry last month?"

A chorus of voices rose up behind Ozzie, people wanting to know the answer themselves.

"When are you building the dam?" someone shouted from the crowd.

Mr. Banks waved his hands in front of him, indicating they should simmer down.

"Yes, federal funding is secured to start construction on a dam that will provide irrigation to 10,000 square miles of farmland east of the Cascades." He gestured to one of the posters with a map of the area in question. "You know it around here as the pumping plan your local commission has been advocating for. Power sales will pay back the construction costs in less than fifty years."

"Where? Here?"

"Fifty years?"

"What about the power company's permit for a dam here at the rapids?"

Mr. Banks continued. "We've selected a location 100 miles south of here with a natural wall that will ease the construction and allow us to back the river up for several miles. There won't be any rapids after that."

A murmur of outrage rippled the crowd.

"How far?"

The men at the table looked at each other.

"How far will the river back up?"

Clearly, this was what they'd come to town to explain. "Past the Canadian border," Mr. Banks said.

Carter heard gasps around him. Kettle Rapids was more than fifty miles downstream from the border.

"The Columbia will back up for several hundred miles, creating a natural reservoir where the water can be stored," Mr. Banks explained. "Unfortunately, this will mean the water levels in the smaller rivers along the Columbia, such as the Kettle River here, will rise significantly."

"You're flooding us? You're flooding the town?"

"To compensate you for your losses," Mr. Banks said hesitantly, "the federal government will provide additional funds to purchase your property from you at a fair market price. Those who own buildings in the anticipated flood zone will be able to move them to higher ground, and the funds should allow you to purchase land elsewhere."

The well-dressed man named Starks spoke up. "This town has not been in its prime for decades now, ladies and gentlemen. I daresay you don't have much to lose by moving up the hill a ways. If anything, the town has a better chance of reliving some of its heyday once the irrigation systems are complete and the railroad tracks are laid."

A man from the crowd spoke and even though Carter couldn't see his face, he recognized the voice immediately as his wife's father, Boone Haufman, who owned a still profitable construction company in town. Carter shrank deeper against the wall, his eyes following the sound of his father in law's voice. Right now, the town going away forever sounded like a relief.

"Will there be roadwork for experienced contactors?"

Starks nodded to Boone in what looked to Carter like feigned sympathy. Starks rose from the table and walked around to the front. Resting his hip against its surface, he leaned forward, opening his hands as though presenting the finale of a magic trick.

"You have to think long term." He addressed the crowd as if he trained his voice for this kind of audience. "This town, this state, and this country are in a situation right now. We all have to think of the long term."

Carter could hear men around him grumbling. Mae looked up at her father while he spoke. Carter's face burned, and he tried to focus on what was being said, but he couldn't stop staring at Mae. This was exactly why he shouldn't have come. Didn't Ozzie know that?

"This is an imperfect moment," Mr. Starks said. "There are sacrifices to be made, and yet there are also great rewards to be had. Many of you have struggled for some time. Your crops suffered from lack of water. Your businesses suffered from lack of customers with enough money. The jobs you once counted on are gone. Years ago, this was a town of opportunity, with gold and coal and a rail line to ship it out. Now, many have already left. Shopkeepers closed their doors. The Grand Hotel that was once a monument to this town's momentum is a museum of its finer past.

"This moment is imperfect because you will have to choose. Do you cling to the past and the memories of what was? Or do you move forward into the unknown?"

Starks stood and looked out the window into the distance.

"Last year, I had the opportunity to attend the World's Fair in faraway Chicago. The day I went, snow dusted the ground, not unlike how it looks outside today. The park and Lake Michigan were grey and blue, the colors of concrete and steel. This entire fair was called 'Century of Progress,' and as I approached the main gate, the archway spanning above my head said in bold letters, 'Science Finds, Industry Applies, Man Adapts.' I stopped."

He arced his hand in front of him like he was running it over the sign.

"Science Finds. Industry Applies. Man Adapts.

"I had to think about that before I entered the Century of Progress. Was I the kind of man who could adapt?"

He looked around the quiet room.

"In the decade or so that engineers and policymakers have been theorizing about how to make better use of the many rivers in this area, one thing has been resoundingly consistent: no one can agree on one clear answer.

"Now you may think this new proposal means the death of your town. I'm not saying I disagree. For certain, you will have to leave some things behind. Your property. Your memories. The shape and proportion of the way it once was. But man adapts. You will either move or be taken by the river."

He took his seat again behind the table and glanced at a sheet of paper. The room was held in a reverent silence, and Carter marveled at the hold this man's speech had on them.

"I will need thousands of men to help me build this dam," Starks continued. "I will need vendors to supply me with materials to build it. There will be roads and bridges to build, railroad tracks to lay. I will need business owners to provide food, supplies, and entertainment for my workers.

"Our president plans to be generous with what he offers to compensate you for your land, and Mr. Banks is correct, there is good land not far from here where you can rebuild your town. Yes, this is all good and useful. What I'm offering is so much more than a new place for an old existence.

"When President Roosevelt came to visit the site for our new dam, he said it was 'the best use of everything for all.' The future is ours to define, and yours may very well sit a hundred miles downriver from here. Only you can decide."

A low grumble ran through the room. Mr. Banks from the Bureau of Reclamation looked embarrassed, but Carter was riveted. He hadn't thought of it quite like that. He looked at Mae, wondering if she heard the same thing he did, about the possibility of a fresh start. He remembered lying in bed with her before the house was built, describing the kitchen to her. Her cheek resting on his shoulder, as she looked up at him with those same wide green eyes. Now she did not return his gaze.

"Either way, the decision has been made, and our crews will start blasting," Starks went on. "Those in the flood plain will receive a letter from the federal government indicating when they are to move and the purchase price the government is willing to pay.

"The president is thinking long term. The farmers of this region are thinking long term." Starks spread his hands wide to emphasize his point. "There's no quick fix here, ladies and gentlemen."

Ozzie Price leapt to his feet, startling Carter even though he'd been expecting an outburst from his father. Ozzie's round body was trembling, and he gripped his hat firmly in front of him.

"Screw your long term. Sure, I care about farmers, but I don't make my living from my farm anymore. And I'm already losing business from the new bridge."

Carter's face burned again.

Another man jumped up, "He's saying there will be jobs, Price. Lots of us need the work!" Several voices rose up in support.

Ozzie looked around the room red-faced and angry. "I own a respectable ferry business, a family business...I supported you pumpers. I opposed the gravity plan for you. I wrote letters for you and donated money to your commission. Now you want me to move my business? How can I do business on the river if you move the goddamn river?"

Mae was looking at the floor again. How dare she be embarrassed of his family when she turned his misfortune into even greater humiliation?

"Sir, please. Be calm." Mr. Banks looked like he was still getting used to the furor these meetings could cause.

"I won't let you do it," Ozzie said. "I'll write to the governor. I'll write to the paper."

"What about the rest of us who need the money they're offering, Price. You're not the only one with a dog in this fight!"

"I'm with Price." Ozzie's friend Jackson, who owned the local gas station, stood in solidarity. "I can't afford to dig up my tanks or buy new ones. I'll have to shut down. Is that progress?"

"You don't know what you're talking about!"

"What about the irrigation? And flood control?"

"I can't get anyone to buy my crops as it is. We don't need more farmland around here."

"Who's going to buy all this power you plan to sell?"

"What about the cemetery? You telling me we're going to dig

up our dead and move them too? My wife is buried down here. You expect me to leave her under all that water?" Ozzie asked.

"Is that true? We're digging up the cemetery?"

Mr. Banks rapped a gavel sharply on the table, but no one paid him any attention. The shouters drowned each other out. Two men shoved and grappled each other, their shoes squealing on the wood floor as the crowd and company men pulled them apart.

Carter knew the kind of man his father was. Once he started on a rampage, it was impossible to stop him until all the steam blew itself out. Mr. Banks tried to calm the crowd, but Ozzie was already on his feet and headed toward the door. "To hell with your long term," he shouted over his shoulder. "To hell with all of you."

Shouts of agreement followed him as men from the town walked out of the meeting before it had officially ended.

As Ozzie passed Carter, his face a burning red, he spat out, "Nice of you to show your face, son."

Carter knew he deserved it and pressed his mouth shut. Ozzie flung the outer doors open, and the blast of cold air hit Carter square in the face like a punch.

The company men hustled the rowdiest of the crowd out the door, while their representatives dismissed the meeting from the oak table at the front of the room.

Carter stared at Mae, but she didn't look his way as she followed her father out of the meeting. Her father eyed Carter with a mixture of curiosity and pity as he passed. Once they were out the front door, Carter headed to the parking lot to avoid prying eyes of the town as they filed out of the meeting.

Carter's cousin Lloyd found him and put out a hand. "Well, that was quite a show," he said.

Carter shook his head. "Let's get out of here."

His sister Ona stopped them, her hands on her hips. Carter

had forgotten about her. "That was embarrassing as usual. Guess I'm gonna need a ride home," she said, and Lloyd waved his cousins toward his pickup.

Harold Burnes from the *Colville Scintilla* rode home as fast as his horse would move to get his story filed:

TOWN'S RESPONSE REVEALS CHARACTER, SAYS COMPANY REP

Comparing the construction of the dam at Milepost 90 off Highway 20 to a Great War battlefield, the representative from Starks Company told the Scintilla *that Kettle Rapids' response to his announcement would "reveal [their] true character." In this exclusive interview prior to the public announcement on Wednesday, M.J. Starks went on to say that outcomes of such a project are "always worth it," apparently ignoring the fact that one outcome is the displacement of more than 500 family homes, businesses and civic buildings. Members of the Colville tribe held a silent protest outside, noting another outcome as the loss of millions of salmon and traditional sites along the river.*

Citing "eventual outcomes" to a surly mob as the prize to keep their eyes on, surely Mr. Starks meant the access to irrigation water and not the loss of land, timber, food sources, traditional lands and structures. Perhaps he forgets sometimes the eventual outcome can mean catastrophic loss of life as well. Take for instance the failure of the St. Francis Dam in Los Angeles, California, a decade ago. Only two years after its completion, the dam collapsed, releasing its reservoir in a flood that killed 600 people.

Kettle Rapid's response? A shouting match.

CHAPTER 3
November 1935

After the meeting, Charlotte finished delivering her apple boxes in town and then turned the Lincoln toward home. The dog pressed his nose against the passenger window, leaving a streak of slime.

She wasn't sure what to think about what she heard. Men liked to talk, but they didn't always follow through. That much she knew. They got too wound up in their own attachment to their side of the argument to listen to other points of view. So why bother trying to rationalize with them.

She'd watched with dismay when they built their irrigation canal a few years before, a canal that stretched through loamy sand and made a mud trickle to nowhere. No one was happy about the outcome of that. At least they'd tried. They built the damn thing. If one of them would take a stand, something might get done right. Instead they hemmed and hawed and tried to satisfy everyone until the plans looked like a crazy quilt of competing agendas.

What frustrated her no end was how long it took these men to agree on a course of action. Pick one, she thought. Pick one and own it. Even now that a plan was in motion, they still argued until they were blue in the face about whose idea would theoretically work better. They dragged out huge sheets of drawn plans and debated endlessly why it wouldn't work.

Gravity dam. Pump dam. Wouldn't they both serve their purpose in their own way? A contract was signed. Why keep arguing about it? She was able to manage okay without institutionalized irrigation; in fact, like most orchardists, Charlotte had more product than she could distribute. They also didn't mention the complication of added competition. If the land around hers was better irrigated, wouldn't someone else want to grow on it? What then?

If she spent this kind of time agonizing over decisions about what kind of tree to plant or which distributor to go with, her business would have failed long ago. This was no time for indecision. The world was unraveling around them. Where the federal money was going to come from to fund these bailout work projects was anyone's guess. Even temperance had failed.

Much of what kept her going these many years was her ability to thrive in a small distribution area—to carve out a small part of the world that she alone could service. Her life had taken such unexpected turns, there was no way to plan for where she was now. From a flapper in her youth, to homestead mother, to a middle-aged widow whose existence relied on the benevolence of the weather, the fates of insects and fungus and blights, the mercy of the markets and price volatility, and now on this group of buffoons and their ego-driven argument. It was as if the massiveness of the river inflated their ambitions.

Charlotte didn't have the energy to expand her business to match any new competitors that might crop up. She hoped to leave something behind for her trouble, not just shut the place down when she was done working.

This turn of events left her perplexed on what to do next. Not that she'd been much more certain before. With no heirs left alive, she put her mind to what to do with her property and business. She could try to sell it, but what would she do with the money? Retire? She couldn't spend it all before she died, and she didn't have anyone to leave the rest to. And who would buy her place? Who had money anymore?

At times, she wondered if it had been a mistake to turn down Oscar Price's proposal of marriage, for the simplest reason of all, that it might have added some financial stability to have a husband and two kids to help out with the orchard—labor she wouldn't have to pay for. It was too late for all that now though. She'd refused him without hesitation.

If he asked right after her husband died, she might have said yes. Would likely have said yes. Of course, Oscar's wife was still living then, so it was the intervention of timing really that kept Charlotte from accepting him. She had been on her own for years by then, learned to take care of herself, with no one else to look after but the old dog, and she loved it. She loved the independence, the satisfaction of sufficiency, and the lack of interference. For the first time in her entire life, she could take action without permission, make decisions without consulting another person. She had the dog for complicit, agreeable company, and she could lie in bed all morning on a Saturday reading until the dog whined to be let out.

It pained her to refuse Oscar, but there was no way she would marry him. It was just unfortunate that he thought to ask, because his rejection was inevitable. Poor Price. He had his good qualities, and for a woman who wanted a crooner and dancer, he had a fun side. He took her refusal in stride, though, his face reddening. He was a hothead, but he didn't express any anger toward her, just a lingering loneliness.

There was still the question of who to leave her place to. The land was the only thing of value she had left, and she'd worked so hard to keep the operation afloat. Her entire life since her husband died was spent keeping the place up.

Adapt. That's what the man at the town hall meeting said. Oh, he was a pompous wind bag, for sure. Something about the size and rush of the river turned men's minds toward an ambition she didn't understand. She knew how to adapt. Was forced to adapt, and it had done her good. The men would do what they wanted. It was up to her to figure out how to adapt to it.

She turned the Lincoln off the highway toward home, and the dog barked at another dog resting in his yard, the two of them yapping at each other until they were out of earshot.

In the weeks after the town hall meeting, Carter noticed Ozzie was quiet around him. His father's typewriter took up residence on the kitchen table, and the clatter of keys filled the room each evening while Ozzie typed letters to politicians and newspaper editors and Ona cooked dinner. No one ate at the table anymore. They carried plates off to corners of the house. Their mother would never have allowed that, and Carter missed her calming presence.

In town, tensions were still high. Angry glares followed them from people who wanted to see jobs come to the area, and still others showed fiery support for preserving the river, inflaming Ozzie even more. Business at the ferry crossing slowed.

As they drove to the ferry landing one morning, Ozzie was quiet behind the wheel. With the light still growing behind the trees, Carter didn't know how to break the silence. They were both still waking up, each unsure what to say to the other.

Carter was staring off into the trees out the passenger window when Ozzie turned the Ford onto the drive and stopped, preparing to unlock the white wooden gate that blocked the driveway when they were closed for business. When he didn't get out and stared, shocked, ahead, Carter looked up.

The gate was smashed to the ground. Ozzie jumped out and ran over to it, like he might save it from peril. He picked up a piece, and Carter could see the red reflector from it that warned night drivers. Ozzie threw it on the ground and kicked the pieces out of the driveway. Carter got out of the car, and Ozzie marched over to him.

"What do you know about this?" he shouted.

"Me? Why would I know anything?"

"Get in the car." Ozzie stormed back to the driver's side and got behind the wheel. Carter stared, stunned, as Ozzie drove through the demolished gate toward the ferry landing without him.

Carter followed on foot, stepping on the smashed pieces of the gate as he passed.

At the landing, Ozzie pulled up sideways and swung the driver side door open. The boxes where they kept supplies on the dock were overturned, the floats they used to protect the boat and dock scattered across planks.

Carter ran out to the dock, his boots clattering on the slick surface. His father stood at the edge of the dock and let out what sounded like the closest a man can get to a roar. Carter looked out past him into the river. The ferry, a flat platform big enough for a half dozen cars, was about 50 feet out from the dock, the portside corner tipping precariously into the immense pull of the river, the cable they used to pulley it across swift water sliced and buoyant in the rushing river, about to sweep away on the vast expanse of the Columbia.

Ozzie threw his coat from his thick frame and kicked off his shoes.

"What are you doing?" Carter called to him.

"I'm going to get my boat!"

"And what? You can't drag it here!"

"Get your shoes off and come help me!"

"It's 30 degrees outside!"

Ozzie stared at him. "I'm not going to let it wash down the river!"

"We'll go get someone from town to help us haul it in!"

A metallic groan came from the river as the ferry strained on its cable. Ozzie splashed into the freezing water, leaving Carter staring as his father thrashed through the current, struggling not to be swept downstream. All he could think of was the day at the mines, his choice to act, to run from the accident leading to a cascade of negative consequences, even though he likely saved their lives.

Carter paced the dock watching his father's arms and head appear and disappear in the dark blue. Ozzie made it to the edge of the flat surface. He grasped the side, and the ferry tilted severely as he hoisted himself aboard. The surface was slick with frost, and his bulk careened overboard with a loud sucking sound that made all other sounds in Carter's ears stop.

In a distant voice, Carter could hear himself calling for his father, too panicked to jump in, his heart beating in his ears. He didn't know what to do. All logic fled from his mind, and he stood there limply hollering into the wind, his voice lost on the wide expanse and loud rush of the river.

Ozzie's face and thick shoulders popped up behind the ferry, and he flopped breathless onto the stern end still attached to the cable underwater. Carter stared, immobile. His father must have found the cable underneath and pulled himself to the back from under the boat. On deck, Ozzie rolled onto all fours, shaking as water dripped from his thick frame, his lips blue from the river, his breath steaming in the cold dawn light.

"Get the canoe!" he yelled to Carter; the sound muffed by the rush of the river between them. Ozzie pulled open one of the hinged boxes on the ferry that doubled as a seat. Carter couldn't think what he meant.

"Carter, go get the goddamn canoe and row out here!" Ozzie yanked a metal weight from the box and dropped it into the river, the boat groaning back somewhere near level as Ozzie anchored it into the rocks on the bottom.

There were no blankets anywhere, no dry cloth of any kind. Ozzie's clothes dripped icy water, and he shuddered as Carter rowed him to shore. Carter got his father into the passenger seat of the car without as much fuss as he expected, throwing his own dry coat around Ozzie's shoulders and his shoes on the floor in front of him. Carter drove Ozzie to the only friendly place he could think of that would be open this early, Jackson's gas station and auto shop on the main highway.

Ozzie's friend Jackson owned the place and lived there alone in a one-room apartment built onto the back of the shop. Together, they pulled the bedding off Jackson's cot and wrapped it around Ozzie, setting him to dry and warm up next to the coal-fired stove that heated the room.

Jackson boiled water on the stove and poured it into a mug with whiskey and gave it to Ozzie.

"You've made a lot of people angry," Carter said, and Ozzie turned a face on fire toward his son.

"And what have you done? You stood there and watched just now while I almost drowned. Stood there like a goddamn statue! You didn't used to be like this. You used to care about something. Now look at you! You make stupid decisions that could get people killed."

"Easy, easy," Jackson said, backing toward the other side of the small room.

"Yeah, you wouldn't know anything about that," Carter threw back, sick of it, sick of the humiliation, sick of living at home, sick of the criticism.

"What's that supposed to mean?" Ozzie's face was now purple as the blood returned to it in force.

"What did you do for my mother when she was dying?"

"What are you talking about?"

"You didn't lift a finger for her. You let her cough herself to death, and you never even knew she was sick."

"You know nothing about it. You were too busy with your

wreck of a marriage."

"I know enough."

"Go get the ferry."

"What?"

"You heard me. Go get our boat and make sure it doesn't wash downriver."

"Your boat."

"The boat that puts a roof over your head. Now go get the goddamn boat hauled in!"

Carter stormed out of Jackson's apartment, slamming the door behind him.

It took most of the day, a truck, and four men from town to help drag the boat back to the dock and chain it up. It could be weeks or months until they could get the parts to repair the cable and take on customers for the crossing again. When the boat was secure once more, Carter drove to the house to pick up clean clothes for his father.

The house seemed eerily quiet. He called for his sister, but she must have gone out with her friends after school. He packed a dry shirt and pants for Ozzie and headed back out.

When he got back to Jackson's, the place was locked up for the night, the closed sign framed in the door's window. Carter drove through town looking for a sign of where his father had gone. As he drove, he imagined the buildings of the town underwater. He pictured them as they would look from above the surface, shadowy and wavering in the cold darkness. It gave him a deep chill. He hadn't thought of the town quite like that before. It was as though it had already died.

His father would never be able to understand why he wanted to see the whole thing wash away. How could you turn a man's mind that way when he was so tied to this place? For Carter, all his failures would be forgotten, buried under the waters of a massive reservoir backed up from the dam, submerged forever from gossiping tongues and pitying eyes. He could wish it burned to the ground, but instead, fate brought its end to him.

There was no doubt the ferry landing would be in the flood zone. His father's ferry business would be lost even if they repaired the boat. His pulleys, his cables, his storage shed and docks on both sides of the river would have to be moved or forfeited to the flood that would eventually envelop it, along with a hundred feet of shoreline the family had owned for fifty years.

Finally, Carter saw Jackson's car with his garage name and address painted on the doors parked outside Ralph's Pool Hall. He pulled into the parking lot, afraid of what he might find inside.

Harold Burnes's face turned a blistering red when he saw the cover of the *Wenatchee Journal* with a photo of M.J. Starks and the headline: "Irrigation at last." Had Starks paid them off? Half of why Harold wanted to criticize the project in the *Scintilla* was to counter the other paper's unwavering support of it. Maybe more than half. They were the bigger town paper in these parts. Did they have any journalistic pride?

In the weeks since the town hall meeting in Kettle Rapids, Harold returned to the town when he could and stayed at the Grand Hotel. Raymond had no funds for expenses, so Harold paid for it out of his own pocket, hoping a new story angle would emerge and catapult his career. Starks was a hard man to get to, especially after Harold's first article, and Starks was surrounded by goons anywhere he went. Harold saw their caravan of company-owned cars outside a place called Ralph's Pool Hall at the end of the workday a few times earlier in the week. Harold wasn't much of a tavern man himself. He preferred to maintain the lucidity necessary to recognize the story in any moment, to remember a quote verbatim, and be the most cogent person in the room. He also was not above shadowing his subject like a Pinkerton tail.

He had a feeling back in Colville. A feeling that something was about to break for him. Every reporter dreams of that moment when they stumble on the key to a story that could only find them by coincidence. As long as the Starks contingent was still in town, he vowed to hang around to see what more he could uncover.

He explored the crumbling downtown and interviewed the few people who were willing. There had to be an angle here no one else had explored yet, something that would get people talking and show those boys in Wenatchee and Spokane that they weren't so highfalutin' after all.

Harold found his way to the far end of the bar at Ralph's. Ralph's was dim inside, and the sun had long since set, the days some of the shortest of the year. Before prohibition, the place had been called Ralph's Tavern, and since the repeal, Ralph hadn't bothered to change the name back. The place was busy but not packed, and Harold found an empty stool so Starks wouldn't see him right away if his entourage came in. Ralph himself came behind the bar and waited in front of Harold without saying anything. Wanting to keep his head clear, Harold ordered his customary black coffee. After Ralph set it in front of him, he swirled the cup, watching and waiting.

Harold pulled his notebook and pencil from his jacket pocket and fiddled with it, looking for the next clean page. His career was ripe for a big story. He could feel it looming out there in his near future, like he sensed a storm coming. He needed one great break, a labor dispute erupting into violence, corruption exposed, public funds mishandled, and he could move on to the big leagues.

Harold surveyed the clientele, which looked like ruffians mostly. Ralph was serving whiskey after whiskey to Mr. Price, a large red-faced older man who caused a stir at the town hall meeting. Harold hadn't run into him since then. Mr. Price seemed to harbor inflamed feelings about the whole affair, though Harold wasn't sure how valuable he might be as a story source. Still, why not take the opportunity to interview Price? Then the man's son came in and took a seat at the bar. The son seemed a more reasonable but morose sort than his father, and Harold suspected the son would wave him off. Better to bide his time. Not seeing much else of interest going on, Harold slapped his notebook down on the bar and swigged the last gritty ounce in his mug.

Inside Ralph's, Carter smelled the familiar sweet and ashy smoke of cigars and hand-rolled cigarettes. The place was lively already, and Ralph had taken the time to put pine and holly swags on top of the piano. As festive as it could have been, they did give the place a life and greenery.

Ozzie sat on a stool next to Jackson, a glass of whiskey, straight up, on the bar in front of him. Carter handed his father the bag of clean clothes and rested his hands on the surface of the bar next to Ozzie, feeling its watery stickiness against his palms. Ozzie eyed him silently, downed his drink, and slammed the glass on the bar, nodding to Ralph to fill it again.

Jackson nodded to Carter in acknowledgment. He looked as though it had been a tiring day of listening to Ozzie, even if they were on the same side of the argument.

"You figure out who sank my boat?" Ozzie asked, as Carter joined them.

The minimal conversation in the back was cracked intermittently by the noise of billiard balls that sounded much like his father clapping his empty glass against the bar.

"You don't know what happened," Carter said softly.

"We all heard what happened in that meeting!" Ozzie's face

was getting color again.

"What did you think about that?" Carter asked Ralph, trying to divert the conversation.

"Don't like the idea of my place being underwater but sounds like they have other plans to make it worth our while."

"Boone Haufmann is signed on to run the road work toward the dam site," Jackson told Carter, and he felt the familiar hot shame any time someone connected to his wife's family was mentioned.

Ralph added, "I hear some of the boys from town want to head down to the dam site. Take a look around."

"Nothing to look at there," Ozzie snapped. "Why don't they head up to the new public roads projects instead? Perfectly good opportunity there."

Ralph hummed in commiseration. "Just saying there's folks on all sides, Price." He turned to wash out the glasses behind the bar.

"If everyone's out of work, where will they get the money to start over?" Jackson said.

"The payouts?" Carter said.

"The payouts won't cover squat!" Ozzie said.

"What will you do then?" Ralph asked him.

"I don't know," Ozzie said. "I'm too old to start over. My business is shot. I can't afford to move if I don't have any money."

"What if I found work outside of town?" Carter asked. "Send money back to help out?"

Ozzie scoffed. "And do what, stand around waiting to get fired? You're not cut out for hard work anymore, and besides I need you here to help fix the boat."

Carter scratched the surface of the bar with his thumbnail, not sure how to react to his father.

Ozzie got up, took his coat off, draping it over his stool, and staggered toward the bathrooms in the back to change into the clothes Carter brought him.

When Ozzie was gone, Jackson turned to Carter. "You got this?"

Carter nodded.

"I'll be heading home then," Jackson said, and gripped Carter on the shoulder as he made for the door.

Carter waited for his father to come back from the men's room. Ralph gave him a commiserating smile and mercifully didn't ask any more questions. The place was starting to fill up. Poverty didn't seem to slow the sale of booze; they were all too excited to have it back again.

A garland tinsel around the top of the bar glistened in the lamp light. Carter glanced around wondering who might have seen something that morning. It could have been anyone really. Kids. Looters. A freak accident. Someone from town angry that Ozzie opposed a payout they wanted. Ultimately, it didn't matter. They were out of business until the damage could be repaired. That meant people would have to drive up to the bridge to cross, and that meant they might get used to that new option. No matter who was responsible, Ozzie's business was going to suffer for the foreseeable future

Carter heard the distinct sound of his father's booming voice over the din of the bar.

"You!" his father was shouting toward the doorway where a group of men dressed in work clothes had come in. Ozzie's face was red and puffed. "It was you!"

The man he addressed was the well-dressed speaker from the town meeting, the one who gave the rousing speech. Carter remembered his name from the meeting: M.J. Starks.

Carter hopped off his stool and pushed through the crowd to his father. Starks tried to brush past Ozzie in the crowd, but Ozzie was having none of it.

"You cut my boat loose!"

Starks ignored Ozzie, calmly taking off his hat and folding his fine coat over his arm, but the men around him turned toward Ozzie.

"I'm talking to you," Ozzie reached out and grabbed Starks's arm, and the men around him jumped to attention.

"Hey, hey, c'mon now." Carter pulled Ozzie back.

"I'm not looking for any trouble here, sir," Starks said, more to Carter than to Ozzie. "Maybe it's time for you two to call it a night."

"Who…," Ozzie started, but Carter shoved him toward the door.

"Let's go," he said. "It's been a long day. Let's go."

Ozzie lunged past Carter at Starks, and Starks's security closed in around Ozzie, grappling until they threw him out the door. He landed with a crack on his hip, his shirt torn. Carter ran after him and helped him up, and Ozzie made toward the door again.

"No! No way!" Carter said.

"My coat is in there, dammit."

"I'll get it. You stay here."

Ozzie kicked at the ground, his gray hair frayed around his face. "God damn it!"

Carter ran back inside. Starks was now at the bar talking to Ralph, and they both turned to Carter as he approached. Ralph leaned back away from the counter, and Starks looked apprehensively at Carter.

"His coat…," Carter said feebly.

"I'm sorry to hear about your father's ferry," Starks said. Ralph must have told him what his father's outburst was about.

Carter didn't say anything. He pulled out his wallet, fished for a bill to give Ralph, and laid it on the bar.

"I hope you know we had nothing to do with it," Starks said.

Carter waited while Ralph made change for him.

"Tempers are high around here I suspect," Starks continued.

Carter took his change, stuffed it into his wallet.

"Son," Starks said, and Carter turned to face him finally. He was older than he looked from across the room, or maybe had the impression of work on him that was hard to see from far away when dressed in rich clothes. "I need men like you," Starks said to Carter. "Strong, experienced workers. Don't rot away here in this dying town. We're building the dam whether your father likes it or not. You can stay here and wish it was different, pine away for what's been lost, or you can join the new world and learn for yourself the magnitude of steel and concrete. We control nature, son." Starks took a business card from his lapel pocket and handed it to Carter. "Don't let yours control you."

Carter looked down at the wallet in his hand, tucked the card into it, and shoved it in his pocket. "I best be getting him home," he said, grabbing Ozzie's coat, nodding to Ralph and turning toward the door.

"If you change your mind, come find me in Electric City," Starks said, and turned his attention back to Ralph.

Outside, Ozzie was gone. Carter ran down the steps and around the corner. The moon was full and high and shone a white beam along the pine trees that ringed the town. Up the road a few hundred yards, his father walked along the side of the road.

Carter pulled the car keys from his pocket, ran over to his father's old Ford, hopped in the driver's side and fired up the engine. He backed out, the gravel under snow crunching under the tires, and then pulled onto the highway, heading toward his father. He pulled up next to him and rolled down the passenger window. Ozzie refused to look at him.

"C'mon, get in," Carter said.

Ozzie kept walking.

"Are you really going to walk all the way home without your coat? Get in the car."

Ozzie stopped and stared at him. "They wrecked my boat!"

"You don't know that. It could have been anyone."

"Whose side are you on?"

"Get in the car, Pops."

They sat there for a moment, the car idling. Carter looked out the windshield, and Ozzie stared stubbornly up the road. The moon shone overhead, bathing them in silver light.

"Let's go home," Carter said, finally.

Ozzie stood reluctantly next to the passenger door, then opened it and slid onto the seat.

Through the dark, headlights shined a thin dual path up the gravel road, the heavy boughs of evergreen trees looming in an arc over them, a strip of starred sky barely visible on the zenith. Carter smelled the rich ponderosa around him, and the damp cold enclosed his face as he drove his father home.

In the morning, Harold Burnes filed his story and smiled when Raymond hooted from inside his office. As Harold hoped, his wait paid off when Ralph's front door had swung open with a swirl of snowflakes and in marched Starks and his detail like a journalistic miracle. Let the Wenatchee boys get a load of their beloved Starks now.

STARKS A SABOTEUR?

If you're wondering why you have to drive down all the way south to Inchelium to catch the ferry or all the way north to the new bridge to cross the mighty Columbia, you may have M.J. Starks and the Starks Company to blame. Or at least the owner of the ferry at Kettle Landing seems to think so. In the wee hours of Wednesday morning, Mr. Oscar Price found his boat adrift and nearly died of hypothermia retrieving it. Mr. Price was overheard that same evening at Ralph's Pool Hall accusing Mr. Starks of the deed, to which Mr. Starks responded by having his company goons toss Mr. Price out into the street without justice. Will the Starks Company go to any lengths to build their dam? Who will be the next victim of this project? Only time will show.

CHAPTER 4
December 1935

Starks pushed his dinner plate aside and reached for his newspaper reading gloves. One of his detail was tasked with gathering newspapers from the area where they had a project, and Starks would scan them at mealtime. He learned to read the headlines with a neutrality acquired over his career, but he hated the way ink stuck to his hands and traveled to his face and clothes.

Back at the home office in Minneapolis, his press secretary was responsible for this job, but here in the field, he needed stimulation and occupation, and scanning the headlines was a productive use of his time.

In his experience, newspaper men typically fell along a spectrum between idealist and opportunist. They weren't so unlike the government workers he encountered, but the journalists had their own nuances. The idealists fancied themselves to be completely objective when reporting on projects like his, but in reality, they often had a bias toward reporting negatively about his work. Their blindness to their own bias seemed a considerable character flaw to Starks, and he kept the most extreme cases of these at a great distance.

The opportunists, on the other hand, would say whatever he wanted them to as long as he greased the wheels, whether that was as benignly arranged as a nice dinner or, for the more corrupt among them, a cash payout. He liked the opportunists best.

Then there was the middle of the continuum. The idealist-opportunist combination, the ones who wanted the personal glory of breaking a story but still believed in the journalistic tenets of objectivity and presenting multiple sides. These were the toughest nuts, and from what he was reading this evening, the kind he currently had on his hands with this fellow from the *Colville Scintilla* lurking about.

Ultimately, though, what Starks came to understand over the years was that newspaper stories only served to sway public sentiment. They rarely influenced the outcome of the actual project unless there was an election coming and someone involved fancied themselves a political candidate. Otherwise, construction went forward with whatever backing was behind it. So who gave a fig about public sentiment in the end?

His press secretary was who. Perhaps it was time to send Fitzgerald a telegram.

On Christmas Eve, Carter stood in the dark kitchen by himself, suspenders hanging at his hips, and poured himself a whiskey. His father had taken his sister to the regional high school pageant in Colville where she was performing. They'd driven the ten miles inland with most of the rest of the families and wouldn't be back until late that night.

Nothing was clear about what happened to Ozzie's boat, and Carter suspected it must be someone from town who wanted to bring work to the area so badly they were willing to go to jail for it. Or pumpers who wanted to scare them.

Carter needed these brief moments of solitude, lack of political rants and judgements. It was humiliating enough to ask his father for work and live in his house again. To be sure, Carter was glad to have the work after being let go at the mine, especially when so many others were unemployed, but one of the sharpest stings of moving back home was enduring his father's boisterous criticisms.

Carter let the woodstove fire burn down. He could feel the cold from the windows, as a handful of snowflakes blew around on the night breeze outside. His mother used to stand like this and stare out the window at the back yard and the barn as if she were thinking of somewhere far away. He missed her still. Missed their holiday traditions, her insistence on family mealtime even though she wasn't the greatest cook. Her absence from the house was an uncomfortable void, as though household operations were on hold waiting for her to come back from a trip.

When she was alive, the house seemed like a machine: meals and chores and people in and out and deliveries and errands. So much action to support the four of them. His mother's nimble hands flying from one task to the next. Now the house was cold and quiet.

The events of recent weeks and his conversation with Starks left him contemplative. The idea of a fresh start became more tantalizing every day, and he thought often of Starks's card in his wallet. He could leave town and show them all he was capable of starting over.

When the near miss happened at the mine and they let him go, the indignity of it all was that in the fleeting moments he had to think what to do when the scaffolding failed; he thought he was preventing an accident. He'd run out of the shaft, leading other men to safety. Then the shaft collapsed, costing them months of work. The company fired him on the spot along with everyone who followed him. Since then, every decision felt tentative.

Mae had not been able to reconcile this failure. She wanted more, she said. She didn't want to be tied down anymore.

He could still picture her in the early days when they first met. She was the new girl in town, a teenager with a wild streak, hell bent on proving she could out-bad anyone. Her hair was lightened blond, and she wore it curled and loose around her face. Her skin was a golden color, not unlike his younger sister, or his mother for that matter, and in the summertime it made her glow.

In the winter it made her look yellowed and unwell. There was always that split in her, those opposites that confounded and intrigued him at the same time.

The unsigned divorce papers were still in his dresser. He'd never known anyone who'd been divorced, and the shame of that second failure was too much. He took a swig off his whiskey and watched the snow swirl outside. Maybe if he reasoned with Mae one last time, she would reconsider. Maybe if he told her about what Starks said, about work and opportunity, she would give him one more chance. Maybe they could wait a little while and see what the payouts looked like before making any lasting decisions. It was electric when she brushed past him at the meeting. That part would never go away no matter how much he knew he should want to be free of it, and as long as it was there, it seemed somehow possible to fix all the rest.

The kitchen smelled of stale biscuits and wood oil, which still reminded him of his mother after these many years. He missed her still but was relieved she was not around to see him lose his job, his wife, his house. Coals smoldered in the woodstove, and a dim candy flame lit anew in the smoky window of the stove's door. He stoked the fire down again, trying to put it out.

For Carter, there was little comfort in the familiarity of home when he didn't have a choice but to move back. There wasn't a lot he could do about it at the moment, except try to make the situation bearable for them all. He and Mae were happy once, in love, eyes full of the promise of adventures together, and then the moment faded and the reality of making a living and maintaining a home sank in. For him, at least. He wanted that old feeling of possibility back.

When Carter told his father that he needed to stay with him for a while, Ozzie stared at him, then shook his head. His father didn't say a word, but Carter knew what he was thinking. Ozzie and Carter built that house together. Carter saved up money working in the mica mines in Colville, and Ozzie showed him how to build it. Then, when things got tough, Carter walked away. What his father refused to understand was that Carter built it for her. It was always for her.

His house, Mae's place, was only an hour walk from here, and he'd managed to avoid it in the months since he'd moved out. It wasn't much of a house, but he and his father built it, and it was theirs, his, now hers. She never seemed to care all that much; the plans only sometimes inspired her, as though it wouldn't be very long until she wanted something better, which was the same attitude she had about their marriage and everything else—a placeholder until she could get her hands on more. In hindsight, he wasn't sure why he'd gone through with building it. At the time, it seemed like the right thing to do. He was a married man. His wife should have a house.

At the meeting, she looked beautiful and sad, and he could still remember how her hair smelled of rose shampoo. He closed his eyes and conjured up a memory of her sitting on the edge of the tub after her bath, rubbing her hair dry. He loved to watch her after a bath, naked, none of her usual pretenses, raw and oblivious.

He went to the hall closet to see if there was a warmer coat than the one he'd been wearing, the winter freeze this year colder than usual. More than a few times when he was young, he'd opened the door to this closet to find his little sister playing in it, her face peering up at him with a combination of irritation at being disturbed and embarrassment that it was odd for her to be playing in there.

It was empty now, a few old coats forgotten on hooks along the back wall. He grabbed a long, grey wool coat from one of the hooks. The coat must have been an old one of his father's. His reach disturbed a layer of invisible dust stuck to the lanolin.

He shrugged the coat on. It was far too big and loose, the sleeves hanging past his wrists. He pulled his knit hat close over his ears, put on his gloves, and tucked his small bottle of whiskey deep in one of the coat pockets.

He kept the money he earned at his father's business in his dresser drawer, and now he took it out, pushing the papers aside, and shoved the cash into his pocket to show her, proof that he was still capable.

Outside, snow covered the ground and the roof of the barn. Carter opened the back door, and a blast of cold air made his eyes water.

The Price farmstead was carved beneath a low ridge above the town. When Ozzie built it years before Carter was born, Ozzie cleared a small gully and field against the hill's rocky face that stood like a fortress behind the property. It shielded the house from some of the stronger winds, but it also provided the perfect spot for drifts, and snow piled with alarming depth along the base. It was not ever a big farm by anyone's standards, only big enough for a house, barn, chicken coop, and a couple of outbuildings in disrepair these days. The long drive from the highway culminated at a massive ponderosa in the front yard. Behind them stretched a small field. Only a few chickens were left, and on the south side of the house was a vegetable garden no one tended anymore.

Carter had walked this path thousands of times as a boy, on his way to school, on errands for his mother, to sneak out to meet his friends and drink hooch in the woods, or with a respectable shine on his way to meet Mae. He knew every family that lived along the road – the Paulsons, the Coopers, the Flannery's—no one seemed to mind they were Irish anymore—and, of course, the Haufmann's, his wife's parents, who bought a piece of land near the Prices back when Carter and Mae were in high school. He shrunk into his father's coat as he passed the driveways, embarrassed if any of them should see him.

The air outside was still and so quiet it amplified everything. It was the sound of impending snow. The ponderosas shivered overhead. The snow squeaked under his boots as they pressed footprints into the powder. It was his fault she had the car. He'd let her have it, thinking at least she had a way back to him, a way to bring him home.

The road led him south, following the path of the river. A car drove by slowly, its headlights shining in the snow, and he recognized the dilapidated limousine Mrs. Powell used for delivering apples in town. Her chains rattled against the snowy gravel.

There was so much he would do differently if he could. It wasn't that he wanted to erase it or wished he'd never done it; he wished they'd handled things better. That they could have come out of their tribulations with something to show for their trouble. Or his trouble. Now that he thought about it, Mae came out pretty well, ahead. He alone had nothing to show for his trouble. Typical of how things went with her.

There was no guessing how things would turn out. She'd come back and left so many times that even a legal divorce wouldn't feel permanent.

Their property line was marked from the road with a low rail, barely a fence, two rows of split cedar resting gently in carved outposts. The fence had been an irritation for him for years. The boards slipped out of the posts all the time, and he finally nailed them in this past spring.

The yard was dark now, the grass pillowed with snow, the drive a soupy grey mash of tire tracks. The drive was a medium grade curve that looped in front of the porch, so you could drive through easily or peel out to make a point, as the case may be.

Mae had a habit of churning up gravel under the tires when she was angry.

There were no cars out front, and the house was completely dark. Icicles hung from the eaves of the house, and Carter's breath pooled in the air. He peeked in the window of the kitchen door. The kitchen table was shoved up against the wall with their liquor collection, a dozen bottles of random sizes jumbled next to a pair of salt and pepper shakers shaped like cartoon pigs dressed as bride and groom, a gift to Mae from his mother when they were first married, when his family was still hopeful and accepting of Mae. There were no signs of anyone. She must not be home.

He tested the knob, but it was locked. She insisted he give her his house keys in their last argument, so he decided to wait in the garage for her to come home. The garage was dark and cold and smelled like motor oil and dust. He pulled off his gloves, stuffed them in his coat pockets, and took a swig from the whiskey bottle, the heat seeping into his brain.

He lit the kerosene lantern hanging in the doorway. His tools were all where he'd left them, scattered across the countertop he built from leftover pine boards. His rifle was hanging by a strap on the wall, and next to it, his collection of fishing poles. She wasn't going to need any of these things. He should pack out what he could carry. His fishing tackle bag hung on a hook behind the door, and he grabbed it, folded two of his favorite poles into it, and slung the bag over one shoulder and the rifle over the other. He took another swig from the whiskey bottle, looking around at the relics of his former life stored in this place he built, and sat on a sawhorse, waiting for her to come home.

After a while, it must have been after ten o'clock by now, Carter heard tires crunching on the gravel drive, and headlights bathed the garage doorway. The familiar hope washed over him. If he could make her see there was so much possibility still ahead of him, that he would find a way to make her proud and want him again, they could make it work. He ran into the yard, whiskey bottle still clasped in his hand.

Their car was parked in the driveway, and she was walking toward the house, her face in profile, backlit in a way that made her look like she glowed. The perfect pout of her bottom lip was silhouetted, a curl fallen across her forehead. Her expression always carried an air of sadness even when she laughed, an air that made him want to reach out to her and hold her, to tell her he would make it okay.

He moved toward her and then saw Roy Carnes, a man he recognized from town, trailing behind her from the car, his hat tipped back casually, laughing as Mae turned to gaze up at him and grab his hand

A red heat shot through Carter's brain.

"What are you doing here?" Carter asked, coming out of the shadows.

Mae gasped, startled as though she thought they'd been invaded by a hobo.

"Carter?" Mae seemed confused, and then he remembered he was wearing his father's coat, a hat pulled down over most of his face, a rifle slung over his shoulder.

"Easy, friend," Roy backed away from Mae, his hands fanned out like he was calming a horse.

"I said, what are you doing here?" Carter asked Roy again, pointing the rifle at him.

Roy looked at Mae for help. "What are *you* doing here?" Roy said with a mocking chuckle that made Carter seethe even more.

"Carter!" Mae said, her voice wavering. He dropped his tackle bag with a thud, and tossed his whiskey bottle in the snow against the house.

Roy edged slowly away from Mae, his hands still raised, and

rushed at Carter, knocking him to the ground, the rifle firing into the night sky and clattering across the driveway. Carter wrestled with him, his back aching already from the fall. A punch landed hard on his jaw, another on his cheek bone, and another and another, the pain renewing his fury. All his pent-up humiliation and anger burst out, and he punched back, he and Roy rolling, clutching, punching, Mae a revolving shadow in the background.

Finally, Carter broke free of Roy and lunged for the rifle, but Mae grabbed it and threw it out of reach.

"Get out!" she yelled at Carter, her expression dark.

Roy backed away from him, and Carter scrambled to his feet. Mae's face was purple with anger, and Roy had red welts on his cheeks and forehead. Carter grabbed his tackle bag and ran down the drive to the road. Roy and Mae stood in the driveway watching Carter run away from his own house, a dog barking in the distance.

Ozzie's drive home with Ona from the high school pageant in Colville was quiet if not a little eerie. A few snowflakes drifted, but no new accumulation landed on the road in front of them. Ona slept with her face against the passenger door, her blond curls bobbing with the dips and turns of the road. What dreams did she see, this teenage enigma? What on earth would a teenage girl think about? Where would she go next?

He never imagined having to raise her alone. It terrified him every day. He didn't pay that much attention to fatherhood until his wife passed. He focused on his business until his children's mother died, after a persistent cough so severe it rattled the house, and left him alone to raise a young daughter and a nearly grown son, who knew even less about what to do with her.

Ozzie never thought his son would be such a source of disappointment to him. Everything started out so promising. Carter was his only child until he was thirteen, and through miscarriage after miscarriage, Ozzie came to place all his hopes on this one boy. He taught him the business. He was even proud, though offended, when Carter left it to work in the mines for extra money. It was only a matter of time before both his children would leave him and he would live out his remaining days alone. He'd tried to remarry, but his words came out jumbled and Charlotte Powell, her manner firm but kind, said no. Since then, he was reluctant to try again.

In the meantime, he and Carter had a lot of work to do to get the ferry back to running condition and to figure out what happens next. Regret panged him that he had suggested one of his children could be involved. This was the first time he needed his son, and even though he knew that's how families worked, he was ashamed. This "getting old" business was for the birds.

Ozzie remembered when he arrived in Kettle Rapids from Missouri. He came by train and then by coach, with not much more than his clothes and a deed to land he'd never seen. Kettle Rapids looked so small to him then, but the town had been his whole world ever since. In its heyday, Kettle Rapids had grown to over one hundred blocks of residences and businesses. There was an airport and a brick plant, two small hotels, a pool hall, and eight family-owned mercantiles. To the west, the town was bordered by river shoreline peppered with ferry operations like his own. To the east, the land followed a steady incline into a timbered ridge that loomed above the town and beyond for a few miles south until it broke open and gave onto rolling farms and orchards.

Ozzie hummed softly along with the radio, remembering easier times with his wife, when he would take her out for a night of singing and dancing.

Ona opened her eyes for a moment—he had disturbed her— looked out the window to see where they were, and then settled back against the door.

He would get to the bottom of it, for himself, for them all. People talked about him being hot headed, but what they forgot was it sometimes takes fire to make things happen.

He pulled up the drive and past the massive ponderosa in the front yard, the house looking unusually quiet in the dark.

Carter sat at the table with Lloyd, breathless and tired from his twenty-mile trek from Mae's through the night. Lloyd's kids would be up in a few hours, two little boys, one less than school age, the other toddling.

Lloyd yawned, his face stretching wide. "Coffee?"

Carter nodded, looking down, and noticed the scrapes on his own knuckles.

Lloyd rustled behind him by the stove, tinkering with a kettle Marie must have put there before Carter arrived.

"You here for a Christmas visit on your way to go ice fishing," Lloyd nodded toward Carter's tackle bag. "Or you want to tell me about it?"

Carter wasn't sure where to start. He stared at the surface of the table, its wood grooved and scratched from years of use. It probably belonged to one of their parents' before they brought it here. Launching in seemed the only way to go. "I don't know what to do about Mae. This divorce business. The house." He stopped, his thoughts jumbling.

Lloyd waited to see whether Carter would go on. The pause let Carter's mind run through the events of the night.

"Look, Carter, I don't know who knocked you around last night or who you knocked around, but that business with Mae was never a good situation for you."

"I know."

"I know you know, but you don't act on it."

"She's my wife."

"*Was* your wife. You have to push that ember deep enough to where it stops sending up smoke."

Carter stared out the kitchen window to the snowy front yard. It was impossible to imagine ever getting her out of his head, even though it would be the relief he needed. The sun would come up soon, its yellow light streaking brightly across every glimmering surface it could find, dark shadows lurking underneath.

Christmas morning, Charlotte walked the edge of the orchard along the gravel road, checking the trees. A light dusting of snow squeaked under her boots, and she pulled her heavy wool coat tighter over her overalls and her cloche hat down over her ears, a plaid scarf looped around her neck. Her place was far enough from the main road that cars rarely happened by, so when the patrol car rounded the corner, she knew the sheriff was coming to see her.

He pulled up alongside her, got out, and stood next to his car, his breath pooling in the chill air.

"What brings you by, Bill?" she asked.

"Dustup at Mae Price's place last night," he said. "Wondering if you might have seen or heard anything."

"Can't say that I have," she lied, but indeed she had. It was well after dark by the time she turned the Lincoln toward home the night before. She knew a little of the Price boy's scandal with his wife. Everyone did. She didn't like to get into anyone else's business any more than she wanted anyone in her own, but when he'd moved back in with his father, tongues wagged all over town. When she saw him in the driveway at their place on her way home, she had a bad feeling. Who was she to pry? For all she knew, they were reconciling again like they had so many times.

When she unloaded her empty crates in the driveway, the gully between her property and theirs amplified shouts and then the report of a rifle that set her dog into a fit of barking.

"Everyone okay?" she asked.

"Shaken up is all," he said. "If you see Carter around these parts, could you tell him I'd like to talk to him? His father hasn't seen him since yesterday afternoon."

Poor Oscar. He must find the whole kit and caboodle embarrassing. For someone who wasn't good at avoiding gossip, he sure took it personally. Did his kids know about his proposal? Had she been the only one to get the offer? She never told another soul, so as not to embarrass him further.

"Carter doesn't come around here really," she said, relieved the situation wasn't as dire as it could have been. She wasn't sure why she didn't tell the sheriff. Would it have mattered? Would it possibly make a lick of difference that she heard what he already knew? She wasn't interested in covering for the Price boy-- or his wife, for that matter-- but she didn't want to get involved.

"How you doing? You holding up okay?" he asked.

"I manage," she said.

"You staying warm? You got someone who can chop firewood for you?"

"I can chop my own wood, Bill," she smiled; and he chuckled.

"All right. You have a good one."

After the sheriff was out of sight, Charlotte whistled for the dog, who bounded over expectantly, and they walked down the hill to the main road. At Mae Price's place, Charlotte paused, looking for signs from the night before. No cars in the drive. An empty booze bottle sat in the snow next to the door. No life stirring that she could see.

Carter slept on Lloyd's couch while his cousin tended his dairy cows. He hadn't slept for long when Lloyd's young sons woke up, excited for Christmas and presents, but at least it was some rest.

The boys made it all the way through presents and breakfast, and Carter wondered if he should wait for the sheriff to find him or if he should try to move on. He'd have to face him at some point or another.

He and Lloyd saw the patrol car coming down the drive long before it arrived at the house.

Lloyd kept his voice low so he wouldn't alarm the boys. "You want to have this chat? Or do you need to be going?"

Carter looked out the kitchen window, watching the car approach the house. "He'll keep looking."

Lloyd nodded and filled up his coffee cup. "Your call," he said.

Carter tried to measure up what his options were. He could sneak out the back door and hide in the woods until the sheriff left, but eventually he'd have to go home. It seemed easiest not to have it hang over his head.

He and his cousin watched as the car pulled up to the front steps, and the sheriff got out, a lithe man in his fifties they'd known all their lives.

Lloyd answered the door. "Merry Christmas, Bill."

"Same to you, thank you. I'm here on business today, though, Lloyd. Looking for your cousin Carter. He here?"

Lloyd looked back over his shoulder at Carter, and Carter nodded to him.

Marie watched as the boys played with their new loot on the living room carpet, oblivious to what was happening in the kitchen.

"He is. C'mon in and have a cup of coffee with us."

"All right," Bill said as he crossed into the kitchen, taking off his hat. "Marie," he said, taking in the boys and reaching out for the cup of coffee Lloyd handed him. The three of them sat at the kitchen table, and Bill smiled at Carter, a kind of fatherly, pitying smile.

Carter didn't know what to say, and a part of him hoped

maybe this was about something else, but he knew the chances of that were slim.

"Looks like you got the better end of things," Bill said, looking over Carter's purple jawline.

"That so?" Carter asked.

"You gave the missus quite a scare," Bill went on. "What were you doing there exactly?"

Carter glanced at the kids, making sure they weren't paying attention.

"Picking up some tools," he lied.

"In the middle of the night?"

Carter shrugged.

"Well, from her perspective, her deranged ex-husband fired a rifle at her for no apparent reason."

"Is that what she said?"

"Pretty much. Pretty much. Don't blame her."

"That is not how it happened." Carter stared at the surface of the table. It had been a while since he felt like a little kid getting a lecture from an authority figure.

"Well, you'll have plenty of opportunity to tell your side of things. "

"You going to take me in?"

Bill sighed and looked out the window. "I've been trying to decide about that," he said. He looked back to the boys on the living room carpet, pushing their toy cars around making quiet motor noises. "I'd like to be home with my family today. I spoke with your father this morning, and I'm betting he'd like to have you home too."

"Is she pressing charges?"

"Right now she plans to, yes, but come next week, who knows?"

"What do you want me to do?"

"You have a telephone here?"

Lloyd shook his head no.

"Tell you what. I'll let your father know you're here, and then seeing as it's Christmas, let's be home with our families today, on the condition that you come down to the station after the holiday weekend of your own volition, and we talk things through. Can you do that?"

Carter looked over Bill's face. He looked tired and disappointed in his life. Carter felt bad adding to the dismay he must encounter every day, but he said, "Sure," knowing full well as the word came out of his mouth that he had no intention of actually following through with it.

Carter and Lloyd watched the sheriff walk back to his car in the cold and drive off down the highway.

Marie looked at Lloyd with intent. "My folks will be by soon," she said. "I best get the food started."

Carter wondered if the time had come for him to get scarce, but Marie called over to him, "You're staying for dinner, I hope."

While Marie dressed a pot roast that would cook all afternoon and Lloyd started a fire for her in the kitchen stove, Carter flopped on the rug and showed the boys how to build a blockade with Lincoln Logs and then ram it down with their new toy trucks. The dog snuffed its cold, wet nose next to Carter's chin, and when he gasped in surprise, the boys shrieked with laughter.

"She's making sure you're one of the good guys."

"Oh yeah?" Carter stacked logs back into a blockade with help from the boys. "What's the verdict?"

"You have to look at her to tell."

Carter looked over his shoulder at her. The dog, a spaniel, with auburn ears and speckles on her white coat, stood back, her mouth open in a drooling smile, her tail wagging slowly.

"She thinks you're okay."

"That's a relief."

Lloyd leaned in the archway between the kitchen and living room, smiling quietly at them, rubbing the soot from his hands onto a ragged towel.

"Carter, you want to join me in the barn?"

Lloyd's barn was a place anyone would want to be. For years during Prohibition, he kept a homemade wine barrel there, big enough to keep himself and his friends in libations when they had occasion. He built a bar area with a card table, chairs, and a pipe-vented woodstove. Out here, no one bothered him, least of all the sheriff, who'd been known to make a visit to the barn himself.

Lloyd and Carter bundled up, and the dog padded along with them, her ears alert as if they were on an errand of grave importance. Even though it was still early, the sky was dark and gray, and the pine trees were silhouettes against the clouds.

Inside the barn, Carter pulled off his gloves and rubbed his hands together, the quickening of blood warming his skin. The cows shuffled in their stalls, and Lloyd stoked up the fire he kept going in the barn to warm the cows. The room glowed a wheat gold, and, down the stretch of stalls, honey-colored Jersey faces peered at them, huge brown eyes black in the dimness, noses raised and curious.

It was more than a year since the ban on alcohol had been officially repealed, but it was still gratifying to enjoy something you'd made yourself.

"It might not be past noon," Lloyd said, "But what the hell, it's Christmas." He set a small cup of homemade wine in front of Carter, and the firelight twinkled in the burgundy liquid.

"Was that a toast or a prayer?" Carter asked.

"Maybe a little of both."

The dog collapsed protectively at Lloyd's feet, and he stroked her ears. Carter took a sip. A cow murmured deep in the barn, and the dog looked alert for a moment, then settled her head back on her paws.

"Do you think the water will come up this high?" Carter asked Lloyd, as he took a sip.

"Hard to say."

"Isn't that unsettling for you?"

"Some. I built it before, I can build it again."

Carter was impressed by his confidence.

"What about Marie? That must really have her turned out."

"She knows I'll take care of us."

Carter thought about this for a moment. Had he taken care of Mae? Had she told him to leave because she didn't have confidence in him like that anymore?

"At least she believes in you," Carter said.

"Are we still talking about me?"

Carter smiled and stared into his wine, took a sip. "I suppose not."

"You and Mae, that was…it was different."

"How do you mean?"

"I know you were happy in the beginning. You were so proud of the hard work you and your Dad did to pay for and build that house for her. Did she even want it?" Lloyd was quiet for a moment, scratching the dog behind her ears, like he was thinking of the right words. "In the end, there was never any place besides each other to aim your focus. Marie and I, we have the boys and the cows and the house. There's always been something else we have to work on together. It changes things when you're supporting lives."

Carter nodded, but the truth was, he'd never been responsible for a life other than his own, and Mae's, to some extent. "Don't you ever wish it was you two?" he asked.

Lloyd grinned, the dog at his feet, the rows of dove-eyed cows behind his back. "Not a bit," he said. "What could be better than this?"

When he put it like that, it did make all of Carter's anguish seem petty and small, like the thin strip of hay floating on the surface of his wine.

Lloyd cleared his throat. "You were wrong to go over there, and you were wrong to do what you did. But at the same time, she's not so right either. It's always been that way with you two. You do something, she retaliates, you fight to get her back, she plays hard to get, and then you start it up all over again. I'm surprised you two don't have a string of kids from every reconciliation."

Carter swirled his wine, watching the piece of hay spin.

"She might drop the charges from this recent episode," Lloyd went on, "but at some point, you're going to have to move on with your life. You can't keep sniffing around until you work yourself up so much that you put yourself in jail. I know you care about her, but sometimes I think it's more your pride than love that takes her back. You don't want to lose her because you don't want to lose."

"What am I going to do, Lloyd, keep living with my dad?"

"Is it that bad? Everyone's hard up right now, you're not alone in that."

"How am I going to start over again like that?"

"You just do."

"Maybe *you* do. I don't know if I do."

"You thinking about heading up to the dam?"

"Would you hate me if I did?"

"Hate you? Why would I hate you?"

"My dad will."

"They're going to flood the river whether you work on it or not."

"He says I'm not cut out for hard work anymore."

"Well, I guess that's for you to decide, not him."

"You make it sound so easy."

Lloyd searched his face. "It sort of *is* easy, Carter. So you had a rough spell. Everyone does eventually. At some point you have to decide what you want and set your mind to getting it and never look back. What does it even mean to be 'cut out' for something? You can change what you're made of. I wasn't born knowing how to tend cows or get a teething baby to stop crying. I had to learn those things. The best test is how you respond to a situation, not how you got there. It doesn't matter if you're rich, poor, strong, weak; it matters what you do with what you have in front of you."

The dog raised her head and barked as if in agreement. Then car doors slammed, and commotion and voices came from the driveway.

"That would be the in-laws," Lloyd said with a grin.

"Should we go in?"

"Guess we better," Lloyd said, draining his wine.

The rest of the day was spent with family coming in and out, more presents, the kids tearing paper, their faces damp and pink. There was so much food, and Lloyd's wine mixed with mulling spices. Lloyd's parents—Carter's aunt and uncle—came by, and Marie's older brother with his family. Carter ate like he wouldn't get a square meal again for a while, which he knew he indeed might not. When he finally collapsed on the living room sofa under a cool patchwork quilt, he was full and warm and exhausted. For a moment, he'd been able to suspend worry about what he would do next.

In the early morning, Lloyd nudged Carter awake and handed him a cup of coffee. It was dark outside and even the kids were still asleep.

His cousin sat in the armchair next to the couch.

"So what do you think?"

"Think about what?"

"You paying the sheriff a visit today like you said?"

Carter blinked, trying to wake up, the wine from the night before still fogging his brain. "I don't know yet."

"C'mon, get up. Come help me with the cows."

In the barn, Lloyd shut the doors quietly behind them. The cows stirred awake.

"Start a fire in the stove. Not too big," he told Carter.

Carter pulled kindling from the box next to the stove and broke it up with his hands while his cousin made the rounds with the cows. Lloyd talked to them gently like they were small children, and they nuzzled him and stepped softly out of his way.

When Carter was done and the fire started to crackle, Lloyd called him over to a work shelf along the back wall.

"I don't know what your plans are, but as far as I'm concerned and as far as I'm going to say to Marie or anyone else who asks, you headed back home this morning."

"Okay," Carter nodded.

"I feel bad we didn't have a Christmas present for you yesterday, so I want to give you some things to take with you."

From a low shelf, Lloyd pulled a small tent, a rolled up sleeping mat, and a folded wool blanket that was peppered with animal hair and hay. "These will do you well during fishing season," he said. "Do you have a good hatchet for firewood?"

Carter shook his head no.

"I have a spare one you should take," Lloyd plucked a small ax from where it hung suspended on two nails hammered into the wall above the bench. It looked a little dull, but it would fit easily into his tackle bag. "You have a gutting knife?"

Carter nodded yes.

"That's good," Lloyd stood with his thumbs hooked in his pockets, looking around the work bench thinking of what else Carter might need for the road.

"You're going to need this," he said, pulling a new flashlight from his work bench. "To see where you're going."

He handed it to Carter, then dug deeper into the shelf. "Take this knapsack to carry everything. You can bring it back later."

Carter loaded up the knapsack. "You think I'll be okay out there?"

Lloyd squeezed Carter's shoulder. "Of course I do. Let's get you some leftovers and get you on your way before the rest of them get up and start asking questions."

The road south down the river was a path Carter knew well. Over the course of his life, he had watched the tree line of ponderosa pines grow and fall along the narrow, winding highway, dotted with small towns, barely more than a handful of houses, people he'd known or met at one point or another. In the dark and the snow, the houses scattered along the road, tiny plumes of smoke rising from their chimneys. He wondered how many of them would be gone once the reservoir filled. The glow of fires in their windows against the deep blue of the early morning reminded him of illustrations on Christmas cards, like the kind his mother used to hang on a red string pinned above the fireplace.

Carter looked up at the shaggy treetops, black against the purple morning. Snow crunched under his boots. He couldn't see many stars; the cloud cover having gathered in the night. He gripped the flashlight Lloyd gave him in his pocket, not ready to use it yet. He wanted to preserve the battery until he got to places he didn't know from memory. Its metal case felt cold against his palm. He was alone now, walking through the landscape he'd known all his life into the unknown.

CHAPTER 5
December 1935

After leaving his cousin's home, Carter walked south along the highway as it followed the Columbia downriver. He found an abandoned barn to sleep in his first night. His daylight hours for walking were few this time of year, and he spent as much time by his fire as he did making progress down the road. It had been cold since he left his cousin's home forty miles upriver, and fresh show made his sleeping conditions, whether in the tent and by a fire or in whatever shelter he could find, much less practical. At least he still had his father's coat for warmth and Christmas leftovers to ration. He'd walked nearly sixty miles altogether since he left his father's house on Christmas Eve, and his boots started to rub places on his feet they never bothered before. The events of the last few weeks swirled in his mind as he walked.

Now it was dusk, and Carter stood where the main highway intersected the road that dropped into a shallow, snow-covered valley and then vanished into a point in the farmland upriver. His boots were coated in fresh snow, and his toes were numb from the cold.

From his vantage point above the valley, he could see a large white gate on the edge of the farm road barely outlined against the snow. He walked the few yards off the highway to read the sign over the gate: *Fort Spokane, Washington Territory, 1880.* He had heard of the abandoned fort but never seen it. The fort might at least have some buildings left for shelter.

He looked around as he passed through the gate, his boots crunching in untrammeled snow. The buildings were shrouded in heaps of white at their bases, and flakes cascaded lightly around him, melting like tears on his cheeks and making a white crust on his shoulders. He was several yards down the long drive before he recognized the smell of campfire. Looking around the fort, he saw lights in the windows of some of the buildings and realized other people had the same thought he did. There were people living in the abandoned fort.

The fort was built on a ridge above tribal fishing grounds, and Carter remembered his father describing it as a boarding school for Native American children that closed several years back, during the Great War. When the troops left the fort, the army first renovated it as a military hospital and then brought children by edict from their homes on the reservations to educate them. The buildings reflected the transitional uses of the place, of lands taken, traditions lost, and livelihoods stolen: a hospital building, a run-down chapel, stables, and on the far side, a row of surprisingly fine officer's houses.

"Help you, sir?" Carter turned around startled. An older man stood behind him, his face barely visible between the broad brimmed hat pulled down low over his forehead and the swath of whiskers that ringed his chin, peppered with crumbs of snow. In the fading light, Carter could see bright orange from the lights throughout the fort flicker in the man's eyes. He was dressed in work clothes, layered with flannel, and loosely held a rifle with the barrel pointed toward the ground, reminding Carter of his altercation with Mae and Roy. Even though this man was armed, his nonchalance with his weapon put Carter at ease.

"Looking for a place to stay the night," Carter said.

"Where you headed?"

"Not sure yet. Looking for work, I guess."

The man grunted and pushed his hat back off his forehead. Carter smelled the sweat and oil in the man's hair on the wind, tinged with the smell of freeze that was dull to Carter's senses from spending days and nights outside.

"You living here?" Carter asked.

"Seemed a shame to let it go to waste."

"And around there?" Carter nodded around the snowy perimeter of the fort.

"Folks like you, down on their luck, passing through, need a place to stay."

Carter's glance veered toward the biggest of the officer's houses across the quad from the main road. Its windows were lit up like the aurora. The man followed his gaze, but quickly looked away.

"You're welcome to pull up a spot to sleep for the night. There are some beds in the barracks, but most folks won't sleep in there since this place was a hospital for the consumptive until a few years back." The man gestured toward buildings in the distance. "Myself, I don't fear it."

It wasn't the threat of old tuberculosis in the walls that made the barracks unappealing to Carter. There was something about the place that made him uneasy at being cornered in a room with limited escape routes, but it was cold outside, and he needed a place to sleep.

As they walked through the snow up the main drive, past the empty stables and armory, Carter learned the man's name was Charlie. His grown sons were living in the family home with their wives and kids in nearby Davenport about twenty miles south. Charlie and his wife had packed up some of their belongings and equipment and come over to the fort, hoping to capitalize on the empty land.

At the barracks, Charlie showed Carter down a long hallway and left him in an empty room, the cot and all furnishings long since removed. Carter unrolled his bedroll on the hard floor and tested if he could see his breath. He couldn't. It wasn't warm by any means, but the windowless room was far back enough from the front of the building and insulated by concrete, buffering him from the cold. It felt a little like a jail cell, but after nights of sleeping in a tent, he wasn't complaining.

He lay in bed thinking about the last few weeks in Kettle Rapids. He really mucked it up with Mae this time. He was so in love when they started out, so hopeful, so ready for a new beginning. He wanted that feeling back again, wanted that sense of purpose, but he couldn't shake the realization that he had lost that for good with Mae. It all amounted to nothing, like water poured out on the ground.

Outside the barracks, he could hear laughter and a radio program coming from one of the nearby buildings. It was strange to think of people out there—he had no idea who or how many and knew nothing about them at all. He got out of bed and slipped on his boots to go see what the noises were about.

From the front porch of the barracks, Carter could see the outlines of men silhouetted in the windows of the biggest of the officer's houses. From where he stood, he could make out the tailgate of a flatbed truck around the back of the house, and for the first time, looking around the quad in the dark, he noticed that some of the fort buildings were being taken apart. Bricks and boards were missing in ways that looked deliberate, not the result of some natural calamity.

Back in his windowless room, Carter slept fitfully that night, despite having four walls around him. The images from his dreams were ominous and blurred. He didn't remember any of it clearly when he shuddered awake before sunrise, but he had the vague sense that he had taken an unpleasant tour of his own mind. He looked around the concrete room in the dark, almost tomblike in this forgotten, blanketed place, an uneasy memory from his dreams like something was wrong. He noticed this tendency in himself when Mae was planning to ask him to leave, even though he hadn't known she was planning it yet. When the circumstances of his waking life were uncomfortable or uncertain, his dreaming life was the same. He remembered once hearing someone say God created sleep as a gift. Judging by Carter's restlessness, God wasn't feeling very generous toward him these days.

Light was barely rising the next morning when Carter rolled up his sleeping mat and shoved it back into his knapsack. The sky had a dark blueness that shadowed the snow, but the trees were already backlit with the faint pink of sunrise. A goldfinch hopped on the snow outside the barracks scrounging for any food it could find. The buildings in the fort were quiet as he stole past the officer's houses along the drive. The crunch of his boots in the trampled snow and the slight rasp in his lungs from the cold sounded loud, and they echoed in his own ears.

As he approached the stables near the main gate, a movement caught his eye, and at first he thought Charlie might have found him sneaking out without a customary thank you. One of the stable doors was moving—not opening but closing—gently, in what seemed like an effort to make as little noise as possible. It closed on the personage of a young woman, fair skinned, black hair cut in a long bob, cheeks pink from the cold, dressed in jeans and a work coat like a boy, bright lavender cat-like eyes staring right at him, not as though he startled her but like she was carefully closing him out of the world she hid inside the stables, hoping he wouldn't see her.

She met his eyes and raised a finger to her lips, as though she wanted him to keep a secret. In the cold, white scenery of the dilapidated fort, her color, her vibrant eyes, reminded him of the first crocuses of spring, popping purple bursts through melting snow. He stopped, his breath fogging between them as she closed the door, holding his gaze until he couldn't see any more of her.

Back at the main highway, the road stretched ahead of Carter into the distance, and he pulled his father's coat collar up tighter to cover his freezing ear lobes. He trudged along the shoulder, his knapsack heavy, his limbs aching from nights sleeping on hard ground. He walked until almost dark, even though it was probably only a little past four o'clock. Where the road from the fort met the main highway from Spokane, he passed the sign for Davenport, where Charlie said he came from, which meant Carter had walked more than twenty miles today in the cold.

Up ahead, Carter saw the lights of a gas station on the other side of the highway. A truck with Montana license plates was parked next to one of the pumps, and several men stood around the building, their heads billowing steam as they breathed into the cold, some smoking, some leaning, talking to one another as if they were on a coffee break.

As he got closer, a few of the men looked his direction, almost suspiciously he thought, including the man he presumed was the driver, who was pumping gas.

Carter crossed the highway and approached him.

"Evening. Where you heading?"

The other men stopped their conversation and looked curiously at him.

"These fellers are off to the dam site," the driver said.

"That so?" Carter shifted the weight of his knapsack and scratched a clean spot with the toe of his boot in the gravel mixed with snow, revealing the bare frozen earth underneath.

He remembered the business card from M.J Starks he'd shoved in his wallet. Maybe this was the directional push he needed, the kind of accidental opportunity you look back on with wonder and gratitude. Or at least he hoped it might be.

"You think I could catch a ride with you?"

The man looked him over, looked at his leather tackle bag and knapsack.

"Cost you a dollar for gas money. No funny business. Everyone's on their own once we get there."

Carter dug in his pocket for a dollar coin, the cash from his dresser drawer still crumpled in his pocket and handed it to the man.

"Much obliged."

"We'll head out in a minute. I suggest you stock up." The man nodded toward the gas station building.

Carter nodded back in understanding and headed over, muttering a soft hello to the other men standing around. He hadn't anticipated a flood of workers heading to the site so early. In fact, it never crossed his mind that so many people from outside the area would be counting on work constructing the dam. It should have. Obviously, the dam needed workers, but how many he had no idea.

He bought a pack of gum and a bag of peanuts from the attendant inside the store and then stepped back outside in time to hear the driver yell, "Let's go, boys," and hang the nozzle at the gas pump.

The men climbed on the truck's bed, some leaning against the cab, some sitting along the plank walls. Carter waited until everyone else was on to throw his bags in and sat on the edge of the truck bed, his legs dangling over the road, and gripped one of the planks along the side, the smell of exhaust ripe beneath him.

The truck pulled into the highway, the men inside leaning in unison with its movement as they headed down the highway toward the construction site. Carter watched the lights of the gas station recede into the dusk behind them. He watched the dim frosted landscape change from woods to farmland. He stared behind them as they drove through miles of snowy wheat fields, flat and grey in every direction, the road cutting a straight, wet, black line down the middle.

PART 2
BLAST
AND HAUL

December 1935
Grand Coulee Dam construction site

The massive construction site on the banks of the Columbia River glowed at night. Miles of brightly lit conveyer belts that ran day and night crisscrossed the site. Generators powered enormous lamps that lit the rock walls, and sledgehammers pinged against the hard surface, echoing into the surrounding black. The night crew was on. Sheeted with ice, the high walls they broke down shimmered in the false light.

To the west of the river, atop the steep bank, the windows in the houses of the federal Bureau of Reclamation's Engineer's Town blinked while the company men sat down to dinner with their wives, nestled inside to stay warm. To the east of the river, where the shoreline was flat, the makeshift homes of Electric City, which housed the skilled workers of the Starks Company, glimmered in the dark. By design, the Starks Company built Electric City to be completely powered by electricity, both to bolster interest in the hydroelectric capabilities of the project and to placate the local power company. South of Electric City, the campfires and woodstoves of Shack Town, a shantytown where the hopefuls waited for work, sent puffs of smoke into the night.

Far above them all, a catwalk made of wood planks and suspended on steel cables crossed the 1,500-foot expanse. It connected the workers' village to the newly formed commercial district of Grand Coulee. B Street, a strip of restaurants, bars, brothels, and shops on a ridge, proliferated beyond the construction site, providing services to the men who came from all over the region looking for work. The catwalk swayed as they scurried across, squeezing past one another to get back to B Street or home to Electric City. Some of them carried bottles tucked carefully into their pockets and waistbands so as not to drop them.

A wind howled up the river, trembling the cables. The men on the catwalk, bundled up against the cold, gripped the handrails to hang on while the gust blew through and then kept moving forward. One of them slipped on the icy planks, his footing lost underneath him. His bottle of booze worked out of where he'd jammed it inside his belt and clattered on the planks, rolling as though in the bottom of a rocking boat. The men near him froze, not daring to risk their own footing to grab him. The man grasped at the cables, holding himself on, and the bottle fell the hundred feet below and splashed into the icy water beneath them. The men on the catwalk laughed in relief and moved a little more slowly the rest of the way.

CHAPTER 6
December 1935

The truck dropped Carter and the rest of the men off close to dark at the Bureau of Reclamation's administration building in Engineer's Town. The truckload of workers that Carter came to town with was not the first or only group of their sort to arrive at the site. A line of them stretched out the door of the building, waiting restlessly in the cold, wanting to know what kind of work could be had.

Carter pressed around them, trying to keep his knapsack and tackle bag out of the way, hoping to see what was happening inside the offices. The room was filled with men like him. Two tables had several rosters, and men from the project sorted the potentials. Locals on one list, Washington residents from outside the area on another. Skilled labor from out of state on one. Black men, Chinese men, and members of the local tribes on a separate list.

A man in a work shirt and suspenders blocked Carter's way. "Line starts back there," he said, pointing several yards down the crowded queue.

Carter looked down the length of the line, the haggard faces anxious for some indication of hope. In Ralph's bar, Starks said they needed people like Carter. In the meeting, Starks said men from the flooded towns would be at the top of the list.

"Mr. Starks told me to come." Carter handed the man Starks's creased business card he'd kept in his wallet.

The man in suspenders looked at the card and glanced over Carter's bags. Carter realized he must look rumpled and dirty from his days of walking and nights of sleeping on the ground since he left home. "How do you know Mr. Starks?"

"I'm from Kettle Rapids."

Carter had no idea if this would help or hurt him, but he was willing to take a chance.

The man took a clipboard from a nail on the wall.

"What's your name, son?"

"Carter Price."

The man wrote on the list. "What are you good at?"

Carter hesitated, thinking of his recent failures, and the man looked up quickly from his clipboard. "I have a long line of people here looking for work."

"I worked in the Colville mica mines, sir. And for my father's ferry business."

The man lowered his clipboard. "Go to the Starks Company offices in Electric City tomorrow, Price. See what they can do for you." He hung the clipboard back up with a sigh.

Carter wandered away from the line, trying to ignore the resentful looks shot his way. The homes around the administration building looked well kept. They lined a ridge overlooking the river and tapered up a shallow hill that butted against shimmering icy rocks. Carter rubbed his shoulders for warmth, grateful he'd taken his father's coat before he even knew he was headed this way. He wished there was a dry spot he could drop his bags to give his back a rest.

He walked toward the river to where the road met a washed-out bridge. The shore on the other side was dotted with a haphazard city of shacks, its alleys muddy and quiet.

He walked back toward the administration building. A cluster of men stood away from the line, smoking cigarettes, their breath puffs of steam and smoke.

"You fellas know where to get a drink and some food around

here?" He would have to watch his funds until he found work, but the walk had left him famished.

One of the men pointed south. "Head up to B Street," he said. "You'll find what you need there." The men snickered, smoke billowing from their mouths.

Carter walked the highway uphill and to the south, watching for cars headed that way to make sure he was on the right path, his bags feeling heavier as he walked. He followed traffic off the main highway to a bustling makeshift town.

Muddy streets, boardwalk sidewalks, falling down establishments propped up against each other. It reminded him of the frontier stories his father used to tell him. A round sign with the words Silver Dollar Club & Cafe written in neon caught Carter's eye, behind it a painted sign for Reno Rooms. He pushed the door open into a long, narrow tavern, the din of conversation coming from men and women clustered at the bar. Tinsel hung from the rafters and bright signs for Olympia and Rainier beer lined the wall behind the bar. An archway into a back room was painted with the words Free Dancing.

Carter ordered a whiskey and sat down, dropping his bags to the floor. The bartender was a short, stout man with a large green bow tie, dark against his light-colored shirt.

"What's a Reno Room?" Carter asked him. "Rooms to let?"

The bartender nodded. "New in town?" He wiped his hands on a towel and then folded it neatly on the bar.

"How much?"

"Five cents a night by yourself. Twenty-five cents includes dinner and a dance. A bit extra if you would like me to arrange the company of a lady overnight."

Carter laughed and took a swig of his whiskey. "Sign says dancing is free." The bartender shrugged. Carter wasn't about to burn any of his limited cash on romance.

He pushed a quarter toward the bartender, and the man gave him a key. "Dinner's at six," he said. "Dancing starts at seven."

The rooms were up a flight of poorly built stairs on the outside of the building. Carter's room was barely bigger than a closet with a cot in it. He tossed his bags in the corner. No stove to keep him warm, but at least he had a place to sleep. He lay down on the cot and pulled the small wool blanket around his shoulders. His eyes were heavy, and his muscles twitched as they finally relaxed from his days of walking. His mind slipped into a light, restless nap, taking him into some other dim place, and he didn't want to fight it.

After about a half hour, music from the Silver Dollar Club woke him, and he wandered back toward the bar for dinner, the evening dark and chilly already. A sharp wind picked up at the top of the ridge above the river, and it penetrated his hair and ears.

Inside, the place was packed with women and men jockeying for a spot at the bar. Carter showed his key, and the bartender slid a plate with a baked potato, bread, and thin slices of beef to him. It wasn't the most remarkable meal he'd ever had, but he was hungry enough to forget his table manners.

When he was nearly done eating, he felt a tap on his shoulder. "Ready for your free dance, mister?"

A woman stood there, blond hair curled around her face, her lips a brilliant red. She was pretty, but he could think only of Mae, her face burning with anger as she threw his rifle into the yard.

He shook his head, embarrassed. The last thing he wanted to deal with was a woman right now, even if it was an uncomplicated tryst. She shrugged and walked away.

Dancing couples bumped against him as the music swelled and the place filled beyond capacity. Tired, Carter wandered out into the snowy gravel road. Men moved quickly through the night, their faces obscured with layers to protect them from the cold.

Two men burst out of one of the bars grappling and slugging each other, pursued by their hollering friends. Cars careened down the uneven, muddy ruts, their headlights cutting frantic swaths across the neon and shining metal signs that peppered the storefronts.

At the end of the road, men poured off a rickety plank catwalk that extended by cables into the dark. Carter walked over to where it attached to the edge of the ridge and stared mesmerized by the sight below. Under the ridge, a vast expanse of brilliant lights and conveyers lit up like a sparkling night city from another planet, the men on the catwalk high above it mere shadows wavering in and out of the dark.

Back in his room, the noise from the club below was like sleeping under wind-shivered conifers. The murmurs from the bar, the muttering of a running river. Their consistent din lulled him to a warm, soft sleep.

Ozzie sat at his typewriter, staring at the keys. *It may interest you to know that no one has claimed credit for sabotaging the Kettle Rapids ferry I operate, a fact I find very suspicious.*

Since the *Colville Scintilla* covered the incident, he included them in his letter rotation, making sure to keep them apprised of any goings on in town. Ona was in the other room listening to the radio while she did her homework, and the noise distracted him. He knew if he asked her to turn it down, she would roll her eyes and ignore him.

He had little doubt where his son had gone. The sheriff came by early Christmas morning looking for Carter and told Ozzie the story. Ona was radiant in her pageant the night before, her cheeks flushed as she sang with her choral group from school. He was so proud to see his singing voice live on in her and hated to see her crestfallen face when the patrol car pulled up to the house the next day. Her moments never got to last long, poor thing.

Ozzie hadn't bothered to go see Lloyd. They were all grown men now. What could he say? Besides, his wife's family always made Ozzie a little nervous. He felt beneath them.

He rattled his fingertips idly across the keys, looking for words to come. He could try to remove himself all he wanted from what he assumed was Carter's decision, but the fact remained that if Carter was at the dam site, they were on opposite sides.

He wished Ona would turn the radio down. He walked down the hall and looked in at her. She stared intently at her notebook, her blond curls falling around her face. He couldn't bear to ask her.

"I'm going to the ferry landing," he said.

"Okay," she answered without looking up.

His long winter coat was missing from the closet. He figured Carter must have taken it when he wandered off wherever he was. Ozzie wore his old pea coat over his work overalls, an army green knit scarf wound around his neck and ears, and a matching knit cap to keep his balding scalp warm. He let himself in through the white gate he'd pieced back together and to which he'd tacked a Closed for Repairs sign. His boat was still chained to the landing where Carter left it. It strained with a groan against the river's current. The longer it sat without generating money, the harder it would be to find the funds to fix it. And was it worth it, if all this would be gone soon anyway? What was he trying to restore?

He started over once before, but he was a young man then, about his son's age. He had resilience and hope back then. How was he going to launch his daughter into the adult world without an income?

While he hadn't been the biggest fan of Mae, he turned a blind eye when Ona started approaching her about women things after her mother died. What could he do? Try to handle it himself? He tried to encourage Ona to reach out to Lloyd's wife, Marie, but she was farther away, had kids of her own, and Lloyd was related on Ozzie's wife's side of the family.

He could see that Ona felt shut off from her one adult female resource in Mae, but he was unsure about Mae's influence on his daughter in the long term.

Long term. Those words stuck in his craw in a new way these days. How dare they lecture him about the long term. He was a father and businessman. The only thing he ever thought about was the long term.

Ozzie realized he was staring off into the river, its current rushing as swift and haphazard as his thoughts. He picked up stray branches that had fallen from the trees and lay in green swags across the front of the landing.

Carter had left the canoe upright on the shore, and it collected snow and pine needles. Ozzie shoveled it out, turned it over, and dragged it up behind the dock. Though he taught his son how to do things right, Carter was still careless.

Tires crunched behind Ozzie on the snow. A dark Packard pulled up the drive cautiously. Ozzie watched the car approach. He must have forgotten to close the gate behind him. He tried to motion to the driver that he wasn't taking people across, but the car kept coming, then stopped.

The driver's side door opened slowly, and M.J. Starks got out and stood quietly next to his car. He was without his usual entourage of security and company men, wearing an expensive-looking brown wool coat that shrouded him against the snow.

"What do *you* want?" Ozzie asked throwing the branches he held onto the ground in case he needed free fists.

"To talk," Starks said. He was wearing his usual homburg hat, his mustache neatly combed.

"What's there to talk about? You already shut down my business."

"I assure you I had nothing to do with this."

"Yeah? Maybe not directly, but you got the town riled up. Even if it wasn't you or your guys, you incited this with your fancy talk at that meeting." Ozzie waved an angry hand in the air.

"If that's true, I'm very sorry for it," Starks said, his hands in his pockets, shoulders and voice relaxed. "I meant what I said in that meeting, but I certainly did not intend for my words to be so divisive."

Ozzie shoved his fists in the pockets of his coat. Starks had not come to fight.

"Well, maybe you should have come here and found out what was happening before you showed up with your hullabaloo speech."

"Fair enough," Starks said, looking out toward the river where Ozzie's boat strained between its tether and the current.

"Is that all you came here to say?" Ozzie asked.

Starks chuckled. "No," he said, looking around the property, the dock, the small building and storage shed, his tone hesitant.

Ozzie was curious. Starks hadn't struck him as the kind of man to be tentative, so he waited for him to start in on whatever he'd come here for.

"I want to make you an offer," Starks said.

"An offer?"

"Yes, for this." Starks nodded around the property.

"I'm waiting for my offer from President Roosevelt." Ozzie squinted at him, his heat rising again.

"I understand."

Starks rocked on his toes and looked like he was trying to remember how he'd rehearsed what he wanted to say.

"Spit it out," Ozzie said. "No use flouncing around about it."

Starks smiled. "You really are one to cut to the chase, aren't you? I like that about you."

"Yes, get to it already."

"Very well, I want to better the federal government's offer. I'm prepared to give you double whatever they pay you."

Ozzie was suspicious. "Better it? How can you double it if I don't know what it is yet?"

"How about you tell me what you want for this," Starks motioned around the property, "and any other land you stand to lose in the river?"

Ozzie knew well enough that Starks would not be making this kind of offer to him without a motive.

"In exchange for what?"

"Your silence," Starks said. "Your compliance."

"Go to hell," Ozzie said, his fists popping out of his pockets again.

"I don't want to see any more agitation. I want the project to go smoothly, and you can help with that."

"I'm not the cause of the agitation. You are."

"Are you sure about that?"

Ozzie let out an exasperated scoff, shaking his head.

"Mr. Price, look, your business isn't going to recover," Starks said. "The dam is getting built whether you want it to or not. Save us both some headaches and take the money." He paused to gauge Ozzie's reaction. "Go build a new life somewhere else for you and your children. Be at peace with this."

Ozzie may have felt some waffling impulses since Carter left, but he was not about to be bested by this man.

"No."

"Please reconsider."

"I will not."

"My offer won't last forever. I hope you'll feel differently before I leave town."

"Screw you."

Starks got back in his car, gave Ozzie one last look, and then backed down the drive until Ozzie couldn't see his car anymore.

Ona watched from the living room window as a Packard drove up the long drive to the house. It might be the fanciest car she'd ever seen, and she wondered what in the heck it was doing driving up to their house. When it stopped out front, she peeked out the front door, opening it enough to see out.

Mr. Starks from the meeting got out of the front seat and stood at the bottom of the porch stairs.

"He's not home," Ona said. She was dressed warm in a cream-colored sweater, a green plaid wool skirt, and thick stockings, her shoes kicked off somewhere inside the house.

"You don't need to be afraid of me," Starks said.

"He's down at the landing," she said, music from the radio playing inside the house. "You can find him there."

"Yes, I know. I just spoke with him," Starks said, placing a foot on the bottom stair and leaning against the railing. "I came to see you, actually,"

She looked at him suspiciously. "What would you want to see me for?" she asked, her cheek resting on the wood door, hand still holding the knob as though she would shut him out at any wrong choice of words.

"You seem like a reasonable young woman," Starks said. "A young woman with some ambition and sense about the world. A young woman who maybe wants something better than to live in a small town in the middle of nowhere."

Ona's grasp on the door loosened, and she searched his face, then unsure of his intent, started to close the door.

"I came here to make you an offer," Starks called out to her before she could close him out.

Ona stopped and looked at him again. "Well, I'm listening."

"I need your help persuading your father to leave my project alone."

"And you think he'll listen to me."

"I think he cares that you're safe and happy, yes."

She stared off into the trees, her cheek pressed against the door frame. "Is that a threat?"

"Of course not," Starks softened his posture in an effort to put her at east. "Look, I offered to double his offer from the federal government if he agrees to leave my project alone, and he adamantly declined. You should understand though, if he takes my payout now, you could move someplace else, maybe someplace bigger, with more opportunity for a young woman like you. He'll have money again, enough to last at least a little while. And how much longer will you be at home? One year? Two years?"

"Three," she said. "I'm fifteen."

"Three years, that's plenty of time to get situated in a new place."

She was quiet, contemplating this.

"You said you had an offer?" she asked, finally.

Starks chuckled. "Indeed. You have your father's directness. I like that about you. Here's my offer. If you can get your father to take my payout, I'll double it. Not to him. To you. No one has to know about it unless you tell them. It's yours to use how you see fit, to get yourself out in the world when you turn eighteen. You could go to New York. Or San Francisco. Or Paris. Think about it."

Ona stared at him for a long silent while.

"You don't have to decide now," Starks said.

"I'll see what I can do," she said, squinting at him, the resemblance to her father showing.

Starks tipped his hat to her and stood away from the porch rail. "Smart gal," he said.

Ona watched from the doorway as his car backed down the long driveway and pulled out onto the main road.

CHAPTER 7
January 1936

The Starks Company gave Carter a spot on a blasting crew because of his experience in the Colville mica mines. They pointed him to their bunkhouses in Electric City and told him about Shack Town, south of the job site, where workers set up shanties and campsites, should that be his preference.

The bunkhouse building reminded him of his night at Fort Spokane. He'd only glimpsed life at the fort briefly, but something about the place stuck in his mind. The men at the officers' house. The woman in the barn as he snuck out. This place, though, with its long room of rumpled cots and the constant traffic of men in and out of the mess hall, seemed to offer a life like the one he'd had at home when his mother was alive, as though the business of living was at hand. He welcomed it but wondered how long he could afford to stay there, his room and board about the same as his paychecks. At least he had a warm dry place to sleep and three square meals a day.

The jobs at the dam followed a hierarchy—not only pay, but housing options and the level of respect you got among the workers. At the bottom were the gravel rakers. At the top were the engineers from the Bureau of Reclamation, who lived in their own town of perfectly arranged houses on the bluff overlooking the construction site. In between were the workers from the Starks Company: the concrete pourers, the blasters, the carpenters who built the conveyer system, the men who scaled cables to install suspension bridges to carry construction supplies across the wide expanse of the Columbia.

Carter's crew foreman was a fit, tanned man in his forties, muscles sinewed in his arms and neck from years of physical work. The crew called him Soop, short for supervisor, and he had a slight accent like he'd come from someplace back east. He most recently came from the massive Hoover Dam project in Nevada, along with many others who had relocated, looking for skilled work now that the Nevada project was nearly complete.

On Carter's first day, Soop sized him up and looked disappointed. "So you're my new pity hire, eh?" It was common knowledge among the laborers who had done this kind of work before that part of the Starks Company contract included giving precedence to workers from neighboring communities. The skilled workers who waited for an assignment resented what they saw as favoritism.

Carter wasn't about to pass up a chance to improve his situation on principle though. If giving him higher priority was compensation for flooding his hometown, he wasn't going to tell anyone he was glad to see it all go.

There were two others on the same crew—a younger guy with light hair and freckles, and a Native American man who looked like he was around Carter's age. Soop pointed to the latter. "Joe Mainzer here is our dynamite man, and you two," he said, pointing to Carter and the young guy, "do what we tell you and try not to get killed."

A lump of apprehension knotted in Carter's stomach. He hadn't banked on getting killed as an option.

"Rules are: Don't keep your crewmates waiting. Don't show up hungover. Keep your rope tied to the person ahead of you. Stay out of Engineer's Town. You can drink and fuck all you want on B Street on your own time, but on my time, you will focus on the job." Soop tapped his forehead with two fingers to illustrate the point. "In spring it gets muddy, in summer it gets dusty, in the fall it gets muddy again, but for now, everything is frozen, and you will be too if you fall in."

Blasting off the rock overburden on the bedrock was the first order of business. The site for the dam was chosen for its geologic history. A natural ice dam had wedged itself between two high rock walls during the Ice Age making an ideal spot to construct a massive concrete barrier big enough to block the largest, unruliest river in the West. To make the plans for the dam work, though, they would use dynamite to blow off huge sections of loose surface rock that couldn't hold the weight of the dam. The bedrock underneath was strong enough to support the tons of concrete needed. That's where Joe Mainzer came in.

Carter learned from the younger guy, Reynolds, that Mainzer was from the Colville reservation across the river, but he was a member of the Palouse tribe relocated many years ago from their traditional territory hundreds of miles away. Joe worked on the Nespelem roads projects and had experience clearing rock with explosives. Most of the men steered clear of him, some simply because he was from the reservation or, worse as they saw it, a Native American potentially taking work away from a white man. For some, his presence at the dam was rumored to have caused bad feelings for his own people. Some distrusted him because Mainzer refused to drink alcohol, and that could be off-putting for those who liked to drink too much on B Street. From what Carter could see at the work site, Mainzer seemed pleasant enough and skilled at his work.

Joe Mainzer did not wear his hair long and braided like the Colville people Carter remembered growing up in Kettle Rapids. Instead, Joe had thick black hair, cut short and slicked back with pomade, which didn't keep it from sticking out in the back. Strands came loose as he worked and swung forward around his face. His eyes were light brown, and next to his dark hair and skin, they looked bright. Anytime they were off duty, Joe kept a pistol tucked in his back waistband, where it swung with his gait, still another reason many of the other workers avoided him.

Reynolds came from Gifford, one of the other river towns near Kettle Rapids that would be flooded. He reminded Carter of himself years ago—hopeful, not disappointed yet.

Every day, the three of them scaled a piece of the rock together, packed it with dynamite, scaled back down, and blew a cloud of rock into the air.

At the end of each day, Soop reminded them they were only there because of his good graces and pointed to the long line of men waiting. "Laid off more than one hundred men since we started. Weather gets too cold? Permits get delayed? Funding gets cut? I shave my crew. Work picks back up? That's when I weed out the weak ones."

The work wasn't that different from the job Carter had in the Colville mica mines. When he was saving to build Mae a house, he spent months at a time at the mine camps. He had been good at that work until the accident, and he forgot how strange it was being the new man on the job. He'd lived in Kettle Rapids all his life until he went to Colville. It was hard to fathom that he couldn't go back there now without facing the sheriff, but it was also a liberating relief that not a soul here knew anything about him—liberation from the fact no one knew anything about his history or situation. He could be anyone with any story he wanted to create.

Once the surface rock was blown off to clear the bedrock, the rubble had to be loaded onto one of the long conveyor belts to move it to Rattlesnake Canyon, where all the detritus piled up. After they blasted the rock, Soop used an electric excavator to load dump trailers with the debris, and Reynolds and Carter drove them to the conveyer belt. The valley was crisscrossed by miles of the conveyer system, its catwalks lit day and night. Carter would dump his trailer onto the belt and watch the rock speed away into the distance on a long section of scaffolding.

Reynolds was surprisingly accurate with his aim, considering this was probably his first skilled job, but Carter seemed to catch the rail of the conveyer with his bumper too often, and then he'd hear it from Soop. More than once, Reynolds helped him nail back up the boards before Soop could see that Carter had knocked them down. It reminded Carter of his fence back at Mae's, which he was constantly putting back together.

Reynolds seemed like a good guy, and although he came from a town that would be impacted by the reservoir, somewhat oblivious to the strife that riddled towns like Kettle Rapids after announcements about the dam.

While they fixed one of the railings Carter had caught with the dump truck, he asked Reynolds what he thought about the possibility of his childhood home disappearing.

"It's sad, I guess," Reynolds said, looking thoughtful while he held a board in place for Carter to tack back up. "There wasn't much there to begin with, though. Hard to see it as a big loss."

Carter could relate to that. Maybe Reynolds didn't have the bad memories of his home Carter did, but he appreciated the sentiment that some things weren't worth saving and wished he could apply it to other parts of his life.

Reynolds jiggled the board to show it was solidly reattached. "Looks good. Next time I'm going to direct you back."

All around them work started to flourish. The cold eased, the ice melted, and everywhere Carter looked now, something new was being built. In the winter, everyone was worried about the river freezing, but now they were worried about high water levels from the snow melt interfering with their work. New restaurants opened, and new temporary homes went up in Shack Town. The rail tracks were laid, ready to haul supplies into all the different parts of the site. In the river, a steam-powered pile driver jacked down the pilings for a new bridge from Electric City to Engineer's Town. The Bureau of Reclamation built a warehouse along the opposite shore. Overhead, men at the end of a crane hung cables for a suspension bridge that would bring supplies to the job site on yet another set of conveyors.

The desolation of Kettle Rapids was nowhere to be seen here in this pit metropolis of steel-laying and cement-mixing. It was exactly as Starks had said. It was a new world, and one they were creating. They were taming nature, after all.

Work days were the easiest for Carter. He had a task. He walked behind Joe and did what he was told. He stood next to Reynolds and kept an eye on him to make sure he didn't get into any trouble and accepted his help directing the dump truck.

On his days off, though, he felt restless. He walked the muddy streets not knowing what to say to anyone and eventually found his way to B Street and blew money on drinks and food. He really should take care not to fritter away his wages, but what else would he do with his time?

One particularly boring Sunday, Carter bought a *Wenatchee Journal* and a *Spokane Review* at the mercantile on B Street. He hadn't read a newspaper since his father started publishing letters to the editors about the irrigation projects. Carter forgot how much he liked seeing what the rest of the world was up to. Germany planned the summer Olympics under Hitler's watch. England crowned a new king at a time of international crisis. He flipped through to the letters page. Nothing from any Prices published there.

Carter folded the paper in a much lumpier fold than he had found it and tucked it under his arm. There was a time before his marriage started to go south, before he was out of work like everyone else, before he left town to make more money to build Mae a house, when he liked to read.

He could remember winter nights at home when the fire burned down to dim coals, and he would sit up late wrapped in an old wool blanket reading books he found—banged up copies of hardbound books that made their way from bookstores in Spokane. Once he even got his hands on books by some new writers, Hemingway and Steinbeck. He'd forgotten how words could transport him from his mundane life.

A spring wind whistled around the rocks as Carter walked from B Street to the edge of the catwalk. Below, the conveyers ratcheted and squeaked as they carried detritus, depositing it in a massive pile at the end of miles of snaking, churning progress. All around him, on the catwalk, on the boardwalks of B Street, along the paved streets of Engineer's Town, speckled across the river below him in Electric City and Shack Town, everyone was after a piece of the action. The humans cranked as relentlessly as the conveyers. They drove, honked, raced, scammed, cavorted, negotiated, and waited restlessly to be part of the machine.

It was hard to know where to turn his attention. On one hand, the pace of life, the competition, was invigorating. On the other, he longed for a simpler time when he could languish by a smoldering fire with a good book and nothing else mattered. He decided his best recourse was to make a new friend.

Behind him, B Street bustled. The sun was already on its descent, and the streets were muddied and thick from rain. Carter saw Reynolds duck into a café and, holding his newspapers over his head to keep off the rain, followed him in. The place was barely more than a shack, made of plywood tacked together.

The pine floor sloped toward one corner, slick with mud from patron's shoes.

Reynolds smiled wide and waved him over. "Price! Have a seat."

Carter sat and picked up a menu, not recognizing the names of any of the dishes.

"You ever have Chinese food before?" Reynolds asked, grinning and picking up the pair of chopsticks on the table. "Tastes like flowers."

Carter had never seen anything like it, so he ordered what Reynolds ordered. It was sweet and sticky, and Carter pushed it around on his plate, trying to make sense of the utensils.

Reynolds scarfed his food down with enthusiasm. He gave Carter an affable grin. "Best food I've had in months."

"How long you been here now?"

"Six months, twelve days," Reynolds said.

"You get back home ever?"

"Not lately. No one's there anymore anyway," Reynolds picked at the last few kernels of rice on his place.

"Where'd they go?"

"My parents went back to Michigan, and my brother is out in Seattle."

"The big city. Did he find work out that way?"

"He's reading meters for the natural gas company. Says he likes it well enough. He told me to come out, but I have a good thing going here."

"Yeah, you like it? This work?"

"Better than the alternatives." Reynolds set his chopsticks down with a clatter. "You should come over to Shack Town with me tonight. Take a break from that bunkhouse you're staying in. It's a whole other world over there."

They finished their dinner and headed to the catwalk. The work lights from the conveyers twinkled below them like stars.

Reynolds jumped on the catwalk effortlessly, his boots clattering on the thick planks. Carter balked at the height.

"You'll be fine," Reynolds told him. "Look straight ahead and keep moving."

Carter tested the catwalk's sturdiness with his foot. Ahead of him, Reynolds trotted along the planks as though it were a boardwalk.

Carter put his weight on the planks, and the catwalk swayed. He gripped the steel cables that served for handrails and gaped down. From this vantage, the catwalk looked like another one of the many rickety conveyers that crisscrossed miles of river shoreline. Carter held on, frozen, the river rushing loud and fast far below.

Reynolds, several yards in front of him, turned to say something but stopped when he saw Carter paralyzed at the end of the catwalk.

"Aw, Price, don't look down, for Christ's sake."

Carter was embarrassed. Here he'd wanted to enlist the younger man's friendship and now he was stuck like a fool on the catwalk men shuttled across day and night.

He mustered his strength and moved his feet forward, willing his weight to cling as close to the planks as he could without getting down on all fours. He shuttled across, like a turtle, his hands never leaving the cables. He scuttled after Reynolds, staring straight ahead, his breath catching in his lungs until he made it to the other side.

"You did exactly what I told you not to," Reynolds said, as Carter jumped gratefully to solid ground.

"I'm fine. I'm good." Carter waved Reynolds to keep walking.

Reynolds led the way, seeming to ignore the incident, or maybe he hadn't really noticed how much the catwalk had scared Carter. He led Carter into Shack Town and down an alleyway rutted with thick mud. Reynolds stopped in front of a makeshift shed with light showing through the cracks where the boards made walls not completely knit together. Voices chattered inside and then stopped when Reynolds knocked.

Joe Mainzer's face appeared in the doorway, and the murmurs and laughter inside resumed, pouring into the dark night. To Carter's dismay, Joe looked perturbed to see them. Maybe Reynolds wasn't the ticket to breaking him into the social scene at the dam after all.

"What do you want now, kid?" Mainzer asked, the light from the break in the doorway casting a golden sheen in Joe's dark hair.

"I want in," Reynolds said.

"We cleaned you out last time," Mainzer said, opening the door a little wider. "Don't you learn?"

"Let me watch then."

Mainzer sighed. "You brought the new guy?" He nodded toward Carter.

Carter tried not to let his face give away how stupid he felt. He would give anything for the comfort of Lloyd's barn right now. He looked back to the dim blue streets of Shack Town, the dark ruts of mud, and the cold, lonely silence behind them.

"I brought whiskey for the guys," Reynolds said, flashing his coat open to reveal a bottle stashed in his inside pocket. "And a Coca Cola for you."

Mainzer let the door ease open and stepped out of the way to let them in. "Fine, but maybe sit out the first few."

Reynolds nodded, and Carter followed him sheepishly into the room, avoiding eye contact with Mainzer. Inside, a handful of men clustered around a table in the center of the room. The shack was maybe ten feet by ten feet, with a narrow cot against one wall and a small woodstove in the far corner, a long pipe fed through the roof. Kerosene lanterns hanging from the ceiling lit the room and cast wavering shadows any time someone moved their chair.

In the center of the table, books were piled next to a stack of cash. Carter wasn't sure what was going on, so he sat quietly beside Reynolds, who poured them each a whiskey.

Joe pulled two books from the stack and flipped each open to a marked page. Carter recognized a few authors from the stack: Faulkner, Orwell, Kafka.

"Will and Jake are up," Mainzer said, and the two men looked alert.

Joe let each man take a look at his page for a few minutes while everyone placed their bets on one or the other.

Reynolds leaned over to Carter. "I would put my money on Will," he whispered.

Carter watched Will as he squinted at his book.

Joe shot Reynolds a look, and the younger man shrugged. "I lost every round last time," he said to Carter.

Will stood up, setting down the dog-eared copy of Orwell's *Brave New World,* and the men who'd bet on him cheered.

Will started on a passage about remorse, that if you behaved badly, to make amends and do better next time. And not to brood or roll in the muck.

Rolling in the muck. How much of that had Carter indulged in these past several months?

As Will continued with the passage, his voice was deep and full, and his recollection of the passage was clear until he got toward the end and started losing the thread, hesitating on his words. Carter was impressed that he'd made it that far before faltering. Will's bettors cheered for him again as he sat back down.

Then Jake was up with a passage from Faulkner's *The Sound and the Fury.* It talked about hope and desire, and suspending time, not to dwell on winning or even fighting, but the revelation of man's own folly and despair. That victory is an illusion. He went on with the rest of the selection but didn't have the depth in his voice that Will had. Jake made it to the end of his passage fast, so fast that the words lost meaning.

Even though Carter used to like to read, he'd never thought about this kind of presentation before. He remembered Starks's speech and the effect it had on the town. It never occurred to him that this could be a finely honed skill. He thought of his father's booming voice and the impact Starks's skill and his father's projection together could have on a crowd.

Joe pronounced Will the winner of best recitation for his delivery, congratulated Jake for his memory, and divvied up the winnings.

Reynolds threw his hands up. "See? I could have won that one."

Joe smiled. "Yeah, if you actually bet on him. Last time, you started betting opposite yourself to stop losing."

Carter laughed. "You're a funny kid."

Reynolds looked hurt. "I've been practicing my recitation skills too."

"Not yet," Joe said, giving Reynolds a look to drop it.

Carter wondered if he would have fared better in life had he put some thought into how he said things. If he phrased it right, delivered it right, like Starks. Like the writers of these books. Like the people in this room.

The kerosene lamps cast a gold glow around the room as Will and another guy looked over the next selections Joe found for them. Carter relaxed into his chair and let the light and the sound envelop him.

The mud and frost warmed as spring wore on, and the *Wenatchee Journal* published an exposé on life around the dam. "Den of Iniquity" was the headline, and the story was full of all the seediest parts of life around B Street. The brothels in town proliferated as "pretty ladies"—enterprising women who saw an opportunity to make a living, some to bring money home to their families, some to gain independence—sought gainful employment providing companionship to the workforce at the dam. The workers laughed the story off at first, but the Bureau of Reclamation didn't like the reflection on their reputation, and rumors hit the camps and bunkhouses that there would be crack downs soon.

On their days off working for Soop, Carter and Reynolds went to Joe Mainzer's recitation club on occasion and tried to stay out of trouble on B Street at night after the new attention from the article. A new two-lane suspension bridge spanned the river, and Carter walked the long way from B Street down a road the workers nicknamed "Speedball Highway" to get across the river without taking the catwalk. He met Reynolds at the edge of Shack Town.

Reynolds grinned at him but didn't give him a hard time about taking the road instead of the shorter catwalk. Carter followed Reynolds into the dark street, and they made their way along the squishy mud road toward Joe's place.

A black police paddy wagon whizzed by and stopped at a shack across from them. Reynolds pulled Carter between two buildings.

"It's a raid," he whispered.

Five men in uniform jumped out, guns pulled, and ran inside one of the shacks. Bright lamplight poured from the wide-open door. Shouts echoed through the neighborhood. Men came out of their shacks to see what the commotion was about.

"Raid for what? Booze is legal again." Carter whispered back.

"Gambling. Prostitution. Anything to make the Wenatchee housewives who read the papers happy."

The police dragged a handful of men out in handcuffs and shoved them into the back of the paddy wagon.

"This is not an open town," one of the policemen addressed the crowd of gawkers who stood in the doorways. "There is law in this town. This is not the wild west."

The gawkers turned, murmured and laughed, and went back inside.

As work progressed, trucks came in and out every day, dumping gravel, sand, concrete mix, and unemployed workers into the construction site. They saw a worker carried out on a stretcher, and Soop reminded them to protect themselves against injuries.

Idle, desperate types hung around the edges of Shack Town and on B Street. Reynolds told Carter he saw a truck with a loudspeaker driving around Shack Town broadcasting, "Fight social diseases!" and handing out prophylactics. Reynolds offered Carter some, and Carter laughed, shaking his head.

One Sunday, Carter went to the Grand Coulee Club to listen to the president's Fireside Chat on the radio. Reactions on B Street to Roosevelt's chat promising jobs and social security were mixed. Some of the men were concerned, and some didn't say much at all but listened sadly. The grumblings around him and the reassurances of the president on the radio worried Carter about morale in Shack Town while many continued to wait for work.

Still, something about the way the president handled himself made Carter hopeful. "It will get better," he said to the man next to him, as much to convince himself as anyone.

"How you figure?" Another man near them, his clothes worn, hem of his pants fraying, asked Carter.

"He'll come up with a plan. You'll see."

The man snorted. "I have a wife at home. What am I supposed to tell her about our house?" The man shook his head and put on his hat.

Wives and houses. Carter used to have one of each himself. He wanted to believe their leaders would be able to turn things around.

The men started to file out, heads hung low, faces fallen.

A drink and a new venue sounded good to Carter at the moment. The Silver Dollar Club where he stayed his first night in town was packed and loud, with a live band and dancing. It was a rough place that made Carter nervous at times, not an easy neighborhood place like Ralph's back home. It could be easy to get lost in a crowd in B Street, unlike Electric City or Shack Town, where everyone knew each other. Carter pushed his way through the room looking for a seat or somewhere comfortable to stand. He found Joe Mainzer sitting at a table against the back wall with a tall blond woman.

"Haven't seen you on B Street in a while. I'll buy a round, if I can join you," Carter said, even though he knew Mainzer didn't drink. Mainzer shrugged at him and said something close to the woman's ear. Carter didn't take it personally. He pushed through the crowd back to the bar and ordered two whiskies and a Coca Cola. He sucked some off the top of each to keep them from spilling. It was a chore getting them back to the table intact with all the drunk elbows in the place, but he made it and set all three drinks on the table.

"Why don't you drink?" Carter asked Joe.

"Makes me mean."

Joe's date excused herself to the toilet.

"I hear you've been getting creative with your dumping skills," Mainzer said, watching the ladies room door for her to return.

Carter's face grew red.

"Soop won't put up with that for long," Joe continued. "You better watch yourself."

Carter knew Joe was right but didn't say anything. He sipped off the edge of his whiskey.

"I heard you're getting shit from your tribe about working on the dam," Carter shot back, regretting it right away.

"You heard about that?" Mainzer tucked a piece of errant hair back behind his ear. "They're afraid of what will happen when the water backs up."

"I still haven't told my family where I am," Carter said, sipping off his whiskey, realizing for the first time how he and Joe faced the same kind of criticism from the folks back home.

"You should. They're probably worried about you."

The woman came back to the table, and Mainzer stood up and, nodding to Carter, steered her away from the table to a dark corner deep in the back where Carter could barely see as they danced, Mainzer pressed up against her, sliding his hand up her skirt.

Carter sipped his whiskey, embarrassed and unable to keep from glancing at Mainzer and the woman while they groped each other in the back corner of the bar. He waited a few minutes, wondering if they would come back to the table, and then he walked down Speedball Highway to his bunkhouse in Electric City alone.

In the morning, Carter bought a postcard at the post office in Engineer's Town. It had a photograph of Dry Falls on it, a geological landmark a few miles south. He filled in his father's address on the preprinted lines. There was no space for a return address for his father to respond, and Carter hoped Sheriff Bill wouldn't come all the way here to look for him. In the blank space, he wrote: *At the dam site. –Carter.*

CHAPTER 8
June 1936

Weeks went by and spring warmed into summer. One day Carter and Reynolds scaled the face of the rock as usual with compression drills. Like any other day, they drilled holes in rock for dynamite, waited for Joe to place it, then scaled back down, waited for Joe to blast it, shoveled and hauled the detritus to the conveyers, then picked at what was left on the wall with their axes until the shift ended.

Landslides happened fairly often, often enough that Carter and Reynolds should have seen it coming, but when they drove the two trucks to the conveyer belt that day, it was the last thing on Carter's mind. Reynolds drove in front, ready to wave Carter into the conveyer without knocking down any railing.

First one rock pinged on Reynolds's cab. Then another. Then a bigger rock the size of a dinner plate tumbled down into the gravel road. Carter leaned over into the passenger's seat to look out the window up the shallow hill to the east. He didn't need to look long. The cascade was on its way. If he honked the horn, Reynolds would stop to find out what he wanted, and then they would both be lost. He only had a moment. He shifted the truck down a gear and rammed into Reynolds's truck. Their bumpers connected, locked, and Carter pushed Reynolds off the road as the cascade of rock pounded the highway behind them.

Carter jumped out of the truck and ran to Reynolds, who looked shocked before getting out of his truck, gripping his shoulder. A pile of rocks taller than both of them marked the spot where they collided.

There was nothing to say in the moment, but watching the medics carry Reynolds off safely, Carter remembered what Lloyd said about the measure of a person being how you handled yourself in a situation you could not control. For the first time in years, Carter felt proud of how he managed something. It was a quiet victory after his recent failures, a victory he needed for himself.

Soop might be a hard man to work for, exacting, precise, but one of his strengths was that he honored success, and when Reynolds told him what happened, he made a thing out of it. Carter was to receive a safety award from a top official.

Carter was embarrassed by the show, but even if he didn't want to admit it, the recognition meant a lot to him, more than he would ever let on. He wished he could tell Ozzie about it, if he would even care. Carter did his best to dress up for the occasion. His suit was still back at his father's house in Kettle Rapids, but this wasn't the kind of place where you embellished your wardrobe.

The Starks Company offices in Electric City looked the same as when he arrived in town only a few months before. On the hill above the construction site, the white words painted against a shaved slab read "Safety Pays."

Inside the lobby, men milled around, sorted into their sections of priority for employment. Carter followed Soop down the hall to the management office, and Soop ushered him in.

Behind the desk, M.J. Starks was seated, signing papers with an air of importance. Carter hadn't seen him since that night at Ralph's in Kettle Rapids when Starks handed him his business card.

Starks set down his pen and folded his hands on his desk.

"Congratulations, son, I understand you prevented a costly accident."

"Yessir."

"Price, right? I remember you. You're the ferryman's son from

Kettle Rapids," Starks said, looking at Carter intently. "I have a certificate for you to take home."

"I know you didn't cut my father's boat loose, sir," Carter said, immediately regretting bringing it up. Starks paused like he was trying to recall what Carter meant.

"Right. Is he back in business by now?"

Carter was embarrassed. "We haven't spoken since I came out here."

"I see. So you took my advice. That's a good sign."

Carter didn't know how to respond, so he waited to see if Starks continued. He wondered if there was any way for them to know about his troubles with Mae, the potential issues with the sheriff waiting for him back home.

"I like that you showed quick instincts on the job. I hear you did well on the blasting crew, and I expect you're experienced working on the water. How are your swimming skills?" Carter's mind flashed to the day the boat was cut, how he froze on the landing while his father swam out to the ferry and was nearly taken downriver in the icy water.

"Decent," he said, watching to see if Starks believed him.

"Good. I need someone like you for a very particular job," Starks continued, and Soop looked at him surprised. Clearly, they had not discussed this before Carter arrived. "As you probably know, there's a catwalk from Electric City to B Street that we constructed so the general labor force could get back and forth without having to cross past the more…how shall I put this…delicate households in Engineer's Town."

Carter nodded, remembering the time he barely made it across the catwalk with Reynolds.

"The workers are a more proletariat bunch," Starks continued. "They like to have their fun on B Street, and I am all for it." He leaned back in his chair. "Sometimes it goes too far, and someone falls in the river. Obviously, that's not good for my business. Retraining workers, insurance implications for injuries, mentions of safety conditions in the newspapers—all not conducive to maintaining our reputation as a beacon of hope for employment opportunities when so many are out of work.

"I need someone, someone like you who's experienced and sure-footed, to keep my workers out of the river."

It had been a long time since Carter was described in those terms, but he liked hearing it.

"How can I help, sir?"

"Price, I want to take you off the blasting crew effective immediately."

"Sir…," Soop started, but Starks waved a hand, cutting him off.

"Instead, you'll be working nights on catwalk patrol. We have a rowboat you can take out into the river and sit underneath. You'll listen for rowdy voices, ferry yourself on the river, and pull anybody out if they fall in."

Carter was stunned. He'd come all this way to find a new occupation and now he was going to be sitting in a boat on the Columbia in the dark pulling drunks out of the river so that they didn't drown or die from hypothermia.

His face must have shown his disappointment because Starks quickly added, "There will be a pay raise, of course."

"Sir…I appreciate that," Carter's mind raced on how to react. "I don't want to seem ungrateful, sir, but I would like to do more."

Soop furrowed his brows and shook his head slightly at Carter, trying to get him to stop.

Starks weighed this surprise reaction. "Like what?"

"I don't know, sir…"

"You don't know? Maybe you'll think of something while you're sitting on the river."

"Thank you, sir," Carter said, disappointed in himself for not having a better answer.

Starks leaned back in his chair and looked from Soop to Carter and then out the window.

"Tell you what, Price. If you do well at this, I might have something more important for you."

Carter thanked him and followed Soop out to learn about his new marching orders, perplexed by this new assignment and wishing he'd been able to ask for what he wanted. But what did he want anyway? Not to sit up all night on the river, that's for sure.

The boat for patrolling the river was barely more than a rowboat, its narrow wooden seat greyed and splintered on the edges. The boat was tied to a small wooden dock on the river's shore under the catwalk, a nearby siren attached to a post. After quick safety training, Carter was left to sit in the rowboat still tied to the dock throughout his shift and told to be ready to row out to any splash. With the river slowed by a partial cofferdam while the crews prepared to pour the cement bases of the dam foundations, the water coiled confused but did not rush through this passage with the same intensity it did upstream.

The stillness was disquieting for someone trying to keep his mind off something, a bright white sliver of moon the only mesmerizing thing to look at as it glistened across the water. The distant pings of pickaxes echoed off the rocks around him, and he could hear the broken reverb of laughter carry over the water from either B Street to the west or Electric City and Shack Town to the east.

The adjustment to staying up all night and sleeping during the day was more difficult in the busy bunkhouse of Electric City. Carter took Reynolds up on his offer to share a place in Shack Town while Reynolds recuperated. The quiet wasn't much better with thin walls and the unemployed milling around during the day. Carter's days were spent trying to get what sleep he could and his nights listening to drunks overhead and fighting to keep his mind from wandering to unhappy thoughts about getting fired from the mine, the demise of his marriage, and his wife's potential trumped-up criminal charges waiting for him back home. Sadness was hard to fight, and he decided, when he was able, that it was time to release Mae, release himself. The divorce papers were still in his dresser drawer at home. While his family knew where he was now, they had no way to reach him, and he could not go home until he was ready to face the criminal charges looming.

At the dam, the removal of the overburden was done now. Joe suspended recitation club meetings during the raids, but Carter ran into him sometimes on B Street on the weekends. On the river at night, a splash behind Carter might make him look around and, seeing only shadows on the shore, pull the field glasses they gave him from the case and peer into the darkness, but it was only someone from Shack Town on the other side throwing a bottle into the river. The security supervisor gave him a logbook to write down everything he found during his night watch on the river. He brought the flashlight his cousin Lloyd sent with him to help see his logbook and to peer into the water, but its batteries were running low. His first few nights on the job, he tried borrowing books from Joe to pass the time, but it was impossible to read in the dark with a flickering flashlight.

In his first few weeks on the water, he logged fifteen bottles of booze, two wallets, seven shoes, twenty packs of cigarettes, three cans of chewing tobacco, a coat, and no men. Carter sat in the boat, the oars crossed on his lap, his back sore from hunching over. The drunks would start crossing the catwalk soon. He let his eyes close, his mind still alert, the flow of the river gently rocking the rowboat. Maybe it was time for him to go home and face it all.

He heard voices overhead and opened his eyes. He'd rather be up at B Street with his friends, but it was clear that Starks wanted him here and Carter wanted to prove to Starks that he could do more. His time at the dam was his first taste of progress in so long, after so many years of feeling more and more like a failure.

He heard a splash, slipped the looped rope off the cleat, and rowed toward the sound. A ripple swirled on the water, but there was nothing there to see. Martins lived in the rocks along the shoreline of the Columbia. He swore they tossed rocks in at night to mess with him. He rowed back to the dock and rested the oars back across his lap.

The laughter above ricocheted off the rocks and glanced off the water. He didn't know how the workers crossed it night after night. His one trip left him panicked enough not to do it again. Shoes rattled on the planks above, and then they were gone into the muddy streets of Electric City.

At least the wind died down. He thought about home. Mae was probably sound asleep snuggled up to Roy, and Ona and Ozzie would be asleep too. Even if Ozzie wasn't running the ferry now, he wasn't the kind of man to sit idle. Carter wished his father could find a more useful way to spend his time. Saving the past wasn't as valuable as creating the future. Carter knew that full well. Although, sitting in a rowboat on the river waiting to pull drunks out of the water didn't seem like he was contributing to that growth.

His back hurt from sitting, and he leaned forward to stretch. It seemed so far away to him now, that day he and Ozzie found the ferry with its cable cut. How he'd hesitated on the shore while his father swam out to secure it. He'd never felt so helpless, so stuck, hesitant to act after his actions got him fired from the mines.

More voices and laughter crossed overhead and disappeared across the river. A steady stream of men came and went for the next hour or so while Carter sat below on the dark water, watching for them without them even knowing he was there. A small martin, hump backed with brown glistening fur, came out of the rocks, looked at him, and ducked back in.

Then Carter heard a yell. He looked up to the catwalk, and the dark shape of a man, his arms out wide, his legs bent, dropped from the sky as if in slow motion. The man almost seemed to float on the night air as his body fell from high above and splashed into the black water. Shouts followed him down.

Carter sprang into action. He dropped an oar into the water, spinning his rowboat around, and then heaved with all his strength across the wide river toward the man. He could hear the man gulping air and trying to stay above the current.

Carter was on him in seconds. The man grasped at the rowboat and it teetered, throwing Carter off balance, its bow starting to spin in the river's current.

"Don't pull," Carter shouted. "Hang on!"

The rowboat rocked mercilessly from the man's weight. Carter grabbed him by the belt and pulled him alongside, flopping him into the port side like a huge fish, balancing their weight against each other to keep from tipping over. The man breathed in deep frightened breaths, his wet hair clinging in chunks to his cheeks while Carter rowed him to the dock and hit the siren for help.

The emergency medical crew came to get the man and took him to the makeshift hospital in Engineer's Town. Carter stayed behind with his rowboat and finished his shift, the din of voices and clattering of shoes overhead more ominous than before. A fall from that height could break bones, split skin, damage organs.

The next morning, Starks sent for Carter. He'd barely fallen asleep when Soop knocked on the door of the place he shared with Reynolds in Shack Town to wake him. The usual line of hopeful workers stretched out of the Starks Company building. Carter pushed past them to Starks's office.

"You're playing the hero again, I hear," Starks said. He sat at his desk, his suit jacket hanging on a coat rack behind him, sleeves rolled up as he pushed a roll of project plans aside.

"That was the idea, right?" Carter said.

"I suppose it was, now that you mention it." Starks smiled.

"When we last talked, you said you might have something else for me if I did well."

"Actually I do. Not that every time you rescue someone means I'll move you someplace else." Starks motioned for Carter to sit in the guest chair in front of the desk.

"How is he?" Carter asked, taking a seat, nervously smoothing his trousers, feeling underdressed.

"What? Who?"

"The man who fell. How is he?"

"Well, that's mighty polite of you, Price. You pull the fool out of the drink, and you still have the good manners to ask after his well-being. I like that about you." Starks pulled a folder from his overflowing inbox.

"Did he make it?"

"Broken ribs and injured spleen," Starks read from the report. "He'll be out of work for a while, I suspect. At least I don't have to add him to my list of deceased workers, thanks to you." Starks tossed the file back on the pile. "The papers have a field day any time we lose someone."

"Yessir. What is this new position you might have for me?"

"You're really coming along, Price. I wasn't sure you'd have the guts to leave home."

"Yet, here I am, sir."

"Lucky for you, I can see what you're made of better than you can. You're handy with the blast, and you know how to move on the water. You already know that when we flip the switch on this dam, it will back the river up for miles, and you're ready for what that means."

It meant every home he'd ever known would be taken by their work, that much he knew.

"Some things have changed though. The feds want us to build a bigger dam now. Bigger! Taller!" Starks waved a hand toward the plans on his desk. "More water for the farmers. More electricity to build airplanes. That's how our world works now, Price. There's no room for small ideas."

"What does that mean? More towns to break bad news to?"

"Don't be so cynical. Your coin came up heads, didn't it? Hot weather is coming, and the water level will be at its lowest in a few months. Surveyors are out now. The Bureau of Reclamation has set a deadline for everyone to move.

"I'm assembling clearing crews." Starks folded his hands on his desk. "We need to get out in the floodplain and start taking down trees, houses, anything that could float up and create a hazard when we turn this thing on."

"Clearing crew? That's where you're sending me?" Carter leaned against the back of his chair, his hands resting on his thighs.

"I have a barge under construction. We're putting crews on the river. Your job will be to take down anything along the shoreline. Burn it. Blow it up. Cut it down. Whatever you have to do to destroy it. Progress always requires the relinquishing of what came before."

"A clearing barge."

"It's a floating camp. Think of it as a bigger version of your father's ferry that a hundred men can live on. There's one catch."

"Of course there is."

"I want the Indian dynamiter on this too. You in with him?"

"Joe Mainzer?"

Starks nodded. "We need him in case we come on any resistance from the reservation side of the river. Get him on board, and I'll send you both. Don't worry, I'll make it worth your while. Barge should be done in a week. Report back here then."

Starks got up from behind his desk and went to the window of his office. He turned away from Carter and looked out over the vast expanse of the construction site.

"This dam is going to be a spectacle for all time, Price. Long after you and I are dead, it will still be a monument to progress so permanent that nothing can destroy it.

"The water we collect in the reservoir, the water that will flood a few tiny towns like Kettle Rapids, will provide irrigation water for 15,000 square miles of farmland." Starks turned back to look at him. "Do you know how big that is? That farmland can grow crops to feed the entire country." He turned back to the window. "Don't you see how important this all is? You think cutting down a tree is a small thing? You think losing salmon in one river is devastating? Think about all that water and what it will bring to hundreds of thousands of people. Irrigation, electricity, jobs. Think of how much fuel and money will be saved. There's always a tradeoff, Price. Always something that must be forfeited or risked for the big payoff."

Starks came back to his desk, resting his hands on the back of his office chair as he continued.

"I fought in the war, Price. I know many men who came back scarred and wrecked. You know what it did to me? It made me see how fleeting life can be, how little time I might have. My brother died over there. My friends died over there. But we did it for a reason. We had to lose some to win.

"I was one of the lucky ones. They shipped me out early because I took shrapnel in my shoulder. I was laid up in the hospital for weeks and couldn't move my arm for months. I spent a lot of time in that bed thinking about what I wanted to do with my life, what kind of person I hoped to be when they decided I was healed enough to leave.

"I waste no time now, Price. I know what I want." Starks turned back to the window. "I want this."

Starks was quiet for a moment, contemplating. Carter stared at his back, waiting for him to finish. Starks turned back to face him.

"The electricity from this dam will power thousands of homes. It will power factories and streetlamps all over the West. I did that. I made that happen. Me. And you. Water for crops. Lights for the masses. Jobs for thousands. That's our legacy."

"Why are you so interested in me?" Carter asked. "There are thousands of men here who want to work and make a name for themselves. Why me?"

"There's a glimmer in you. It's faint, but it's there. You wanted something once. You wound up disappointed, but you know how to want. I can see it in you. I can see it in the way you react to crisis with the quickness of someone who desires good outcomes. You're the one who's going to have to figure out how to put some purpose to it. I can only point you to the path."

"What about the catwalk?"

"We'll have someone else do that for now. In the meantime, take a break, talk to your friend for me, blow off some steam at B Street."

It wasn't too hard to find Joe Mainzer on B Street. Carter wanted to secure his participation, make sure Starks followed through on his offer. Joe was holding court at a table in the back of the Silver

Dollar Club with pretty ladies and his recitation buddies.

Carter worked his way to their tables, and as everyone was saying their goodbyes on the boardwalk of B Street, he told Joe about Starks's proposal.

"You're not a snitch, are you?" Joe asked, rolling a cigarette.

"No."

"I want to show you something," Joe Mainzer said, taking a drag off his cigarette and reaching a hand back to ruffle the hair on the scruff of his neck. "Can you pack a bag for overnight?"

"Right now? Tonight?"

"No, tomorrow. I have a counteroffer for you."

The next morning, Carter hitchhiked with Joe Mainzer to the dock for the Brewster ferry. As they approached in the back of the pickup, Joe told Carter the trip wouldn't be long, but the boat ran only a few times each day across to what used to be scattered tribal villages, mixed with homesteads. A decade or so before either of them were born, the United States government moved members of twelve different tribes in the region onto a consolidated reservation, the biggest in the state, then appropriated much of the reservation and their traditional land for homesteaders. Joe explained that where they were now in Brewster used to be the Okanogan tribe's territory, but over at the dam used to be the Sanpoil tribe's territory.

"What about your people?" Carter asked, remembering what Reynolds told him months ago about Mainzer's history.

"My people, the Palouse, are scattered all over now," Joe said. "I was born on the Colville reservation, but my people come from downriver. We had no lands around here, and when they moved us, we mixed in with the other tribes who still lived on their original territories."

When they got to the crossing, Carter was amazed. The boat that crossed the Columbia River here wasn't anything like his father's small cabled operation that Carter was used to in Kettle Rapids. It was more like a floating dock the size of a small steamboat, with a low wood railing around the edges that powered livestock, cars, and foot traffic across.

Mainzer walked up to the ticket taker with a wave, and he and Carter got in line for the next scheduled run along with sheep and a few cars. This close to the river, the rush of water was loud enough that you had to raise your voice to have a conversation. It reminded Carter of his father's unique ability to project his voice across the rushing river.

Carter and Joe waited silently in the line for their turn to board. The passengers waiting in cars seemed at ease, but the sheep shuffled restlessly as they backed up from the high gauge chain that hung heavily between the wooden planks serving as sides of the boat.

The sheeps' shorn coats looked dingy with road dust, but Carter knew if he touched them, he'd feel the oil from their wool despite the dry weather. He watched them bump against each other uncertainly. Either they were too dumb to understand that a man-made device could bend laws of nature and take them safely across the river or they were smart enough to know better than to believe a man-made invention was infallible. Carter couldn't decide which made more sense. As he looked across the rushing water to the other shore, Carter thought of what Starks said at the town hall in Kettle Rapids months ago about the inventions at the World's Fair in Chicago. Someone at some point must have thought crossing a river this wide was as impossible as flying cars.

When they finally boarded, Carter felt the familiar awe of the river. He'd been on the river countless times, but after the chain was pulled back, the sheep chased on, cars parked, and he and Joe had settled against the wooden slats, watching the ferryman unloop the ropes from the cleats and jump the gap from dock to boat as the engines moved them away from shore, the Columbia felt massive and wide in a way that could only be fully understood when one was in the middle of it. A massiveness that inspired ambition and innovation. It was like stepping into the wake of a turbine, the way the wind tunneled through the canyons cut by the river but with barely a ripple on the surface of the water other than the churn of wake alongside the ferry itself.

Crossing the Columbia always made him feel small and inconsequential in the scheme of things. Putting boats, bridges, and dams on this river was like fleas saddling a dog.

On the other side, an older Native American man, named Moses, waited in a pickup truck, its paint worn and fenders adorned with rusty dents.

"I thought your folks didn't approve," Carter said to Joe.

"Moses is from the Nespelem tribe," Joe told him. "He's a business partner."

They rode from the ferry dock in the truck, and when they reached a village, Moses pulled up to a collection of small buildings, hopped out, disappeared into one of them, and came out leading two bridled horses by their reins.

Joe and Carter left Moses in the village and rode the horses up a narrow trail to abandoned outbuildings and shaft of a mining operation that predated the consolidation of the reservations.

The manganese mine was deep in the hills, long forgotten and off any well-traveled path. The idea, as Joe explained on the ride up, was to work the mine that had been abandoned on what was now reservation land. With everyone focused on the dam project, Moses and others from the Nespelem tribe hoped no one would notice they were recovering stashes from abandoned mines. Joe and Carter would work the mine, bring what they found back to the village in exchange for cigarettes, chewing tobacco, gum, candy, whiskey, anything valued back in Electric City where the two of them would trade or sell it to the workers.

Carter had no idea where the Nespelem got the candy, cigarettes, fireworks, and everything else. Joe didn't offer, and Carter did not ask. The answer seemed irrelevant like it was an ancient trade system that didn't need meddling from him.

According to Joe, they wanted to add Carter to the operation for palatability with the white workers at the construction site, not so different from what Starks wanted from Joe on the clearing barge.

When Carter and Joe got up to a cluster of rundown buildings in the dry forest of the ridge, they tied up the horses, and Carter followed Joe past the sagging village and into the shaft itself, his time in the Colville mica mines flooding his memory with an oppressive wave. The narrow entrance opened into a small platform area. Beyond that, they could see very little with only two kerosene lanterns. The mining cart inside the shaft was on wheels but not on tracks, which struck Carter immediately to mean that this was even in its best days a small-time operation.

Carter ran a hand over the damp, rough wall of the cave. Being underground was a feeling he'd never much liked and had more reason to dislike now.

Joe Mainzer hung a lantern on an iron spike above their heads and leaned against the rock wall with one foot up to brace himself.

"You've been doing this for a while then?" Carter asked him, looking around at the old equipment and chipped walls.

The light from the lantern glowed in Joe's eyes and refracted around the shimmering walls.

"Not so long," Joe said.

"How do you get the manganese out?"

"Truck it into Canada."

"What's it used for?"

"Steel manufacturing. Bombs. Airplanes."

Carter looked at his friend to see if he was joking, but Joe was straight faced.

"Don't worry about that part," Joe said. "Your only job here is helping me get the stuff down the hill."

"Okay." Carter said, his hands on his hips, nodding as he surveyed the site.

"Okay, you're in?"

"No, okay, I won't worry about it."

Joe chuckled and ran a hand through his hair.

Carter looked out toward the entrance. The small opening was so bright compared to the inside he couldn't see anything distinguishable outside. He did not want to keep spending his nights on a rowboat pulling garbage—or people for that matter—out of the river, and partnering with Joe on this and the offer from Starks were his best options.

That night, Moses made them elk steak and beans for dinner. Carter never spent time on the Colville reservation before, despite living his whole live across the river. He spent plenty of time with members of the Colville tribe in town at Kettle Rapids, watching them catch salmon in baskets at the falls. He always pictured life on the reservation as shown in the few cowboy movies he'd seen at the theater in Colville. Visiting with Joe, he was surprised to see how similar life was to back home. He was also surprised how welcome he felt compared to how Joe was treated back at the dam.

The three sat in Moses's kitchen around a homemade pine table and worked out the details of their plan over dinner and rounds of barn-stilled corn whiskey for Moses and Carter and small bottles of Coca Cola for Joe. Joe would work the manganese mine with Carter's help. Moses would make the swaps with members of the Nespelem tribe. Carter would be the white face of the enterprise at the dam site. In exchange, Joe would come with him on Camp Ferry.

When it was all agreed, Moses stood up from the table and said, "It's a Bing moment," and then walked into the next room.

Carter looked at Mainzer, hoping for an explanation.

"He likes Bing Crosby," Mainzer shrugged. "Knew him in Spokane."

From the other room, the initial squawk of the phonograph turned into crooning. Moses came back to the table shrugging his shoulders in time to the music, and the three men toasted whiskey and Coca Cola to their new venture.

PART 3
THE
TAKING

Summer 1936
Camp Ferry, Columbia River

Camp Ferry was a massive floating structure that could house nearly a hundred men and weeks' worth of supplies. Or rather, it was three floating platforms with a two-story building on each of them encircled with a walkway and metal railing. The white buildings with green trim reflected the style of the Starks Company dormitories in Electric City. On the bottom floor of the center building was a compact mess hall and recreation room for the men to use in their off hours.

A barge they called "The Blue Ox" towed Camp Ferry upriver to the next work site.

The survey crews measured the high water line on the Columbia to 1,290 feet above sea level, an estimate for when the dam went into operation. Then they added another 20 feet for the "taking line," the line where the government would purchase land from its owners at an as-yet-undetermined amount.

Clearing crews worked in two-week stretches and then traded out with another crew, transported in and out by truck. They were to clear to the lower elevation, leaving a slim strip of what would be shoreline below the taking line. They pulled down trees and stacked them on the shore. They found fishing shacks and docks, and if there wasn't anything worth salvaging, they burned them.

The three connected barges and their crew meandered length-wise upriver like a languid juggernaut, clearing the shore of anything that could eventually float downstream and stick in the spillways of the dam.

CHAPTER 9
June 1936

Carter and Joe watched the budding landscape float by, the trees and shrubbery along the shore blooming and green, as Camp Ferry sailed north to where the reservoir had already started to fill in behind the dam's foundation, the water level rising daily. The Columbia was at one of its widest spots here, its currents already slowed by the rising water.

"Don't fill your pockets, boys," the captain told them their first day. "This is government property now and stealing here is a federal offense. I don't want to have to send any of you off to the clink for palming silverware."

Carter and Joe's plan was to work the two-week shift on Camp Ferry and then use their two off weeks to sell their traded goods back at the dam site. It didn't make sense for Carter to keep paying rent on his place with Reynolds in Shack Town while he was gone, and since the weather warmed into summer, he and Joe planned to camp or stay in Moses's barn when they needed.

On Camp Ferry they had small beds in long dormitory rooms and their meals were taken care of. Space was cramped, though, and they didn't have room for more than a change of clothes and a few personal effects. Joe packed a few paperback books for them from his stack of recitation books: Kafka, Dostoyevsky, Hemingway. Everything else, they left with Moses.

The work was hard, not unlike their earlier assignment on the blasting crew. They would anchor close to shore and drop a gangplank, sending the crew off to clear anything they could find that might create a hazard in the reservoir. They mostly took down ponderosas with axes and saws and used hatchets and machetes to remove any of the bigger brush that might come loose and float downriver. Joe would set his explosives on larger structures that remained: fishing shacks, houses, outbuildings. As the days grew warmer, Carter ended them sweating and dusty, bits of bark and ash clinging to his skin, hair, and clothes.

As they sailed, Mainzer pointed out important sites for the tribes, places they used before the government consolidated the reservations on the other side of the river and relocated many other tribes, including members of Joe's family, who settled into the unfamiliar land of the Colville Reservation only a few decades before Joe was born. As outsiders in this new reservation, Joe's parents insisted he learn all the history and dialects of the surrounding tribes.

"Where the dam is used to be Nespelem territory," Joe said. "And this here was Sanpoil." He pointed out fishing sites, former villages, burial grounds, and monuments on the shore. Even though the barge moved slowly, the wind off the water ruffled Joe's pomade, and his short hair fanned in a stiff plume.

Carter heard from someone on the crew that there was a clearing encampment on land near Kettle Rapids. His father was sure to be stirring up trouble. Since the "declaration of taking" and the deadline to vacate had been announced, Ozzie must have had to face facts. Carter wondered what his father was offered for his land or what Mae would be getting for their place.

For now, his days were filled with crashing, burning, and heat, and the nights were still and cool on the river, the men in Camp Ferry's bunkhouse lulled by life on the water. Carter and Joe played cards with the other workers in the recreation room to pass the evenings or read their paperbacks by lamplight on their beds. Carter poured with fascination through a dog-eared copy of *Crime and Punishment,* remarking how multiple lives could change in a single day.

In their off weeks from Camp Ferry, Joe and Carter met Moses in the reservation village to trade him the manganese they were mining for the goods to take back to Electric City and Shack Town. Carter had the sense from his Okanogan and Nespelem compatriots that what they were getting was rightfully theirs and belonged to them regardless of the law. He understood and respected that. Carter was kept in the dark on specifics, but from what he could see of the men who showed up from nearby communities to make deals, there wasn't a shady element, despite the discretion around their operation. In fact, there was a reverence in the way the men addressed members of the multiple tribes now located on the Colville Reservation, a blistering difference to the way Joe was treated in town.

At the mine, Carter helped Joe dig and haul. They began in a section already scaffolded and picked at by the previous operation. It was strange to be back underground again, their arms and faces lined with dirt and flecks of rock.

While the men back at the dam found places to sleep and waited for work in the dust and heat, the cool depth and damp of the mineral-leached walls inside the mine were somewhat of a relief, despite whatever danger might lurk below. The smell inside reminded Carter of river water and the iron scent of blood, like some common source of metal, fundamental to all natural things. At night they slept on the floor of an abandoned outbuilding.

It didn't take long before Carter and Joe were able to trade enough from the mine to borrow Moses's truck to take into town and test out their sales. They rigged the sides of the truck with hinges and folding two-by-fours so that they could flip a side rail down like a tabletop and set up their merchandise—cigarettes, chewing gum, canned food, home-stilled corn whiskey, nudie cards—then toss it all back in and fold the sides back up and cover it with tarps when they were ready to close up shop for the day.

Their first day, Carter loaded up Lloyd's knapsack with his tent and sleeping mat and jumped into the passenger seat next to Joe. In town, they found a spot to park the truck not far from where the catwalk to B Street started in between Electric City and Shack Town. Business was surprisingly good.

Reynolds found them, his face cracking in a wide smile, his arm secured tightly in his sling. He still had a bruise on the bridge of his nose where his face hit the steering wheel when Carter collided with Reynolds's truck, pushing him out of the way of the avalanche.

"You back for good?" Reynolds asked, rifling through their merchandise with his good hand

"For a week or so," Carter told him, stacking packets of gum and candy, happy to see Reynolds on the mend. "Then we head back to Camp Ferry."

Reynolds nodded and jiggled his slinged arm. "Maybe I'll be able to join you soon."

Carter wondered how Reynolds would fare with the work they were doing on Camp Ferry.

"Is Soop keeping you busy?" Carter asked, turning his attention to the cigarettes and nudie cards.

"Mostly. Mostly running errands or doing my best to drive things to the other end of the site with one arm," Reynolds told him, grinning.

In a few days, Carter and Joe sold or traded most of their merchandise to men they knew from Shack Town and to some unfamiliar faces that must have shown up while they were on the other side of the river. They set up near the catwalk during the day and stayed in the camps of Shack Town at night.

In the camps, other small tents dotted the strip of loamy ground. Some men slept in pairs: friends, brothers, and those too poor to provide their own tents, and they came from all over the state—Spokane, Walla Walla, Yakima—even from the nearer parts of Idaho and Montana. Carter expected, as work progressed, that more would show up from farther away.

They were all looking for work, if not on the dam site, then on surrounding road works, laying rail, or any of the other projects that had been planned to facilitate the excavation for the dam. Many of the men at the site had been able to sell or trade what they'd brought for things they needed, but how long they would last, he didn't know.

When their merchandise was mostly gone, Carter sat in the passenger seat of Moses's truck watching the crowd disperse, while Joe sat in the driver's seat, counting and dividing the cash, handing Carter a fistful of bills and coins.

"Pretty good," Carter said, unballing his share to count it.

"Pretty good, indeed."

The first few rounds of clearings on Camp Ferry were relatively easy. They involved mostly trees and shanties—nothing of a community, only random structures, temporary and often unused. As summer cooled into fall and Camp Ferry sailed upriver toward the small communities that clustered on the Columbia's shores, the clearing became more complicated.

First, the crew walked through any structures they found, looking for anything useful to take back with them. Whole buildings were lit on fire. Once, one of the crew missed a gas can in a building, and the blast lit up the sky in a black and red fireball. Joe watched it burn and shook his head.

Carter recognized the shoreline near Gifford, where Reynolds was from, homesteads scattered around the banks. They found a schoolhouse, where Reynolds likely went, weighed down with sandbags, water already pooling around its foundation. Clearly, the community hoped to move the school but ran out of time before the deadline to vacate arrived.

As Joe set the school with explosives, Carter walked through the building looking for anything left behind. He found a few tools and an empty beer bottle, but nothing else of real value. Outside, he sloshed around the exterior, checking for anything that might be in the puddles on the ground. A gleam caught his eye, and he reached a hand into the muddy water. He pulled out an arrowhead, turning it over in his hand, admiring the chiseled craftsmanship. He fished around and found another and another, likely buried by school kids and disturbed by the rising water.

He showed them to Joe, who took them from Carter and shoved them in his pocket.

"What are you doing?"

"Taking them back." Joe said.

"Back to Camp Ferry?"

Joe didn't answer him.

"The captain said this is federal property now," Carter said, confused.

"These don't belong to the feds," Joe said, lighting his fuse, the school building imploding into the puddling water around it.

As Camp Ferry continued north, they encountered more abandoned tribal sites, and whenever they stumbled on an item, Joe discreetly hid the baskets, pottery, and jewelry in his belongings to take back to the reservation. He wanted Moses to get them to their rightful owners. Carter understood where his friend was coming from, even though he knew the captain would not.

North of Inchelium, Carter spotted two men on horseback watching them from the banks on the reservation side of the river.

He almost wouldn't have seen them, but one of the horses raised its head and its brass bridle caught sunlight. Carter turned to see if Joe had seen them, and his friend looked worried. They sailed past slowly, the workers on the barge staring into the brush as the horses sprinted off, carrying their riders into the trees.

"What do you think that was about?" Carter asked Mainzer.

"We're sailing into fishing grounds," Joe said, his eyes scanning the shore.

"Do you think it will be bad?"

"Don't know. Could be. The salmon won't be able to come upriver here to their spawning grounds once they close off the river at the dam."

Carter remembered how important the salmon were to the tribal communities around Kettle Rapids and the massive amounts of fish they caught each year. He watched behind Camp Ferry where smoke pillars faded into the distance, behind them chunks of shoreline crashing into the river. It looked like an army razed a country of its structures.

As they sailed closer to Kettle Rapids, Carter felt a growing sense of foreboding. For one thing, what would happen if he ran into the sheriff? And eventually, they were going to encounter buildings he knew. Like his friend who'd recognized tribal sites along the way, Carter had memories of these places up river. Though he'd been eager to see it all underwater, now that it became more real to him, he started to understand how his friend and his father could want to preserve a place. Starks said we destroy in order to build. That it was inevitable. Maybe there was truth in that, but this business of taking from people was difficult for Carter to stomach.

Camp Ferry continued slowly up the river, leaving piles of felled trees in its wake. All around them, the leaves were starting to turn yellow, orange, red, darkness coming on earlier this time of year. The land around the river this far north was more mountainous, the hills in the distance a blue green.

One afternoon, around a bend in the river, they saw Native American men on horseback, their war gear on, headdresses brilliant against the sunlight, brown chests flanked in fish bone armor. Instead of spears and arrows, they all held rifles.

The clearing crew clustered around the rails to look at the men on the shore. The line of horses was at least twenty-men long and flanked the shore several feet away from where the boat moved at a snail's pace in the water.

Joe Mainzer took a sharp intake of breath and let it out in a long, quiet sigh.

The captain approached Joe. "They don't look friendly."

"What do you want me to tell them?"

"Nothing. Find out what they want."

A skiff was tied alongside the barge. Joe hopped into it and started untying the rope that held it.

"I'll come with you," Carter said.

"No, stay here. It's better if I go alone."

Joe waved to the men on the shore and, calling out a greeting in their dialect, started rowing toward them. Before he could make it to the shore, one of the men fired a shot into the air. Joe dropped to the floor of the skiff, and the clearing crew on the barge ran inside and huddled under benches for cover.

"These are our burial lands," the man called out across the water in English.

The captain came out of the building with his rifle trained on them. "Let my man come back," he called out.

Joe and the skiff drifted downriver on the current.

The man nodded and held up his hand signaling the others to stand down.

"Come on back, Mainzer," the captain called out to Joe, who was still hunkered down in the hull of the skiff. "I've got two shells ready for these fuckers."

Joe rowed back to the barge and clambered aboard. The captain stood on the deck of the barge with his rifle trained on the men on shore until the barge slowly cleared the bend after what seemed like a merciless eternity.

That night, Joe seemed restless, pensive, and Carter didn't know what to say to make him feel better.

The next day, as they cleared along the shore, Carter cut down brush with a machete while Joe demolished what had appeared to be a small cluster of outbuildings. Dirt burst into the sky, raining down with unusual heft, surprising them both. They walked closer to the blast site and found bone fragments littering the loose dirt where they had inadvertently blown open a native burial site.

Joe sucked in a sharp breath, looking over the human remains, his face tight with regret.

"It was an accident," Carter said, trying to reassure him.

Joe walked a few yards away and stared at the river for a moment before turning back to Carter. "We should move them," he said.

"Move them where?"

"Anywhere but here," Joe said, and walked back to the skiff.

That night, Carter sat on the deck of the barge with Joe, and they stared out at the twilight, clear skies awash with stars, the moon casting a brilliant light across the water.

The taking work, the clearing, the confrontations with the tribes wore them both down.

"I can still smell the smoke from today," Mainzer said.

"It's hard to get used to all this," Carter said, looking across the dark water.

"I've been through things like this before," Mainzer said. "We get moved all the time. There's no declaration for the taking with us. They simply take it. We get moved. All that land along the river where the construction is happening? That used to be tribal villages. All these sites along the river? All our things left behind? Our dead? It's the order of things, Price. Someone always pushes us out."

They stared out at the moonlight on the water together, the toll of the past few days sinking in.

"Starks says we have to destroy the past to create the future," Carter offered.

"You listen to the boss now?"

"He likes to talk."

Joe chuckled sadly and looked up at the sky. "He does indeed."

"I don't know how much farther up the river I can go either," Carter said. "I have family up there."

Joe nodded, looking back at Carter again. "Let's go to the reservation and think on it. I don't want to get in line back at the dam again."

Carter nodded and stared out over the water. He didn't know what to do next. He couldn't go home. He remembered his walk to the dam from there. How listless he felt. How purposeless. Starks had given him purpose and now he felt the cost of it. When he was at the construction site watching the concrete pours and clearing bedrock for where the dam would go, it was easy to forget about life upstream. Now that he was on the river, tearing down its shores, it was impossible not to think about the reality of seeing his hometown destroyed forever.

He heard from other crewmembers that townspeople along the shore were getting restless to know what they would be paid. The deadline to move passed and still no one received a letter from the federal government. Now that he saw that destruction with his own eyes, completed it with his own hands, he wasn't sure he could still be part of the taking once they started taking from people he knew.

When it was time to go back to the mine, Carter wondered how long he and Joe could sustain their arrangement. Joe brought the tribal artifacts he found to Moses, and Moses agreed to return them to their rightful owners. Joe advocated moving graves. Moses told them the federal government promised to move native burial sites before the reservoir filled in, and he was hopeful they would make good on it.

The leaves were falling, pinecones dropping from the ponderosas. Eventually the work they did from Camp Ferry would be complete. The reservoir would fill in, and the workers would move on to the next opportunity.

As work at the mine progressed, Joe led Carter deeper into the shaft, bringing back memories of his near accident at Colville. The deeper Joe led, the more hesitant Carter became. Joe seemed to sense Carter's discomfort, leaving Carter in the dim corridor, doing the deepest work himself, leaping, sometimes crawling, down into the caverns with his lamp to find what was down there.

One early fall night on the reservation, Joe invited Carter to come with him and Moses to a celebration. The air was crisp, the sky dark and clear. Carter rode in the bed of Moses's truck, steadying half a dozen gallon jugs of corn whiskey, his breath pooling around him in clouds, the temperature still not too cold to be outside, while Joe sat in the cab, the driver's seat loaded with elk jerky. They drove along a clattering country road pocked with ruts and rocks. The glass jugs jangled together in a sing-song clanging.

An old crank-start Model T rattled past them, driving across a meadow to meet the road. Moses slowed and waved, and the car pulled in front of them with a sputter and honk.

Moses pulled up to what looked like a falling-down barn. Its siding was weathered into a bright silver from years of wind and snow. There was no paint left on it to speak of, and the few remaining strips were bleached white from the sun.

In the dimming light, the windows of the barn lit up the night with an effervescent orange. It almost seemed to explode from inside out. Dim strains of music floated down the road.

Carter hopped out of the truck and looked through the door with wonder.

"What was it before?" he asked Joe.

"White man's barn? Storage?"

Inside was nothing like he'd ever seen. Carter expected a longhouse or something of the kind he'd seen in the tribal villages near Kettle Rapids. There were tables arranged in cabaret style with couples sitting at them. Everyone seemed to glow from the warm lamplight. There were Colvilles in traditional dress. There were Nespelem in plain clothes. There were black folks clustered together at tables with instruments strewn around them. There was even a Chinese man by himself. No white person other than Carter.

Volunteers in the kitchen set out baskets of fried fish with fry bread. Carter and Moses set out the whiskey jugs on long tables lining the wall, lifting their heavy weight.

The performances were varied, from native drum songs to blues ballads. No matter what, the crowd beat time with them, clapping and pounding their feet on the floor.

"You going up?" Moses asked Joe.

"You're going to play?" Carter asked, made incredulous by the whole scene around him.

"No, I'm going to recite." Joe flashed him a grin.

"Of course you are."

Joe went over to the bandleader, crouched next to him to confer, then came back to the table where Moses and Carter sat.

"I'm on last," he said.

The place filled up as the hours wore on. The more people drank, the more they clapped. Cars and buggies pulled up outside, silhouetted against the field. Now Carter wasn't the only white person anymore. The nearby towns had caught onto the joint as well—mostly young people, barely more than teenagers. He could picture Mae waltzing into a place like this looking to cause a stir. He pushed the thought from his mind.

The stage was close enough that the band filled up the room with sound. At last Joe took the stage. The bandleader nodded to the drummer, and they started a beat with brushes. Joe grooved in time with them, waiting to start.

"April…" he started. The drummer whisked his snare, and Joe shimmied in time with him.

"April is the cruelest month." Carter recognized the line but couldn't remember where he'd heard it, faint memories from high school bubbling up.

Joe didn't sing exactly. He spoke in a poetic rhythm while the band played behind him.

> *Lilacs out of the dead land, mixing*
> *Memory and desire, stirring*
> *Dull roots with spring rain.*

Joe paused, letting the band play, while the crowd ate it up.

> *Winter kept us warm, covering*
> *Earth in forgetful snow, feeding*
> *A little life with dried tubers.*

Joe waited, letting the verse settle, swaying to the music behind him, his hair loosening in the warmth of the barn.

The crowd tapped their feet, snapped their fingers, clapped their hands. It was mesmerizing to watch. Joe continued for a few verses that sounded familiar to Carter.

Then Joe's voice rang out in the room.

Hurry up please it's time, Joe sang, landing a phrase Carter recognized.

Hurry up please it's time, the band sang behind Joe.

Hurry up please it's time, Joe sang again.

Hurry up please it's time, the crowd sang back, surprising Carter, as he looked around the room.

> *The river bears no empty bottles, sandwich papers,*
> *Silk handkerchiefs, cardboard boxes, cigarette ends*
> *Or other testimony of summer nights.*

Joe's voice took on almost a trancelike chant while he recited. It reminded Carter of his father's noteworthy voice, which could carry across a rushing river, and he thought of the last time he'd seen Ozzie, packing his sister off to her Christmas performance. He closed his eyes and let Joe's voice wash over him.

> *I sat upon the shore*
> *Fishing, with the arid plain behind me*
> *Shall I at least set my lands in order?*

Hurry up please it's time! Joe sang out one more time.

The crowd roared for him, the last performer of the night. Joe laughed, elated, shaking hands with the band members as the crowd went back to drinking whiskey, the warm barn filled with conversation.

On their way home in Moses's truck, the three of them crowded into the front seat, windows cracked, letting in the cool night air. Joe was coming off the high of his performance, and Carter had a buzz from the whiskey and the joy of the evening. Carter watched the stars streak over the pickup as they headed back to Moses's place.

Moses had a serious look as they drove. He let the truck bounce through the unpaved roads for a while, his expression taut, not saying anything as though he didn't want to be the one to spoil the mood.

Joe caught his expression in the rearview and finally asked, "What's wrong?"

"My buddy back there says the Bureau of Indian Affairs has been hanging around, asking questions," Moses warned them.

"The feds? What does that mean?" Joe asked him, looking alert in the cab of the truck, the night dark outside the passenger window.

"Might want to lay low, head back to the dam for a bit," Moses said, holding the steering wheel lightly, his eyes trained on the road.

By the time fall cooled toward winter, Carter had saved enough money to feel covered for a while. Back at the dam, he felt the burn of the money in his pocket and was nervous that someone might rob him. They were now doing enough business in the streets of Electric City and Shack Town that they were getting noticed.

He met Joe and Reynolds at the Grand Coulee Club instead of Joe's usual table at the Silver Dollar. President Roosevelt was giving another Fireside Chat and people gathered on B Street as usual to listen to the live radio broadcast. Carter recognized some of the customers they'd been selling to out of the truck and noted the extra attention it brought to Joe and him compared to their relative anonymity before—Carter's at least. People in town were aware they had cash.

President Roosevelt spoke about drought in other parts of the country and his plans to help out-of-work farmers. He talked about how factory workers depend on farmers' business, and how farmers count on factory workers to buy their food. Carter thought of all the roads and rail lines and bridges built to support the dam. He thought of the B Street businesses thriving while serving the dam workers. "We are members of one another," was the way the president put it. Carter wondered what Starks would think of that sentiment.

After the program ended, Joe and Reynolds wanted to head to the Silver Dollar Club, but Carter was spent. The weeks on and off Camp Ferry and working in the mines had worn him out, so he headed back toward their campsite alone, wary of anyone he passed who looked at him with interest.

On his walk back to his tent in Shack Town, he remembered the day a few years before he came to the dam when he heard there was an assassination attempt on President Roosevelt. Carter had been in a grocery store in downtown Kettle Rapids when the radio erupted in an emergency bulletin. A man had opened fire during a speech by then president-elect Franklin Roosevelt.

Carter stared at the clerk, listening to the radio announcer as he continued. What would they do without a leader? There was already so much chaos, what next?

Carter ran out of the store in a panic, forgetting his groceries, and ran into Ralph's where his father and others were poised on the barstools.

"Roosevelt's been shot!" he yelled breathlessly to the group.

At the bar, still under the last months of Prohibition, Ralph turned on the radio and the men gathered around, faces grim, their eyes searching one another's faces, a watery fear rising among them.

Back then, Carter wasn't much of a radio listener, preferring newspapers or dusty hardbacks whenever possible and guidebooks for hiking and even scouting books. There had been a moment during the election, where politics caught his attention, if only for a moment. Will Rogers, expert roper and cowboy picture star, briefly made a run as a candidate for the Democratic Party, and Carter, even knowing the roper wasn't a serious politician, wanted him to win, maybe because it annoyed Ozzie so much, maybe because Rogers was the kind of man who made you want to root for him—in any ring—or maybe because there was a farcical nature to the whole thing that captured Carter's attention. Ultimately it didn't matter, as Rogers's bid was short-lived and potentially lifesaving.

After that, Carter watched the banks tank, watched jobs vanish, watched developers promise change and men he knew and respected fall apart. It could turn ugly, the way his father described anarchists at the start of the Great War, blowing themselves up with tacks and jacks and coffee cans in city parks.

Over the day they learned President Roosevelt had almost been shot—not shot but almost shot—in an attempted assassination. Roosevelt had been up at the podium, newly elected, not even sworn in for another month, and someone took a swipe at him. In the meantime, Will Rogers was safe; Roosevelt, a married father, rumored to be disabled or at least well past his prime, was shaken up; the mayor of Chicago, the guy shaking Roosevelt's hand on the platform in Miami when the pistol was fired, was fighting for his life in the hospital, and a random woman from the crowd was dead. Everyone in charge of the country was alive, but only by luck. After Roosevelt dodged the anarchist's bullet, the new president promised jobs and set up the Conservation Corp to create new opportunities, and a new hope was in the air.

On Carter's walk back to Shack Town, he thought how easily

everything could have taken yet another turn for the worse that day, right when it seemed like it was getting better. When the assassination attempt happened, Carter felt a sense of connection with his father and the men, of shared concern with the people around him.

Carter wandered back to his campsite without Joe, stars blurry above, crawled into his tent, and pulled his boots off, tired and feeling something between hope and despair in the darkness. President Roosevelt was right that they were members of one another. Carter was a member of his father, of Starks, of Mae, of them all, whether he liked it or not.

Winter came on quickly and parts of the river froze, making work on Camp Ferry impossible. The barges were anchored upriver, and the crew sent back to Electric City. The weather slowed work on the dam as well, and tensions rose on B Street as men were laid off from the project and spent their time in the bars and brothels. Snow in the foothills made trekking by horse to the mine more precarious, and Carter and Joe divided their time between Moses's barn and Shack Town, waiting out the freeze.

One cold morning, Carter woke to a muffled clanging coming from the new company store and food shack a few yards away from where they camped in Shack Town. His ribs ached when he took a deep, cold breath, and there was no way he could fall back asleep with the background music of metal on metal. The cook was making breakfast to sell the campers, and the smell of grease already hung in the air.

Carter dug deeper into his bedroll, listening to the men rustle in their tents. He dreaded leaving the warmth of his wool blanket, but if he didn't beat the rush for firewood at the company store, he might run out that night.

He reached for his wool pants, suspenders still on from the

day before, and shoved them down under his blankets. He pulled them on to let them warm up inside his covers and then did the same with his coat. He shivered there for a moment and then finally slunk out of his blankets and stepped into his shoes.

Outside his tent, the camp was quiet other than the noise from the food tent. Only a few fires sent whiffs of smoke up into the grey sky. The company store was south of the camps where the washed-out bridge met the road that led to Engineer's Town.

Since Carter came back to town, not much had happened at the excavation site besides the blasting and chipping of the rocks. The rail extension still needed to be finished, once the weather warmed up, to get the rest of the equipment in for the next phase of construction on the dam. For now, they only needed men for construction and repairs on the conveyers that took the rock away from the job site. Reynolds was fortunate enough to secure a job with Soop again, now that his arm was mostly healed, and Carter met him on B Street when he could. Reynolds still had a place in Shack Town with some other members of the crew. It looked like everyone else in the camps would be waiting for a while for the work to resume.

The company store was in a brand-new building, one of the construction projects that had taken place while he and Joe were gone. It was a low one-story shack with vertical siding, painted a fresh white. The clerk was stacking firewood outside next to the front door, his hands protected with thick leather gloves.

"You're up early," he said, straightening up when he saw Carter.

"How's your supply today?" Carter asked.

The man chuckled and tossed Carter a small bundle of sharp-smelling, freshly split pine pieces that were held together with a twisted piece of wire.

"What else you need?" The clerk gestured toward the front door as though to say, have a look for yourself.

Carter went inside, the little bell on the door barely making enough noise to be heard over the radio. The shelves were bare compared to the mercantile back home. A few canned goods, basics someone might need for a camping trip. Carter didn't really need anything, but the inside was warmer than out, heated by a small iron coal stove that vented out the back of the building.

"What do you got for me?" the clerk asked, coming through the front door and tossing his gloves on the chair behind the counter.

Carter dug in his pocket for cash to pay for the firewood, tossing it on the counter.

"You and your friend still selling goods out of your truck?" the clerk asked.

"Oh you know," Carter said, wanting to appear nonchalant. "Wintertime is tough all around."

"Hope you're not planning to give me any trouble," the clerk said.

Carter tucked the bundle under his arm, saddened by the man's suspicion. "Thank you for the firewood," he said, ignoring the man's question.

Back at his campsite, Carter squatted in the V-enclosure of his tent and rifled through his minimal wardrobe. He should get some laundry done. He was more interested in having clean duds now that he was sleeping outside on a consistent basis and the frozen dirt of the camp and worksite had developed big patches of thick, silty mud like Soop warned them about many months ago. The frozen mud tracks slowly thawed into boot-sucking pits, and Carter was trying to keep the ashy crust off his attire as best he could.

He found that anytime he was alone, his mind would wander to Mae and their early life together, guilt and shame pooling back in a hot rush to his brain. This thing with asking for a real divorce, taking the house, and pressing charges against him when clearly she and her friend were as much at fault—that was new, not like all her backs and forths over the years. It was as though she'd finally found a way to close him out of her world. It was so long now since he last saw her, so long since he left home with barely any word. He wondered what she was doing. If she might let him come home now after so much time had passed. Maybe they could still start over.

Laundry was only a moderately effective distraction from these kinds of thoughts. He took his undershirt to the river and washed it in the cold water. He could only keep his hands in the icy stream for a few seconds at a time to swish the fabric around in the shallow murk.

"They're going to freeze," Joe Mainzer came up behind him in the dark from downriver a few yards. Carter hadn't noticed anyone nearby and was alarmed that his guard had come down enough to be surprised.

"I've got a method worked out," Carter said, wringing out his shirt and shaking it open. He had strung a short clothesline from the peak of his tent to a railroad spike in the ground. The triangular space created between the tent door and the clothesline made a screen of sorts with enough space for a small fire. Under his bedroll, a tarp kept the clothes sealed in and dry from his body heat while he slept.

Joe sat on rock next to Carter and watched as Carter shook out as much of the water from his shirt as he could onto the muddy shore.

"The clerk at the company store asked me if we were going to be a problem," Carter told Joe.

"Allies are always good to have," Joe said, palming a rock from the riverbank and tossing it in the air before plunking it back down in the sand.

Carter hadn't thought of it that way, but he liked the sound of it.

Eventually, everything thawed again, and spring returned to the basin. Camp Ferry unmoored from its winter storage. The horse trails to the mine were clear, work on the dam picked back up, and with it, the cash flow in Electric City. Carter and Joe resumed their rotation from Camp Ferry to the abandoned mine, back to Shack Town, then Camp Ferry again. More than a year had passed since Carter left home. The shifts of their rotation started to blur together from constantly being on the move.

Back in Electric City, Reynolds told Carter there was a telegram waiting for him. Carter stood in line at the post office in Engineer's Town, a spring drizzle wetting the steps. He hadn't heard anything in almost a year since he sent the postcard home, but then, there wasn't an address where his family could reach him. He'd been deliberate about that.

He braced himself for the tirade he expected from his father, but when he sat on the edge of the post office porch to read the telegram, it was from his sister:

Mae says she won't press charges if you finalize the divorce. Stop. She wants to get remarried. Stop. Love, Ona.

Carter crushed the paper into his pocket and let the mist soak into his shoulders as he crossed the street from the post office to the bluff above the river. He knew his sister's friendship with Mae had continued discreetly since they'd split up, but it still felt like a betrayal.

The proliferating tents of Shack Town looked tiny from the heights of the opposite shore as they sprawled along the thawed and muddied banks with more and more unemployed men, the spring rain steaming off their campfires.

Fine, she could have her divorce. Fine, she could marry…

who? Roy Carnes? That jackass? It could finally be over. No more back and forth. No more games. No more late-night visits. No more pitying looks from other people. No more what ifs. If she was going to go, he wanted her gone for good this time.

Carter turned back toward the road. It seemed like a very good time to walk up Speedball Highway to B Street and get stinking drunk. The Silver Dollar Club was nearly empty that early in the afternoon. The only patron sitting up at the bar was a young man with reddish hair. He seemed barely old enough to be there, but who was Carter to point that out? He didn't care. The kid looked glum, and Carter nodded hello as he took a stool near him.

Carter pounded a whiskey and then another, his glass clapping on the bar as he finished them. The sound reminded him of that day at Ralph's with his father after they dragged the ferry in. Here the juke box was playing "Night and Day," a sappy Cole Porter love song. With everything going on, it felt too pathetic to be sitting in a bar listening to a lovesick crooner pining over a woman.

"You mind if I put something else on?" he asked the kid at the bar.

"I played this actually," the kid said.

"Ah." The kid could have his song, Carter supposed.

The kid hummed along quietly with Fred Astaire. Poor sap. Seemed like anyone of any age could get turned inside out by love.

"You ever had a dame leave you?" the kid asked.

"Oh, sure," Carter made his tone nonchalant. No use telling the poor kid how many times. It would only make him feel bad.

"Yeah?" he seemed relieved. "Is that how they are then?"

Some of them, Carter thought. He certainly hadn't had the best luck so far, but that wasn't what this kid needed to hear.

"I really don't know," Carter answered him. "Sometimes they should leave us, sometimes they shouldn't."

The kid nodded as though he was thinking of reasons why his gal should or shouldn't have left.

"So how do you know which it is?" the kid said. Carter thought this probably wasn't the best time for him to get into the advice business. He stood up and pulled a few coins out of his pocket and tossed them on the bar.

"I don't know your gal, but it seems to me you can either go after her or let her go," Carter told him. "Try to figure out which one you'll regret the least later."

The kid seemed to mull this over as Carter headed out the front door and back to B Street. He felt invigorated by the news from Mae as he walked the boardwalk, and it surprised him with its intensity. The unsigned papers were back in his dresser at his father's house. He could go home again. She wanted to play one last game? Fine, he would give her what she wanted.

Who knew where she would go. Kettle Rapids would be underwater soon. All his failures and humiliation forgotten, buried under cubic tons of river, no longer a part of his life. He was in a new place with a new cast of characters, and for the first time, he felt as though he could rewrite his own story. He wanted to yell it out loud. He wanted to hammer something, tear something down.

Out on B Street, Carter saw Joe Mainzer coming out the door of the dry goods store onto the porch. He jogged across the street to him, remembering the gun Joe always kept in his waistband when off duty

"Can I fire your pistol?" he asked Joe. His brain was hot with whiskey, relief, aggravation, frustration. A tangle of emotions that wanted release with some kind of bang.

Mainzer looked at him, his arms full of canvas bags.

"No way," Mainzer told him. "You got too much fight in you right now. I don't know what you're fired up about, but I'm not going to arm it. What you need is a woman."

Carter didn't argue. His brain felt swollen from thinking about Mae's proposition and inflamed from the whiskey he drank. Still, he couldn't shake the faint regret that he hadn't had one last chance to make things right. Mainzer was right; Carter needed to get his head straight.

Mainzer led Carter to the door of a run-down house on a side street. He left him on the porch, saying, "Welcome to the Red Rooster. Go work it out," and pressed a bill into his hand.

"Come find me when you're off this kick," Mainzer said, and Carter watched Joe walk away, pistol safely tucked in the back of his waistband, as he disappeared into the foot traffic on the sidewalk.

Mainzer was right about Carter's agitation being physical in nature. When he knocked, the door was opened by the same blond he saw Mainzer with at the bar months before. "I'm Colleen," she said, smiling up at him through the open doorway, taking him by the hand. He thought of Mae at the town hall meeting, her face and hair perfect, her green eyes fixed down where she didn't have to look at anyone. This woman couldn't be more opposite. Her face was soft and open, her hair shaken loose, her manner warm and welcoming, kind.

He'd been with working women before, but not since he was married. It was the same as he remembered: benign, emotionally detached but with warmth and connection. Deep wants colliding in human form. Afterward, he hugged her close, grateful for her touch, his despair over his failures with Mae somehow less important.

"You're so sweet," she said, running the tips of her fingers down his face. He kissed her warmly on the cheek.

"Thank you, Colleen," he said, holding her a little longer, then handing her their agreed upon amount. He left B Street and walked back on the road to his tent, spent and relieved.

Back at the mine site one morning, Carter woke to find Joe already at the campfire, heating coffee in a bright orange pile of coals. The trees were in their greenest flush of the spring, the morning still damp and steaming in the ascending sunlight.

Carter felt a new relief knowing he could soon be free of his marriage and the potential criminal charges waiting for him at home. He'd written his sister, letting her know he was agreeable to Mae's terms and arranged to receive mail at the Silver Dollar Club.

At their camp, the coffee smelled lightly burned. Carter grabbed a tin cup from a nearby log that doubled as their table and sat across the fire from Joe.

He looked around at the dilapidated buildings and remembered his night at Fort Spokane and told Joe how the people there were taking the buildings apart.

"Maybe we should take a break from all this, head over there and see what they're up to," Carter said taking a sip of his coffee.

Joe looked alert and held his hand up for Carter to be quiet. They both sat silently for a moment.

"Someone's coming," Joe said.

"Someone you know?" Joe didn't answer him and poured the percolating coffee into Carter's cup.

Joe's manner didn't reveal too much alarm, so Carter assumed it was business.

Carter left his coffee in the dirt next to the fire and walked to the edge of the hill. Beneath them in the ravine, a work truck was parked at the trailhead leading to their camp.

He looked at Joe, but Joe sat quietly next to the fire, waiting patiently but not without tension for what might come next.

"Should we clear out?" Carter said, finally.

"Calm down."

"What about the horses?"

"What about them?"

"Should we hide them?"

"Where?"

"I don't know. In the shack over there?"

"What for? Sit down and be quiet."

Carter hesitated. Wasn't there some way they could cover up what they were doing or hide or get out of the site? Joe was still sitting glued next to the fire, but he adjusted the pistol in his waistband to make it easier to grab. Carter grew more disturbed.

It took a while for a man dressed in a Bureau of Indian Affairs shirt to arrive in their campsite and show them his identification. It must have been the same man Moses's friend warned them about at the barn event.

Once he was there, Carter felt a sobering calm take him over. You never knew what you might find up or down any trail anymore.

"You gentlemen have permission to be up here?" the man asked, once he'd established his authority by showing his badge.

"Passing through, sir," Carter said, shooting a look to Joe Mainzer in hopes of getting his equally reassuring assent, but Joe stared into the fire. Carter hoped there weren't any artifacts here from the clearing that would incriminate them in some way,

"Passing through a remote reservation ridge on horseback in the era of public works and motorcars?"

"Times are tough," Carter said, and gave a commiserating laugh.

"I hope you boys aren't up to no good."

"No, sir," Carter said, and stared at the man as unwaveringly as he could. Joe Mainzer kept his eyes on the fire, and Carter wished he wasn't acting so suspicious. Carter wasn't sure if they were or weren't up to no good. Everything they'd taken out of the mines or from Camp Ferry rightfully belonged to the tribes, but nothing seemed black and white to him anymore. The man left without incident, but the message was heard loud and clear: I'm watching you.

As spring eased into a dry summer, Camp Ferry continued upriver toward Hellgate, a part of the river blocked by small islands that made sailing the barge more precarious. The afternoon was hot, the water level still low from the dry weather.

Carter and Joe took the skiff to shore to do the next round of clearing, checking to see if there was anything left. They trampled over a concrete foundation cut deep into the ground and no longer supporting any walls. The remnants of outbuildings, tumbled into flat piles, littered the field around it.

"This family must have moved their house," Joe said, smoothing his hair back and surveying the property.

"I wonder how they got it out of here," Carter said, looking around at the empty expanse of grass. Most of the property was already cleared of trees, probably when they'd originally home-steaded the place.

They rowed the skiff farther along the shore, looking through the trees to see if there was any other sign of human life. The white peaks of a house glinted through green limbs, and they macheted through the underbrush to clear a path to it.

Something felt wrong to Carter. He sensed a presence, like eyes were on him. He looked at Joe, and Joe seemed nervous too. Something strange was in the air.

At the house, Carter pushed the front door open carefully into a kitchen. A cold pot of beans was still on the unlit stove, like someone made dinner, remembered an errand, left suddenly, and didn't return.

Joe followed him quietly down the hallway. Carter peered into the first doorway. Nothing. An empty room, no bed, no nothing. At the end of the hall, Carter pushed open the door to the last bedroom, Joe trailing behind.

Carter jumped back into the hall, and Joe stared into the room, frozen. A man sat on the floor between the bed and the wall with only his face showing above the white bedspread. He looked up startled at them and clambered to his feet. He was holding a shotgun.

On the wall behind him, Carter saw a spray of blood. A woman's shoes and skirt hem stuck out behind the foot of the bed.

"I couldn't finish it," the man cried out and started to shake. The man had shot his wife, but not himself. He sank to the floor and sobbed into his hands, his shotgun rattling on the floorboards. "This house was all we had left. I couldn't finish it."

Joe staggered out of the room and down the hall. Carter ran after him. At the porch, Joe leaned over the rail and puked into the matted brown grass.

A shot rang out from inside the house, long and resolute, echoing around the farm. Their witness of what the man had done led him to finish what he'd intended.

Joe and Carter stared at each other silently, the sound of the blast ringing in their ears. They sat in the grass and waited, for what exactly Carter wasn't sure, but it seemed right. For the peace to take the man. For him to complete his dying. For his soul to leave the house. To make sure he'd succeeded. They sat quietly in the brown grass for close to an hour before Carter broke the silence that engulfed them and the house behind.

"We should burn it," Carter said to Joe, and his friend nodded, wiping his eyes and mouth on his sleeve.

They retrieved a can of gasoline from the skiff and poured it in a circle around the house. It lit easily in the warm afternoon, and the two friends watched as the house burned, the flames making a mirage around the walls as the house and everything it contained collapsed on itself.

In the weeks that followed the man's suicide, Carter woke with dread on Camp Ferry. He thought of Starks's idea that they needed to destroy to build and remembered President Roosevelt's words about being "members of one another." How could both be true when lives and homes were at stake? It had been easy to think of destruction when he only saw it from his own perspective of wanting a fresh start. It was not so easy now. From the back of Camp Ferry, he looked out at the pink sunrise as it came up behind the tree line and glistened across the water. Everything looked harmless in the morning. In the distance, tiny plumes of smoke faded into the clouded sky. Behind the barge, they left a wake of stumps and charred underbrush.

He hoped his father wouldn't get any wild ideas like the man they'd found. Or do anything he couldn't undo.

Carter continued to work uneasily with Joe in the reservation mine. Every snapping twig he heard while they were in the ghost town of the mining village startled him. Badges, guns, and desperate people standing to lose money, or their homes, did not sound like a winning combination of factors.

Carter's nervousness must have shown because one night on the Brewster ferry on their way back to Electric City, Joe Mainzer broached the subject.

"You thinking about quitting?" Joe asked.

Carter stared out at the water, the closing distance between them and the opposite shore an advancing relief. So much had happened since he arrived, and still his business at home needed to be resolved before he could ever feel free to move forward. The river rushed in his ears, compounding the chaos of his thoughts.

"Thinking about it. Thinking it might be time for me to settle things back home."

Carter didn't want to let Joe down, but truth was he knew he needed to take care of things.

"Not a bad idea, really," Joe said.

"What about you, though?" Carter tried to read Joe's face. "I don't want to leave you shorthanded."

"We're getting deep into the mine," Joe said, his tone even. He looked back toward the north shore of the river and the ridge above them. "I'll need more skilled help soon." He grinned as though to suggest Carter wasn't up to the job.

Truth was, he wasn't. Even though he'd done this work before, the dark caverns—small spaces, rich and limited air, the memories—felt more oppressive the longer he worked in them. The heaviness of their work on Camp Ferry and attention from the federal government wasn't sitting well with either of them. Carter knew he was in no position to be picky about work or working conditions, but it was time to keep an eye open.

CHAPTER 10
August 1937

Ozzie's offer letter from the federal government finally arrived. He tore open the envelope and read the amount and the deadline to vacate, enraged at how little he was offered for what amounted to his entire life.

There was only one thing left to do: fight the buyouts. The president was coming for a dedication ceremony at the dam, and this might be his chance. He stopped by the auto shop to see if Jackson received a letter yet. He had.

The two sat outside on metal chairs and watched the cars drive by along the highway, occasionally stopping to fill up at Jackson's pumps.

"I don't know what you think you're going to do," Jackson said, handing Ozzie the letter he had received, with the dollar amount he was offered.

According to neighbors who received such notices, there was no rhyme or reason to the amounts. Some thought it was adequate, others generous, and still others, like Jackson and Ozzie, knew they would never be able to move their businesses or open new ones with the money.

"I can't move my gas tanks for that amount," Jackson said, refolding the letter back into the frayed envelope.

"There has to be a way to stop it."

"Don't you read the papers? They've finished the foundation of the dam already."

"We'll demand more for our land, stall them a bit."

"What if they won't agree? Then what?"

"I'll write to the governor again."

"The governor is for it." Jackson watched as a car pulled up to a pump.

"Maybe he needs to know more about how it affects us."

"You're not going to do something crazy, are you?"

Ozzie squinted at him. "Crazy, how?"

"I don't know, crazy like what-happened-to-your-ferry crazy."

They still didn't know what happened with his ferry, but if it wasn't the Starks Company, it had to be someone who stood to gain by shutting him up.

"Would you blame me?"

"No, not at all, but you're no good to anyone in jail."

Ozzie's mind flashed to Ona. "True. I'm heading down to the dedication. You in?"

Jackson shook his head. "I have to keep things going here, Price. You go."

On his way to the dam, Ozzie pulled off the highway and took out his field glasses. The clearing camp at Kettle Rapids had more than two hundred men in tents camped out in a field not far from the shore. He searched in the trees, the images large and bleary. They looked like a military encampment spread across the meadow. He'd give them a war.

Men moved around the camp in the black circles of his lenses, small puffs of blue smoke emanating from their campfires. In the trunk of his car he had chunks of chum on ice. He'd stopped by the fish monger on his way out of town and asked for whatever bait they had left. He knew he'd never get the smell out, but it was worth it. Let the river give them back a little of their comeuppance for their part in the charade. He slung his rifle over his shoulder, in case, and hiked into the woods. He placed chunks of chum at regular intervals around the periphery of the camp, knowing the smell would attract cougars, bobcats, coyotes, and maybe even brown bears and wolves. Give these guys a little scare. See if it was worth tearing up the shore if they were surrounded by hungry carnivores.

Carter was relieved to get back to Electric City after his time with Joe on Camp Ferry, even if they had to camp out here for a while. Since the man from the Bureau of Indian Affairs showed up at the mine, they decided to spend more time in Electric City to see if his attention might blow over. They would wait to hear from Moses if people on the reservation continued to see the man around. Carter still thought about the man they'd found during their time on Camp Ferry, and sometimes dreamed about him and his wife, the final shot ringing loud in his ears like it was yesterday.

Camp smelled like sweat and oil and hot canvas, and there was a constant clatter of idle busywork everywhere they went. They both wanted to see the dedication event with President Roosevelt. Carter's sister wrote again saying she was hoping to come down with her high school friends and would bring the papers with her. He wondered if anyone else from home would be there, if his father would come or Lloyd or even Mae.

He hoped his father would stay home. Carter didn't want to have to argue that he wasn't cut out for this work anymore. That he wasn't a man of purpose. He hoped his father would be able to let go of the fact that Carter was working on the one project Ozzie was most adamantly against and see that Carter was finally getting his purpose back, like Ozzie wanted.

The morning of the dedication, Carter and Joe went to see the preparations in town. Carter looked for Starks around the administration building but didn't see him anywhere. Starks was no doubt entertaining the president somewhere. Did Starks have a house in town, a wife, little Starks?

Starks could see purpose in Carter in a way his father could not and had the objectivity to look at things from all angles while appreciating the truth in each of them. Ozzie would never be able to do that. He refused to do that. Maybe his conviction was admirable, but nothing was ever so simple as to be completely right or completely wrong.

It was already hot, and the mud Carter remembered from when he first arrived two winters ago, then frozen, was now hard and cracked. Men from the Starks Company built the grandstand in Electric City on the hard mud, laboring in the heat for the past week. There seemed to be little interest in passing the meager construction work for the event on to others, and a crowd of bitter men gathered slowly in the scant shade to look on. Now it was completed and festooned with red, white, and blue bunting, its open back urging viewers to look in awe at the concrete foundation they'd built, spanning nearly a mile long across the swirling Columbia River.

Carter and Mainzer wandered down the road to Shack Town, staying off to the sidelines, watching people pour in by the carload. Cars drove past them looking for a place to park, pulled in along trees, bounced over dusty dirt ruts.

Already, merchants were setting up tables along the road, getting ready for the crowds that gathered in the area.

"Where would be a good place to set up the truck?" Carter asked Joe, looking around for a space big enough but also close to the road.

"Somewhere with some shade," Joe said, looking up at the sun, and they headed over toward a stand of poplars.

Charlotte looked in the rearview mirror of her beat up limo, watching Ona Price and her friends in the back. The dog panted blissfully in the passenger seat next to Charlotte, his tongue lolling, nose pointed up to the crack in the window. In her wildest imaginings, she never would have thought she'd be driving three snickering teenage girls a hundred miles to see President Roosevelt. When Charlotte ran into the Price girl with one of her high school friends while making rounds delivering apples in town, she was surprised how mature Ona seemed since she last saw her. A little lady almost, with an edge of cunning to her. Not surprising really. Ona had a shrewdness when she worked for Charlotte that struck Charlotte as potential for something bigger than Kettle Rapids.

When they met in town, Ona asked after Charlotte's land—would she be affected?—and Charlotte assumed Oscar must have received his letter. Charlotte received one as well, but the impact was minimal, an offer only for a narrow strip at the lower end of her property across the road from Mae Price's place. Shoe money, she thought with a smile as if she cared about anything but practical work shoes anymore. The majority of her acreage, including the orchard, was on a plateau well out of reach of the Columbia.

Ona's question was posed as politeness, but Charlotte read something underneath it, a kernel of an idea, but she didn't know what. Maybe Ona heard of Oscar's proposal. It did get Charlotte thinking again of what to do with her place when she was gone. Could Ona handle it in a few years? A girl of twenty or so by then with a sharp mind? Did she have hard work in her? Independence? The fortitude to go it alone? She might. Or she might have a better idea. Lord knew Charlotte figured it out by the seat of her pants with pluck and determination. Maybe Ona could improve on what Charlotte was able to do.

The girls' little heads were cocked together, their lips bright with red lipstick, like babies who'd eaten too many Bing cherries. Charlotte chuckled to herself.

After she spoke with Ona on the sidewalk in town, Charlotte unloaded her apples and overhead Ona tell her friend that she wanted to see the president speak, wanted to join their high school friends for the dedication event, but she was too embarrassed to go with her father and didn't have another way to get there. Poor Price. A soft prickle of motherliness stirred in Charlotte, and she thought of her son at that age, tall and gangly, so worried about what everyone thought.

"I can take you," tumbled out of Charlotte's mouth. Why not? Heck, why shouldn't they all go see the president speak.

Starks surveyed the grandstand from his office window with concern. President Roosevelt was coming up for a dedication ceremony after a visit to Bonneville Dam, and the scene below looked like general buffoonery. The weather was dry, and the site was dusty. Workers wet down the dirt around the grandstand to minimize the chance of a dust storm, which turned everything to mud. Starks's press secretary from the home office in Minneapolis was still en route by rail and would have his work cut out for him getting the event under control. He would need to deal with the president's new Secret Service detail the White House created after the many threats the president received since implementing the New Deal, and he would need to coordinate the numerous newspaper and radio reporters who would be covering the dedication event in the next several hours.

Starks cared about the reputation of his company, but he preferred to leave these matters to others while he focused on the future. More pressing were the threats of labor protests that were brewing among the workforce. The last thing he needed was any kind of mob scene at the work site, especially when his primary federal funding source was making an obligatory visit.

Harold Burnes parked his car on B Street and walked into the Silver Dollar Club. The *Colville Scintilla* was paying for his travel this time, and he felt a new sense of pride and self-respect booking a room on his editor's dime. He'd left Colville early, hoping to be one of the first newspaper men to Electric City, but from what he could tell, the area was already filling up with people eager to see President Roosevelt.

"I'd like a Reno Room, please," he said to the barkeep, surveying the signs around the place.

Since his coverage of the new dam began, Harold had saved money, sold his mare, and upgraded to an older automobile. Things were looking up for him. His coverage of the Starks Company earned him new favor with his editor, and he was shocked but elated when Raymond chose him to cover President Roosevelt's visit to the dam. This could be a game changer, the story he'd been waiting for.

The stakes were high though. Reporters from the Wenatchee and Spokane papers would surely be there. This was the president, after all. Papers from Seattle and Portland would be there. Radio stations throughout the country would be broadcasting the speech live. Harold had to find some way to break through the clutter, some angle to get his name out there.

Ozzie cranked down the driver's side window of his Ford and let the wind blow in, knocking his hat into the back seat. The foothills rose up in majestic purple in the distance, trees whizzing past as he drove.

Ozzie was ready to give the president a piece of his mind. It would only take him a few hours to drive the hundred miles of highway.

A truck passed on the opposite lane, its engine roaring in his open window, and was then gone. He planned to publicly refuse the payout offer in front of all the newspaper men who would be there covering the event.

He'd typed out what he wanted to say to the president when he saw him. He also made several copies on carbon paper so that he could give them to any reporters who were there to make sure they printed his comments with complete accuracy. He held one of the sheets against the steering wheel so he could review and rehearse on the road.

"Sir, I come before you today to tell you you're a hypocrite, a shyster, and a thief."

He cleared his throat. He was known for a voice that could carry across the river when needed, but public speaking was not his strong suit, which was why he tended to stick with letters where he could revise and rework until his thoughts were perfectly captured. When he tried to say them aloud, his feelings got the best of him, and he would derail into angry and less articulate tirades. His outburst at the town hall meeting was evidence of that, and he was as embarrassed by it as his children were, although he would never admit that to them.

If only he could have known what the men in that meeting were going to say, he could have prepared his speech in advance. He knew the letters embarrassed his children too, but he didn't care. They would thank him later if he were able to preserve their lives. They were young still. They didn't understand how complicated and difficult it is to start over.

Carter would learn soon enough because indeed he'd put himself in a position to start over from nothing. He didn't have to. He could have stayed home, helped save the business, tried to reconcile with his wife or at least work on getting the house back. He didn't have to wander off to God knew where. Carter would have to learn that starting from something is better than starting from nothing and that holding on to what you have is the only way to survive.

"You're a hypocrite, a shyster, and a thief. I decline your paltry offer of payout for my lands and buildings."

It was Ona who worried him the most. She kept quiet on the issue. Her mother and he had tried to protect her from grown-ups' business. He wondered sometimes what went on in her mind. Where she was when her eyes looked far away. He'd tried to give her a stable life, a roof over her head, and to make sure she never had to worry about the basic things in life.

Now his ability to do that was uncertain. He was living off what little savings he had. His business was in shambles. They would soon have nowhere to live. He had no choice but to fight to save those things. For her. For them. Where would he take her? Would he find heavy labor somewhere and work until he died or he was able to marry her off? He couldn't leave her alone. He could go back to Missouri and throw himself on the mercy of his family. A family he'd barely spoken to in thirty years. At least they'd take pity on his daughter if not him. He could leave her with a generous aunt or cousin and go find work wherever he could.

None of these options were good. His best chance of maintaining their life, their family, was to fight for what he'd already built. And he couldn't tell if she understood that.

Maybe it was time to sit her down and explain it to her, a thought as frightening to him as losing everything.

When Ozzie got to the site, he followed the other cars and then walked through the crowd toward town, the smell of hot chum residue wafting from his hands and clothes. Everyone was sticky with the heat, silt clinging to their damp clothes and dusting their hair.

He left his car on the outskirts of a shanty town, in a field full of other cars, a man in overalls collecting a parking fee. There were cars and people everywhere, more than Ozzie thought he'd probably ever seen assembled in one place in his entire life.

The walk to the ceremony site was long and hot, and Ozzie stopped and fanned himself with his hat. It was times like this that he wished he'd been born a more svelte man. He rested under the shade of a lone poplar seedling, barely tall enough to cast a shadow, and wiped his neck, forehead, and the bare parts of his scalp with his handkerchief. Beyond the road, brown, rocky hills, their craggy spines threaded with crisscrossing transmission lines that powered the new communities along the river rose under a cloudless blue sky.

His daughter was here somewhere meeting up with her high school friends, and possibly his son too, although he didn't know if Carter would care enough to show up.

As Ozzie neared the site, he encountered makeshift tables of souvenirs, popcorn, candies. "The Eighth Wonder of the World," they were calling the dam now. He picked up a promotional pamphlet that estimated the number of employed at six thousand men, not including the Bureau of Reclamation staff, as well as numerous public utilities employees and all the service providers that had cropped up for the community's supposed "spiritual and material welfare." The pamphlet claimed the Eighth Wonder would be as tall as a forty-six-story building and would contain more than twelve million cubic yards of concrete.

"Bah," Ozzie said, and tossed the pamphlet back on the pile. The young woman staffing the table looked offended, but Ozzie didn't care what she thought of him.

Closer to town, Ozzie heard chanting and saw bobbing, handwritten signs on sticks ahead.

"Wake up, Mr. President!"

"Fair wages for all!"

"Safer work conditions!"

One of the signs was scrawled with, "More than 60 dead laborers."

"Fair treatment for all!"

Ozzie limped in the heat as fast as he could to the picketers, his excitement building.

"Fair wages for all!" one of the men shouted almost in Ozzie's face.

He was so happy to find fellow agitators that he forgot for a moment that they were promoting work at the dam.

"How about fair payouts for people losing their land?" he said to the man, waving his carbon copies in the air.

The man stepped back from Ozzie. "Fair treatment for all!" the man repeated to the crowd of passersby.

Ozzie poked him in the chest. "You should see the ridiculous amount Roosevelt offered me for my property."

The man looked interested at last. "You're getting a federal payout?"

"Well, I'm here to refuse it. Take a look." Ozzie pulled a carbon copy of his speech from the sheaf of papers and handed it to the man. "I'm going to read this to the president during the ceremony in front of all the radio microphones and newspaper men."

The man took Ozzie's paper and read it with interest, then handed it back to him. "'You're a shyster and a thief'?"

"You come on up there with me, and you'll see," Ozzie told him.

After securing his Reno Room for the night, Harold Burnes crossed the rickety catwalk from B Street to Shack Town, marveling that the workers crab-walked this height and expanse over the deadly rushing water of the largest river in the West on a daily basis.

On the other side of the river, booths with souvenirs, cigarettes, nudie cards, cotton candy, candied apples, applets and cotlets, kettle corn, fresh fruit—even lemonade—littered the dusty roadway to the massive grandstand built for the occasion.

Harold bought a paper bag of cherries, and wandered the stalls, spitting the seeds into the dry, trampled grass.

A booth, clearly set up by either the Bureau of Reclamation or the Starks Company, was handing out pamphlets titled, "The Grand Coulee, Eighth Wonder of the World," with an artist's rendering of the finished dam on the cover. Harold flipped through it, chewing on a cherry. Nothing incendiary, although pure propaganda. He folded the pamphlet and tucked it into his notebook.

He wandered along, perusing trinkets and candy, until he heard heated voices. Naturally intrigued as a newspaper reporter, he followed the sound of shouting and found labor organizers in hot debate with a familiar face: Oscar Price from Kettle Rapids.

Ozzie recognized him straightway. "You're that newspaper man from Colville," Ozzie said.

"Harold Burnes, *Colville Scintilla*," Harold said reaching out for a handshake, but Ozzie didn't seem to notice his outstretched hand.

"I've been writing you letters," Ozzie said, a whiff of offense in his tone.

"Yes, I've received them," Harold said, smiling as diplomatically as he could muster. The letters were essentially long rants about any and all of the infrastructure projects taking place throughout the area.

"You haven't printed any," Ozzie said, squinting at Harold in the bright afternoon sun.

"I'll be sure to mention that to my editor," Harold said, trying to defer any hostility toward his absent editor, who was safely back on his horse ranch outside Colville.

"Hmm," Ozzie hummed, and pulled one of the carbon copies from his stack. The picketers behind him continued waving their signs and chanting. "Here's one for you." Ozzie said.

Ozzie handed the copy to Harold, who read it with amusement.

"I'm going to confront President Roosevelt with this today," Ozzie said.

Harold looked back at Ozzie to see if he was joking. "He's surrounded by a security detail at all times," Harold said.

"I'm not going to try to hurt him," Ozzie said, exasperated. "I want everyone to know that his offers for our land aren't enough. I have a daughter to care for. I can't move my business and my home for this amount. I can't start over with a pittance. The world needs to know how unfair he is."

"You're going to call the President of the United States a 'shyster'?" Harold folded the carbon copy into quarters and slid it into his notebook next to the pamphlet. "Why not a 'charlatan?'" Harold joked, but Ozzie was barely listening.

"My land and assets are worth far more than what he's offering me. He's got millions to build a dam, but he can't pay me what my land is worth? Just because he's the president, he thinks he can take my property with a low-ball offer? Hell, no, I say," Ozzie pointed a finger in the air for emphasis.

After paying to park the limo in a field, Charlotte made the girls line up against the Lincoln before they disbursed. The dog sat patiently on the grass next to her watching the instructions.

"Ladies," she said, looking each of them pointedly in the eyes. "This is an exciting day. We may never see a President of the United States in the flesh in Eastern Washington again in our lifetimes. Watch yourselves, keep your purses close, and your dignity closer. Meet me back here at the car by eight o'clock so we can get home around dark."

She thought of a phrase her husband used to repeat from his time in the service during the Great War. "We'll leave no girl behind, so keep track of where the car is." Charlotte gestured around the parking lot. "Keep your wits about you and watch the sun. When it gets close to that ridge to the west, make your way back to the car."

They nodded solemnly, which surprised and amused her. She chuckled as they scampered off in the dust and heat. Let them have their fun. Why not? Soon enough, they would be saddled with husbands and babies and laundry and all the regret and disappointment that might come with them.

Charlotte meandered up the road after the girls, the dog trailing dutifully as always. She looked at the many booths along the way and stopped at the Liberty Orchards table. She knew them well and supplied their factory in Cashmere with apples from time to time for their aplet confections. She bought a small paper bag of the apple candy, having long since stopped caring about her figure, and snacked on them as she walked, the powdery outer layer sticking to her lips as she chewed on the firm apple gelatin, walnuts crunching.

She came upon a booth with pamphlets for "The Grand Coulee, Eighth Wonder of the World," and chuckled to herself. There were pennant flags, scarves, spoons, ash trays, patches, plates, postcards, and all kinds of useless garbage. Yet she bought a small souvenir spoon with a tiny crest that said, "Grand Coulee Dam," with an artist's rendering of what it would look like when the spillway was done. She tucked it into her pocket.

Up ahead, she heard angry voices and could see picket signs, so she moved to the opposite side of the crowd that was making its way up the roadway to the grandstand, purposely avoiding whatever mayhem that was on her way to where the president would be speaking

She'd never seen a president live in the flesh before and was glad the girls had given her a reason to make the trek.

As soon as Joe and Carter flopped the sides of Moses's truck down and put out their merchandise in the shade, a crowd of curious onlookers quickly swarmed around them and continued to swarm despite the dust and heat. Carter saw Reynolds in the crowd of shoppers, his hair damp and sticky, a grin wide across his face, as he approached the truck.

As the crowd filled out, Carter scanned the faces for Ona.

"I'm looking for my little sister," Carter told Reynolds.

"What are we looking for? What does she look like?" Mainzer asked, searching the crowd of faces and automobiles. Reynolds nodded, looking around.

Carter had never thought about how to describe Ona before.

"Small," Carter said, and his friends both laughed. Carter panicked for a moment that they might find Ona pretty but didn't say anything about it. Raising the subject might plant the seed in one of their minds.

A group of Native Americans in ceremonial dress approached on the road, some on horseback, some on foot, some carrying drums. They stared at Joe while he handed a pack of cigarettes to a customer. Joe nodded their way, listening quietly to them converse with one another as they passed.

"Sanpoil tribe," he said to Carter and Reynolds after they passed. "From across the river. Likely here to protest the dam closing off their salmon runs."

Carter remembered Joe pointing out the native sites along the river during their time on Camp Ferry, the men they'd encountered on the shore, and how important salmon spawning season was to the tribes who lived around the Kettle Rapids area when he was young.

When Carter finally spotted Ona, she was screening the crowded road for him too, her face swarmed by the shoulders of the people around her. In flashes, he saw her. She looked like their mother, dark blond waves, deep gold complexion, and bright blue eyes. She was wearing a pale-yellow cotton dress that showed off her figure but didn't look quite right on her yet. Carter glanced quickly at his friends to see if they were looking at his sister with interest.

Joe Mainzer's attention was safely occupied by customers. Reynolds, on the other hand, looked alert and shoved a hand at Ona, "Pleasure, miss!" he said a little too excitedly.

Ona seemed taller now, or older since Carter last saw her. Maybe he hadn't noticed it before, but she didn't look like a kid anymore. There was something new in her posture, in her face, unlike the teenager he'd seen his last Christmas at home. She had on a straw hat to shield her from the sun, and when he hugged her hello, she held onto the crown to keep it from falling in the dirt.

"Where'd you get the duds?" he asked and pushed her away gently, jostling her by the shoulders, wishing she was still a little kid. This womanly Ona made him want to tousle her and remind her and himself that she was still his kid sister, that time wasn't passing so fast.

"It was Mama's," she said, crossing her hands to opposite shoulders and smoothing down the short sleeves. "I found it stuffed in a drawer. You like it?"

The crowd pulsed in and away from them as though they were a small snag in a stream. Carter stared at his sister, another face among so many strange ones, one he'd seen nearly every day after she was born and still barely knew.

"You seem different," she said, her expression quickly turning to suspicion, and he remembered how suddenly her demeanor could cloud over. Her friends came from behind the crowd, and she gave them a huge red smile as she introduced two giggly girls to him.

"How'd you get down here?" he asked her.

"Mrs. Powell drove us."

"Mrs. Powell? Where's Pops? Is he coming?"

"He's here somewhere with a letter for the president," she said, squinting at him in the sun.

Carter rolled his eyes. "We'll see how that goes."

"I suppose we will."

"What about Lloyd? Mae's not here, is she? Gonna have me arrested until I finally sign her papers?"

His sister's face clouded. She rifled in her purse and pulled out a sloppily folded sheaf of papers. "This is what you wanted, right? You can't really blame her," Ona said. "You came over to her house with a rifle."

"I didn't come over with it, it was already there," Carter said, taking the papers from her and tossing them into the bed of Moses's truck.

"Still. And you punched Roy."

"You're friends with Roy now, too?"

"She's my friend."

Carter scoffed at this.

"You're like our dad," she said, shaking her head. "You make Mae out to be such a terrible person, but you didn't think she was so terrible when you fell in love with her. You didn't think she was terrible when you were trying to talk her out of leaving you. She's not a new person all of a sudden because she doesn't want to be married to you anymore. Why is she now a bad person?"

Carter didn't have an answer for that. His sister had a point.

"You can say what you want about her," Ona continued. "Yeah, maybe she likes to live a little faster than most women, but who was right there with her? You were. She's never been anything but kind to me. Who was I supposed to talk to after Mom passed? You? Dad?"

Carter stared at the ground. He'd been so caught up with his own feelings about Mae and his dad's criticisms, he never thought how any of this might have affected his sister.

"Then all of a sudden, you move back in with us, and I'm not supposed to treat her as my friend anymore?"

"I'm sorry, kid," Carter said. "I didn't know you were that close."

"Well, she got lonely. You were gone to Colville all the time working. She didn't have a lot of company while you were gone, especially in the wintertime when the roads get tough to drive. I could walk the highway after school and spend an evening with her. She would have parties sometimes. She even helped me with my homework when I asked."

"I didn't know, I'm sorry."

Carter was perplexed by this. It was as though his wife had a secret life while he'd been away working to finish their house. If he didn't know about the depth of her friendship with his little sister, what else did he not know about?

"Did she have men over?" he asked Ona.

Ona sighed in disgust and turned to head up the road.

Carter ran to catch up with her. He grabbed her arm and stopped her. "Did she?"

"I don't know, probably," she said, shaking off his hand.

"What do you mean, probably?"

"You were never around."

"Did she or didn't she? What do you know?"

"Fine, there was a guy."

"You knew about this?"

"I never met him or anything; she talked about him sometimes."

"What? What did she say?"

"I don't know. It was a long time ago. I don't remember it well."

"Ona, spit it out. Did he come over to the house while I was gone?"

"I don't think so. I think they went out in Ephrata a few times."

"Like friends? Or like lovers?"

"Carter, what difference does it make anymore? You're not together."

"I want to know!" he raised his voice at her. "Tell me."

"I don't know what happened between them," Ona raised her voice back. "Ask her yourself."

"Maybe I will."

"Good."

Ona stalked off toward the grandstand, and he let her go.

He had upset her. He'd seen this look of hers many times. It reminded him of an incident when she was a girl of maybe five and he was a teenager. They'd been walking back from the ferry dock to where their buggy was parked. These were the days before Oscar bought them a car, when rickety wood wagons broke wheels on the rocks and holes in the roads by their farm. Carter had convinced Ona to walk along the riverbank, a shortcut over an uneven shoreline, rather than the long way up the road to town. She complained she was tired, but he convinced her to follow him even though she was small and not surefooted. She could have easily stumbled into the river and been swept away by the current. He'd wanted to get back quickly, wanted to get her home and not be responsible for her anymore. He couldn't remember now why he was in such a hurry, but he remembered his frustration with her as she picked her way unsteadily along the rocks as he hollered back, "C'mon!"

Eventually, he left her trailing behind and wasn't too worried when she was no longer in sight. He paused along the shore, waiting for her to catch up around the bend.

"Carter!" she called from someplace invisible to him.

"Up here! Follow the damn river!" he called back, uncertain if his voice would carry backward over the rush of the river.

"Carter!" she called again, only this time her voice had a sharp waver of fear, and he groaned and made his way back to where it sounded like she was.

When he came around the bend that hid her from view, he saw her standing frozen on the rocks, staring into one of the kettles swirling in the deep holes of the bedrock by the river rapids.

When Ona looked up and saw him there, her voice became even more panicked, "Carter! Carter!"

He was confused. She was clearly fine, but as he stared where she was staring, he saw what troubled her. A river otter was trapped in the kettle. It scratched at the rock walls of the kettle as the water spun and dunked it. As he got closer, he realized she was crying. What in the world did she expect him to do? Dive in the racing water and rescue the thing? Now he wished he'd at least tried something. Instead he made fun of her. She cried harder then, blame and incredulity in her eyes. He left her on the bank to probably watch the animal drown and walk home by herself.

Back at home, she never said a word to their parents about him leaving her alone, but she looked at him with mistrust after that, a look he'd seen plenty more from his wife after he was married.

Now, as she stalked off from him up the road toward the grandstand, her face red under her summer hat, her jaw set, eyes bright but hardened, her firmness unable to fully hide her fire, he recognized finally that it was a result of all those experiences.

He watched her yellow dress push through the crowd, saddened by his role in her transformation. Reynolds wandered up the road behind her, his slinged arm hung like a broken wing.

Mainzer nudged Carter with his elbow, and they both watched silently as the man from the Bureau of Indian Affairs who approached them at the mine wandered past their truck on the road, raised his hat when he recognized them, and kept walking.

"Is this area in his jurisdiction?" Carter asked Joe.

"I don't know," Joe answered.

Surveying the debacle below, Starks became anxious. The president and his Secret Service contingent would be arriving within the hour, and Starks wanted to rehearse his remarks before Mr. Banks from the Bureau of Reclamation and his team showed up. Starks's press secretary was still on the train from Minneapolis and had wired draft remarks the day before. If Starks was being honest, though, he preferred to speak in his own words. Not that he didn't appreciate the support of his public relations team. Certainly he did when there was a labor issue, death, injury, or other company inconvenience he needed them to handle for him. For these big press events, though, he enjoyed preparing what to say on his own.

He watched the scene below, mentally chewing on his own rhetoric, until his secretary, a lanky woman in her forties originally from Moses Lake, interrupted his reverie, looking over her glasses at him.

"A Miss Ona Price here to see you, sir."

Starks turned from the window, perplexed.

"Miss Price?" he asked, trying to think who she was.

"I can send her away, sir, but she said you would want to see her," his secretary said.

"Miss Ona Price," he said, nodding as he put it together that she was the daughter of the Kettle Rapids ferryman he'd offered to pay out and whose brother was one of his employees. He remembered the day he spoke with her on the front porch of her father's house.

"I'll send her away, sir," his secretary said, moving toward the door.

Starks reached a hand out to her. "No, no," he said. "This could be interesting. Send her in."

"Sir?" his secretary said. It wasn't customary for him to accept impromptu visits, but he was curious what the young Price girl wanted and impressed by her nerve to show up and ask for a meeting.

"I'd like to speak with her," Starks said, and settled into the chair behind his desk.

Ona Price swished into his office, a tiny vision with red lips and in a yellow dress that was too big for her, chin stuck out to overcompensate for her nervousness, her hands trembling on her huge hat and a small white handbag she kept clutched in front of her.

"What can I do for you, Miss Price?" he asked, fascinated by this unexpected visit.

It had been many years since a teenage girl tried to railroad him, and a long-forgotten fatherly instinct was intrigued, impressed, and curious what she would say. He leaned back in his chair and folded his hands over his abdomen. He noted with interest that she instinctively leaned forward when he did this.

"Well, sir," she said, working to still her hands and her timbre. "When you came to my house before, you said you would give me double what you offered my father."

"Indeed, I did," Starks said. "And since then, he's sent dozens of letters to the local papers criticizing my project."

Ona furrowed her brow and sighed. "Yes, I know."

"The deal was you would stop that from happening."

"I have a counteroffer for you," she said, her voice wavering.

"Really." Starks leaned forward with interest, forgetting his usual poker face in this turn of events.

"I believe my father plans to make a scene at your event with the president today."

"That's not too surprising, I suppose." Starks leaned back again in his chair. "We have security ready for outbursts of that kind."

She eyed him for a moment, the corners of her eyes puckering like she was offended he wasn't taking her more seriously.

He relented. "What makes you think that?"

"He left copies of his speech around the house."

"And what makes you think I should be concerned?"

She handed him a creased carbon copy with jagged typewriter marks on it.

"He's brought copies with him. I'm guessing you don't want his speech in all the papers or on the radio programs. I'm guessing you don't want the president embarrassed by your event. I'm guessing you would like today to go as smoothly as possible." She stared at him wide-eyed but straight-faced, folding her hands on top of her handbag again.

She wasn't wrong. The president would be there shortly, and Starks and his press secretary would need to shepherd him and Mr. Banks through the event as seamlessly as they could in the dust and heat of an Eastern Washington summer afternoon. They had enough problems with the labor organizers picketing and protests about upsetting native burial and fishing grounds.

"You have my attention," he said, leaning against his desktop and folding his hands on the piles of plans and project files.

Her hands trembled atop her handbag. "If I can stop him from making a scene, you'll give me the same money you offered me before."

Starks nodded, thinking about this. Did he really want to get into a negotiation with a teenage girl right now? He really didn't. The money was there. This girl, though, she had a future ahead of her that she would need to fire in the kiln.

Before Starks could answer, his secretary came back in, and he and Ona both turned to see what she wanted, "The president has arrived, sir. And Mr. Fitzgerald is here from the home office."

Ona turned back to face him with a look of panic. "Do we

have a deal?"

"Sir, they're waiting for you," his secretary said from the doorway.

Starks feigned reluctance, unable to stop from smiling at Ona Price's awkward brazenness. He knew he couldn't resist her. "We have a deal," he said.

She sighed with relief. "I'll be by after the event for my money," she said meaningfully.

"That won't be necessary," Starks said, turning to his secretary. "Draw up a check for Miss Price for double whatever her father was offered by the federal government for his land."

Starks stood and shrugged on his suit jacket.

"No," Ona said standing too, and squaring her shoulders. "Four times. You said double what you offered my father, which he said was double the government payout. The amount of the payout is in his speech. He has the offer letter with him."

Starks smiled, checking himself in the mirror, and straightened his tie. He couldn't help but admire her grit.

"You're right." He turned to his secretary.

"Make a check out to Miss Price before she leaves for four times whatever her father was offered for his land."

He turned to Ona. "If the event today goes smoothly, that check will clear," he said. "If it goes smoothly."

The Price girl watched him quietly as he left the room, as though shocked at her own success.

Starks hustled over to the makeshift accommodations his team set up for the president and his Secret Service team in the administration building in Engineer's Town, careful not to break a sweat in the heat, even though he was in a hurry. Starks had offered his own security as a gesture, but the White House insisted on having their own detail since the assassination attempt on President Roosevelt a few years back and several recent death threats. They also wanted everything to be carefully coordinated to prevent the press and the public from seeing the president coming and going in his wheelchair.

Mr. Banks and his team from the Bureau of Reclamation were there, and the hand pumping and "how do you do's" were going strong. Starks hung back, letting the bureau make their lap first.

His press secretary from the Minneapolis office was attached to his side. Mr. Fitzgerald, a tall, remarkably calm man with a dark curling pompadour, his suit rumpled from train travel hanging off his lanky frame, handed Starks a dossier that was propped on top of Fitzgerald's perpetual clipboard.

"All the Seattle and Portland papers and radio stations are here, sir. And of course the locals."

Starks rifled through the folder, mostly talking points and back up documentation if he should need it.

"The Secret Service is very insistent no one is to see the president in his wheelchair. They will prevent anyone from taking photos of him in it and confiscate the film of anyone they think might have photographed him. They've asked us to instruct our men to do the same."

Starks stared at Fitzgerald. "How in the world is he going to make his speech?"

"They want to prop him up at the lectern."

"Why did we build a grandstand?" Starks asked, knowing Fitzgerald did not have an answer for that. "He'll never make it up those stairs."

"Maybe we can drive him up close and have him speak from the car. We can drag the microphone wire out a few feet longer. They're driving him to Spokane right after the event anyway."

"Better make it a convertible so people can see him," Starks said.

"Where will we find a convertible in an hour?"

"There are thousands of cars out there today. You'll find one."

Fitzgerald made a note on his clipboard. "I'll get with the other press secretaries to rewrite the flow on stage for you and Mr. Banks."

"Better do it fast," Starks said. "What about crowd control? Any risk assessment?"

"We have labor representatives picketing on the road into Electric City. They are citing unfair wages and racial discrimination among their rationales for union organization."

"Expected that," Starks said.

"Also members of the Colville Reservation expressing concerns about salmon and burial lands, but they seem peaceful," Fitzgerald continued.

Starks nodded. "Anything else?" he asked.

"Drunks, heat, dust…" Fitzgerald stopped and motioned with his head past Starks's shoulder, prompting Starks to turn around.

Mr. Banks was waving him over to meet the president, who was seated in an armchair with two Secret Service men flanking him, the president's own press secretary hovering close by.

Without getting up, President Roosevelt took Starks's outstretched hand in both of his, shaking it warmly, and Mr. Banks looked on, smiling.

"Thank you for being here today, sir," Starks told the president. "It means a lot to me, my workers, and to the community that has sprung up around the construction site."

"I go back a long, long way in my interest in the Grand Coulee," the president said, raising his eyebrows and peering up at Starks through his spectacle lenses. "I remember very well that in the campaign of 1920, when I was out through the Northwest, it was a very live subject."

"Yes, of course," Starks said, feeling self-conscious that he was towering over one of the most powerful men in the world.

"We are in the process of making the American people 'dam minded.' I know you intend to continue to do your part in that."

"I will do my best, sir."

"As we were coming down the river today, I could not help thinking of all that water running down unchecked to the sea, and all the territory now unused but destined someday to contain the homes of thousands and thousands of citizens."

"As you said yourself before, the 'best use of everything for all,'" Starks said, repeating the phrase he'd read from the president's speech during his last visit to the site years earlier.

"Indeed. We are going to see, I believe, with our own eyes, electricity and power made so cheap that they will become a standard article of use, not merely for agriculture and manufacturing, but for every home within reach of an electric transmission line."

Mr. Banks chimed in, "I certainly think that's a possibility now that you signed the funding bill for the high dam extension, which we greatly appreciated."

"I want to leave you with one suggestion," the president said, pausing for a moment and checking his wristwatch to see how much time he had before their expected start time for speeches. "There are parts of this nation that are not as favored as the Northwest. Mistakes have been made. They have cut off their timber, their land is played out, or they plowed up prairie land, which is now blowing away. You have room for them here in the Northwest, where they can make homes, where they can live happily and prosperously. I am asking for your hospitality in helping your fellow Americans, who are less favored than you are, to make a new start in life."

"We will do what we can, sir," Mr. Banks said.

"I knew you would," President Roosevelt said, motioning to his press secretary, who escorted Starks and Mr. Banks out of the room, closing the door behind them.

Fitzgerald and the press secretary from the Bureau of Reclamation were waiting for them with a new plan for the event.

"Well, ain't this a pretty picture."

Carter recognized his father's voice in the crowd before he saw him. He finished taking cash from a customer for a pack of cigarettes and turned to Ozzie as his father sauntered over from the road.

"Is that all you have to say to me after not seeing each other this long?" Carter asked, hands on his hips, squinting at his father in the bright afternoon.

Joe looked at them with interest. It wouldn't be hard to guess they were related based on their facial features, even though Carter had his mother's slighter build.

"You out here selling nudie cards and cigarettes because you got shit-canned from the dam?"

Carter gestured to the rumpled sheaf of papers Ozzie held that were now damp with sweat, remembering what his sister said about a letter for the president. "You're not about to do something stupid, are you?"

"I don't see how that's any of your concern," Ozzie said, taking his hat off and wiping his scalp and forehead with his handkerchief again. "What kind of candy you got?"

Carter stared at him for a moment, amazed that this was how he would want to carry on after everything they'd been through and how long since they'd spoken.

"Life savers and red hots," Carter told him.

"Mmm, I think I'll pass," Ozzie said. "I'm in more of cotton candy mood today." He put his hat back on, its rim showing a ring of sweat, his insult clear and satisfying, and kept walking.

"Suit yourself," Carter said, turning back to their customers. Joe raised concerned eyebrows, but Carter shook his head to let his friend know he was fine.

Carter tried to focus on work but couldn't help but see his father's bulk moving through the crowd, the second family member today to walk angrily away from him on this same road.

"You got this?" Carter asked Joe, looking around at the crowd. "I should probably head into the ceremony in a bit and make sure he doesn't try anything."

"Of course," Joe nodded.

Fitzgerald and the other press secretaries were franticly directing reporters to the fenced off area they'd designated in front of the grandstand speakers. Between the heat and the last-minute changes to the program, they were all sweating and anxious. Regional and national radio stations had their microphones positioned in front of the speakers for live broadcasts, and the newspapermen were gathered into a pit area, pencils sharp and elbows sharper.

Harold Burnes looked around the press pit, fighting the feeling of a small fish in a big pond. Sure, maybe he worked for a smaller town paper, but he was still getting started and determined to go places. And he might be the only one in the pit who knew Oscar Price of Kettle Rapids planned to make a scene in front of President Roosevelt. Harold scanned the crowd until his eyes landed on Ozzie, agitated and sweaty, fanning himself with his hat and still clutching his stack of carbon copies under one arm.

A meager clapping started in the crowd, and Harold looked up. M.J. Starks from the Starks Company, Mr. Banks from the Bureau of Reclamation, and their security people filed on stage.

Starks surveyed the crowd as he walked out onto the grandstand with Mr. Banks. Fitzgerald and the rest seemed to have the press under control in the dusty pit below. The crowd of spectators spread out all the way to the road to Shack Town, people milling around and half paying attention. He scanned the crowd for the

Price girl or her father but didn't see them. It would be time to move on soon, time to bid this job adieu and win the next construction contract. It would be more cost effective to sell and surplus the equipment and other assets they'd accumulated here than to move them. His head of finance was negotiating to sell some of their steel and other scrap metal to Japan, presumably to help them with their war effort in China.

For his part, he would head back to the home office in Minneapolis when they were done here, check on his estate, visit his children and grandchildren, and calculate his next move. Many of his crew, including Soop, were headed down to the Friant Dam project in California, capitalizing while they could on the nation's "dam mindedness" as President Roosevelt called it. As long as there was funding to support jobs to drag the country out of the Depression, he and all the rest of them would dam any river they were paid to.

At the designated time by their wrist watches, Mr. Banks went up to the microphone to welcome the crowd.

Carter pushed through the crowd, looking for his sister or his father. A tapping on the microphone came through the loud-speakers on the stage, and Carter looked up to where a man he recognized from the town hall meeting back in Kettle Rapids took the microphone to address the crowd. Starks was sitting behind him. Along the periphery of the stage were security people, but Carter couldn't tell who was from Starks Company and who were with the president.

"Today is a great day in our nation's history," Mr. Banks said, reading from the talking points his press secretary prepared. "Our president is here today to celebrate the most impressive feat attempted by mankind yet. The construction of the largest hydroelectric dam in the world on the biggest, wildest river in the West."

The crowd clapped, obviously more interested in hearing the president.

Mr. Banks gestured Starks up to the microphone. Starks looked out over the crowd, faces blurring in the heat.

"When we started the Grand Coulee Dam project, we made you a promise," Starks said. "We promised you water for irrigation, thousands of acres of previously unusable land. We promised more jobs, more industry, more development in this region. We promised you electricity to power cities for generations to come. Today, our president is here to mark the day we fulfilled those promises."

Many people in the crowd clapped, but Starks knew they were here to see the president and kept his remarks short. Fitzgerald and the press secretary from the bureau stretched a long red ribbon across the stage, and Starks and Mr. Banks cut it awkwardly with a giant pair of dull scissors, bulbs flashing as reporters photographed the occasion.

Fitzgerald dragged the microphone out to the convertible, where President Roosevelt was positioned in the back seat, Secret Service men all around the vehicle keeping the crowd back. Earlier, Fitzgerald sent a staffer out to find a convertible, and the staffer intercepted a motorist coming off what Fitzgerald learned the locals called Speedball Highway. The motorist was looking for parking, and the staffer offered him five dollars for the use of his car. The motorist declined and then reconsidered when he learned it was for the president to use, an occasion he'd probably brag about the rest of his life.

Mr. Banks went back to the microphone, reading from his prepared remarks. "Thank you, Mr. Starks. My colleagues and I want to thank our president for being with us today. Please turn your attention to President Roosevelt," Mr. Banks motioned to the road where the convertible was waiting, "who will be addressing us all from his motorcade as he is heading directly from our event to Spokane for an important meeting with our state house and senate representatives."

Fitzgerald clutched the long stand of the microphone, holding it at an angle, the hot end toward President Roosevelt where he could hold the circular device with his hands to steady it while he spoke. The massive speakers at the grandstand squawked, and the crowd cheered, which made the President grin, the skin around his eyes crinkling behind his spectacles.

President Roosevelt gripped the microphone and started his remarks: "Coming back to Grand Coulee after three years, I am made very happy by the wonderful progress that I have seen."

The crowd cheered again for the president, and he smiled, waving from the back seat of the convertible to them.

Starks surveyed the crowd, looking for any trouble and making sure he had eyes on Fitzgerald.

President Roosevelt continued, "I cannot help feeling that everybody who had anything to do with the building of this great dam is going to be happy all the rest of their lives."

More cheers, a few boos, Starks noted, spotting Ozzie Price in the crowd.

Ozzie scoffed and looked around to see other reactions.

Harold scribbled notes in his notebook about the crowd.

"Someday we will have a 'Grand Coulee Association,'" President Roosevelt went on, "for those people who had something to do with this construction. Membership in that association will be like a badge of honor because we are building something that is going to do a great amount of good for this nation through all the years to come."

More cheers from the crowd.

Charlotte pushed her way closer to the grandstand, keeping an eye out for the girls in her care. She spotted Ona up toward the front, not far from the press pit, and navigated through the crowd in her direction.

"My head is full of figures," President Roosevelt continued, gesturing a hand toward the massive expanse of the construction site. "The easiest way to describe those figures is to say that this is the largest structure, so far as anybody knows, that has ever been undertaken by man in one place." He waved a hand widely as though capturing all of the world.

The crowd cheered, "Eighth Wonder" pennants waving. The president beamed at their approval.

"Superlatives do not count for anything because," President Roosevelt pounded his fist in the air between words, "It. Is. So. Much. Bigger," he paused for effect, "than anything ever tried before. There is no comparison."

The crowd cheered again, and Starks was relieved.

Ozzie looked around the crowd, annoyed that none of the picketers followed him or were anywhere to be seen.

President Roosevelt leaned against the back seat of the convertible, clearly pleased with himself and waited for the crowd to calm.

"We look forward," President Roosevelt said, cradling the microphone Fitzgerald still held for him, "not only to the great good this will do in the development of power, but also in the development of thousands of homes, the bringing in of millions of acres of new land for future Americans."

Ozzie booed as loudly as he could muster and shouted to others in the crowd. "Future Americans? What about the rest of us? What about my land and my business?"

President Roosevelt continued over the loudspeaker: "In the State of Washington, there is a splendid understanding of one of the objectives in the development of the acres that are going to be irrigated."

Ozzie turned to anyone who would listen. "Here's what President Roosevelt offered me," he said, attempting to hand his carbon copies out in the crowd, but no one was interested. "Here's what this thief is offering me for my land."

The president went on, "There are thousands of families in this country in the Middle West, in the Plains area, who are not making good because they are trying to farm on poor land."

Starks noticed the crowd murmured at this and did not cheer. He spotted Ona Price finally in the crowd, her attention keen, her big hat shading her from the worst of the afternoon sun, her lips freshly bright and red.

Ozzie cupped his hands around his mouth to call into the crowd and up to the motorcade, "You're a charlatan, a liar, and a thief!"

Ozzie had a moment of panic realizing he said his insults wrong. He shuffled through his papers again making sure he had the right words for his next opportunity. *Hypocrite, shyster, liar. Hypocrite, shyster, liar.* Although maybe *charlatan* was better. Too late now.

Carter pushed his way through the crowd looking for his sister. He spotted her not far from the stage watching the unfolding events and glancing around nervously, and he angled toward her direction.

The president continued, "I look forward to the day when this valley, this basin, is opened up, giving the first opportunity to these American families who need some good farmland in place of their present farms."

"Opened up?" Ozzie grew more agitated. "You're going to take my land from me but then open up the valley?" Ozzie shoved his way toward the radio microphones.

Charlotte spotted Ozzie headed toward the reporters. Oh, Price. So unnecessarily hot-headed. She started making her way toward Ona to make sure her young charge wasn't overly embarrassed by anything Ozzie might say or do.

President Roosevelt went on. "They are a splendid crowd of people and it us up to us, as a nation, to help them to live better than they are living now."

Harold Burnes watched as Oscar Price pushed through the crowd toward the press pit.

Ozzie shouted into the crowd. "Oh, they're 'splendid' are they? How nice."

Ona heard the distinctive sound of her father's voice coming toward her in the crowd and bristled. She scanned the faces around her but could not spot him. She looked quickly to the stage where Starks was standing, and the two of them locked eyes. Ona raised her eyebrows to Starks, and he nodded ever so slightly to her left to indicate where Ozzie was, a calculated complicity between them born from interest in a mutually agreeable outcome for this day.

"There is another phase that I was thinking about this morning," the president continued. "When the dam is completed and the pool is filled, we will have a lake 155 miles long running all the way to Canada. You young people especially are going to live to see the day when thousands and thousands of people are going to use this great lake both for transportation purposes and for pleasure purposes."

"Pleasure purposes! Pleasure purposes!" Ozzie yelled into the crowd, still moving toward the press pit, ready to toss his carbon copies like ticker tape into the air. "They're drowning my business on this lake!"

Almost to his sister now, Carter recognized his father's voice shouting above the crowd.

Harold watched Ozzie with interest, wondering how this would end up for him.

Ona searched the crowd, looking back to Starks, who tried to give her clues from the stage. Finally, she spotted her father coming her direction, and she fought through the crowd, her tiny body no match to his hulking frame, determined to make this go her way, the check from Starks burning in her handbag.

Charlotte pushed against the crowd, trying to get to Ona who was moving toward Ozzie. At last, Ona reached her father. He looked genuinely shocked to see her, as though in his outrage he had forgotten she was there.

"Daddy," she implored, her hand on his arm. "Please don't. Whatever it is you're planning to do, please don't."

Ozzie looked confused for a moment, looked toward the press pit, then back at his daughter's face.

"Why are you wearing her dress?" he asked, breathless.

The president continued on the loudspeakers. "There will be sail boats and motorboats and steamship lines running from here to the northern border of the United States and into Canada."

Ona gently took his carbon copies from him. "Please don't do it."

"It is a great project—something that appeals to the imagination of the whole country," the president went on.

"For my sake, please don't," she said, tears welling in her eyes.

Ozzie stared at his daughter. She was a tiny vision, who looked so much like the woman he'd loved and married before hardship broke them both. He never wanted to disappoint her, only to protect her. The words *sailboats and motorboats* rang in his ears, and he started toward the press pit again.

"Pops!" Ozzie felt hands on his shoulders, and then Carter was there, and Charlotte was pulling Ona away from him. Ona looked over Charlotte's shoulder to Starks who nodded to her and looked away.

The sight of Carter and Charlotte rattled Ozzie anew. He pointed to Charlotte, "Don't you patronize me. Don't you judge me. You could have helped me with this. You could have been a second mother to them."

"Pops, what are you talking about?" Carter said, and Ona looked at Charlotte, who pursed her lips.

"She didn't tell you?" Ozzie shouted at them. "I wanted to marry her, but she said no," he said, wagging an accusatory finger at Charlotte. "It's me, you and you," he said, pointing to Carter and Ona. "No one else is going to help us. Not your dead mother," he pointed at Ona, "and not your ex-wife," he poked Carter in the chest, "and not anyone else," he said, waving a dismissive hand at Charlotte.

Ozzie broke out of Carter's grasp and started toward the press pit again. From the crowd, Secret Service men dropped on Ozzie. Carter, Ona, and Charlotte watched, their eyes wide, as the Secret Service swiftly and quietly scurried Ozzie out of the crowd. In mere seconds, he could not be seen.

President Roosevelt went on from the back of the convertible: "I am always glad to see a project in the construction stage because when it is finished, very few people will realize—they won't be able to visualize—all the difficult work in the actual construction."

Harold Burnes watched the scene with Oscar Price unfold, making notes in his notebook while all the other reporters remained focused on the president, unaware of what happened. Starks too kept an eye on the situation.

"I hope to come back here in another two or three years," the president said, concluding his remarks, "and see this dam pretty nearly completed. When that time comes, I think we had better, all of us, have a reunion of rejoicing."

The crowd cheered louder than before, pennants waving wildly.

With that, to Starks' relief, President Roosevelt's team whisked him away to switch cars and drive to his event in Spokane.

After the scene Ozzie almost made, Charlotte hustled Ona through the crowd, still gripping the sheaf of carbon copies, Carter following closely behind them. When they got to the stand of poplars where Moses's truck was parked, a crowd of shoppers still pressed around their merchandise, handing Joe their money.

Charlotte went to look for the dog, whistling for him in the parking lot.

Ona's face was damp, her dress rumpled from the crowd. Carter searched his sister's face not sure what to say to her. She didn't look upset or angry but stunned and resigned. He was saddened by their conversation earlier, that their father didn't do any better by her. He wanted to help her, wanted to erase the many ways he'd hurt her.

Carter dug in his pockets, and Joe watched with mild interest as Carter counted his bills.

"Everything okay?" Joe asked. "What are you doing?"

"What do you have on you?" Carter asked.

"Why?"

"What do you have?"

Mainzer looked from Carter to Ona and back to Carter again. Joe's hair had come undone from its pomade in the heat. He handed Carter a fistful of bills and coins.

Charlotte came back with the dog. "I should get her home," she said to Carter, and he nodded.

He gave his sister a hug goodbye and forced the cash into her hand.

Ona paused as though she might not take it, and then shoved the wad into her handbag.

Charlotte led a quiet Ona down the dusty road through Shack Town, past the picketers to the limo, and the two of them waited, Charlotte anxiously, Ona in a shocked state of calm, until her friends arrived back at the car. Charlotte hugged the girls in relief, grateful that they'd actually listened to her instructions.

"Let's go home," she said, and opened the door for them to pile in.

On the drive back through the winding wilderness, in the dark summer night, all the windows open, and the moon and stars firing overhead, Charlotte glanced nervously in the rearview at her wards. She wondered where the Secret Service whisked Oscar off to and how long they would keep him. Ona would be fine alone for a day or two, but much more than that, Charlotte wasn't sure. She might bring the girl to her place until he was able to come home.

Ona's friends jostled quietly against each other in the back seat on the drive and eventually fell asleep, while Ona looked alert to the world, her adorable white handbag with its patent leather bow clasped tightly on her lap.

Charlotte let them be. It seemed the right thing to do. When they got closer to Kettle Rapids, Ona told Charlotte where to turn to let her first friend out. The girl clambered out like a sleepy deer, saying, "Thank you, Mrs. Powell." And when they got to the other's house, that girl did the same.

Charlotte and Ona were alone in the car. "Do you want to come up front?" Charlotte asked her.

Ona hesitated, but then said, "Okay."

Charlotte sat patiently in the driver's seat, shooing the dog to the back while Ona climbed in next to her in the front passenger seat. They sat quietly outside the house for a moment, Charlotte not wanting to pressure Ona but give her the opportunity to say whatever was on her mind.

Ona took a deep breath and looked down at her handbag. Charlotte waited, that motherly thing burbling up again.

"Is it true what my father said?" Ona asked.

"You should probably talk to him about that," Charlotte said gently.

Ona nodded.

"Mrs. Powell?" Ona asked finally, looking at Charlotte.

"What is it, dear?" Charlotte said.

Ona opened her purse and fumbled inside, pulling out a check.

"How much of your land could I buy with this?" Ona asked, handing Charlotte a check from the Starks Company.

Charlotte looked at the check in the dark trying to get her middle-aged vision around the numbers.

"Good gracious, girl, what would you want to buy property from me for?"

"Because you're out of the flood zone. We could move our house up there."

Charlotte stared at Ona, trying to determine if she was serious.

"We could move other houses up there too," Ona continued. "Make it a new town."

"I think your father might have something to say about that once they release him," Charlotte countered.

"See, that's the thing though. I owe him."

"After what I saw today, I don't think you owe him much."

Ona looked up at Charlotte, her eyes welling. "I'm the one who did it."

"Did what?" Charlotte asked, tired and confused by the events of the day and wishing she'd eaten more than candy. And then it dawned on her what Ona was talking about.

Ona looked back down in her lap. "I'm the one who cut his boat loose. You're the only one who knows."

Charlotte exhaled, not knowing what to say and taking it in. The stars looked farther away than usual, like they had taken a step back from the spinning earth she was on. She turned to Ona.

"You can never tell him that," Charlotte said. "No one will be better off for him knowing. Not him, not you, and not your brother. You unburden yourself to me tonight, you give me those copies now, and we will figure this out. Then we will both take this to our graves, do you hear me?"

Ona's voice wavered as she said *yes,* handing the sheaf of carbon copies to Charlotte, the tears at last trickled down Ona's cheeks.

"I didn't mean for it to happen the way it did. I was tired of his letters and his ranting and raving in town. This was going to be an opportunity for all of us to find someplace new, to start over. I don't want to live in the house where my mother died. I don't want to walk the streets of town and know that people are judging me because of my father's politics and my brother's situation. Every time I see someone carrying a newspaper, I cringe. Did one of his letters get published? Is there some new story that's going to set him off today?"

Charlotte stroked Ona's shoulder.

"I didn't mean for the ferry to be so damaged. I wanted to scare him. Make him think that maybe there was more at stake, so he'd stop. I asked Mae if I could borrow her car, and I drove through the gate. She was always running into things and beating up that car, I knew she'd never notice. The gate smashed to bits across the front grill more easily than I thought it would. Then I tossed whatever I could on the ground. Nothing too important, made a mess.

"I never realized how heavy those cables are. I only meant to let it drift a little. Even if he couldn't move the landing and the cables, the ferry will still float, right? Maybe if he saw a threat to the ferry, he'd back off. I guess I didn't think it through as well as I should have.

"The crank for the cable was hard for me to move. I had to put all my strength behind it to even get it to budge. I finally climbed up on it and bounced my full weight on it. And then it gave and knocked me onto the dock."

Ona's voice broke, and Charlotte squeezed her shoulder. "You could have been hurt."

"The cable whizzed like a fish line out into the water, and I heard a groaning and ripping sound. I didn't want to be caught there, so I ran back to the car. I didn't even stop to look to see what happened to the ferry. I had to get out of there.

"I drove back to Mae's, but I didn't tell her what I had done. I didn't think she'd tell my family, but I didn't know who she else might tell. She might be afraid someone saw the car and would blame her. I didn't tell anyone. I kept quiet.

"At first I hoped he'd be able to fix it, but then it occurred to me that this might make this move easier. He has nothing to preserve now. It's already done and gone. Maybe he would give up the fight."

Charlotte sighed and looked out the windshield into the dark landscape, her hand still on Ona's shoulder.

"Do you feel better now?"

Ona nodded again, dabbing at her eyes and face with the hem of her dress.

"You understand that you can never tell anyone else about this?"

"I want to make it right," Ona said, her voice soft and wavering.

"By buying some of my land?" Charlotte said.

Ona nodded, "And making a new town."

"Why a new town?"

"Other people need to move too, don't they? Not just us?"

"Yes, I suppose that's true. Everyone down along the shoreline." Despite the surprise of Ona's revelation, Charlotte was intrigued by this idea. It certainly was a possible solution to what to do with her place when she was no longer able to work and eventually when she passed on. Lord knew she'd reinvented herself before when she needed to, she could do it again.

Ona looked at Charlotte carefully and shuddered a teary sigh of relief.

"We could call it Powell Creek," Ona offered, her tears subsiding.

No offense to her late husband, but if Charlotte was going to do this, she wasn't about to give the credit to her husband's family on any maps or highway signs instead of herself.

"We'll call it Charlotte Creek," she said, smiling at Ona and patting her hand, then turning the Lincoln back toward home.

The morning after the Grand Coulee Dam dedication ceremony, Harold returned the key for his Reno Room to the bartender and made the drive back to Colville. He went straight to the office to type up his notes and left his story on his editor's desk before going home.

FDR'S SECRET SERVICE TEAM EARNS THEIR KEEP

Local pot stirrer Oscar Price put the President's new Secret Service team to the test this week. At the dedication ceremony for the beloved Grand Coulee Dam project, Price was seen trying to distribute anti-dam, anti-government propaganda to attendees of the event, spurred on by labor agitators protesting the employment practices and working conditions of the notorious Starks Company.

Price was last reported about in this paper when he accused the Starks Company of tampering with his ferry business in Kettle Rapids and their security team tossed him into the street.

In a letter obtained exclusively by the Colville Scintilla, *Price revealed the purchase price provided for his land and assets by the federal government. Addressed to President Roosevelt, Price referred in his letter to the mastermind of the New Deal as a "shyster, hypocrite, and a thief." Before he could deliver his letter, however, the Secret Service escorted a belligerent Mr. Price out of the event.*

PART 4
SALVAGE

Late summer 1937
Washington State Route 25

In the corral behind the stables at Fort Spokane, a half dozen or so spotted Appaloosa horses and dove-eyed dairy cows grazed, grasshoppers pluming at their hooves any time they stepped. Outside the fence, wooden apple crates full of plates and other tableware were set out on the ground like a buffet.

In the failing light of dusk, the main officer's house was lit bright, men coming in and out of the front porch, screen door squeaking and slamming, drinks and guns held with equal casualness, laughter and serious conversation mingling as though celebration and business, fun and violence, were equally at hand.

The surrounding buildings lingered in various states of disrepair, some from the elements, some from human hands, piles of lumber, brick, and other useful resources stacked nearby.

In the orchard beyond, the sound of more laughter and music floated into the dimming summer evening, specks of kerosene lanterns lighting up the apricot and peach trees. The trees trembled, their underleaves silver, clusters of golden fruit dotting them, shuddering as though about to drop to the ground from ripeness.

CHAPTER 11
August 1937

The morning after the dedication event, Carter got up early before anyone else in the camp was awake. The night before, everyone was drunk and celebratory, and they would be sleeping it off for a while. The town was feeling elated and hopeful after the ceremony. Carter and Joe sold more than ever before that night. After Mrs. Powell took his sister home, the crowd got even rowdier as the temperature cooled off. Joe Mainzer grabbed a tackle box full of merchandise from the truck and walked the crowd selling junk to drunk people like a cigarette girl in a movie theater.

Carter, on the other hand, after arguing with his sister and seeing his father hauled off by the Secret Service, was even more depressed by the enthusiasm around him, the exuberant crowds leaving him jostled and claustrophobic. He should have done more for Ona and his father. He felt a pang of guilt after she handed him the papers and stormed off to the ceremony, the look on her face after their father was taken away still lingering. There was something in those moments with her, something she wasn't saying, an ambitious determination to improve her situation without ever letting on that there might be imminent economic catastrophe awaiting her household and so many others.

His father was likely detained somewhere in Engineer's Town. Carter wanted to be far away from the false joy in town. So much had happened since he left home, and it had all culminated in a strange burst the night before. Nothing productive was likely to happen in the next day or two, and Joe Mainzer would be fine without him for a few days, as long as the man from the Bureau of Indian Affairs didn't cause trouble for him. Carter wanted to slip quietly out of town to think through what to do next.

Carter packed his cousin Lloyd's knapsack with what he needed for a couple of nights, careful not to wake Joe or anyone else in the camp. He stashed the rest of his things in the cab of Moses's truck, including the divorce papers his sister brought the day before, and took some cash from the locked metal cashbox, tucking it inside his boot. He wrote a quick note for his friend, saying he needed a break and would be back soon. It would be hot again before noon, morning and evening the best time to be on the road this time of year.

He headed north on the highway, the same way he'd come from home so many months ago. It seemed like a lifetime since he left, since the winter day he pulled his father's ferry in from the river, since Christmas Eve when he fought with Mae and Roy, since he'd seen his cousin Lloyd on Christmas Day or even had someone like Lloyd to give him advice. Home seemed like a distant, foggy memory, like a dream from someone else's life.

After a couple hours of walking, he cut in on a trail that led to one of the many coulees, lakes carved by glaciers that split the craggy hills. The landscape here was nothing like what he was used to. Coulees cut through miles of copper-colored rock pocked with pothole lakes and patches of sagebrush but had no forests or fields.

The trailhead to the water was barely more than a coyote trail, a narrow tramp between rocks. Carter stepped carefully past the craggy orange tumbles. When his dusty boot touched down on the trail, he heard a whipping in the sagebrush and froze. He had been careless and didn't check for rattlesnakes while stepping into the rocks, and as he peered cautiously into the underbrush, he was relieved to see the smooth glistening brown of a gopher snake, thick and long as a man's arm, shrinking into the prickly, yellow-blossomed underbrush.

When he was a boy, he and Lloyd charged farmers to catch gopher snakes in the brush outside town. One of them would grab a snake behind its head to avoid the snake's bite—painful but not poisonous—and the other would grasp it by the belly. Together they dragged the snake, thrashing, into a pillowcase, where it flipped inside the smooth cotton sheath until finally subdued, resigned, and then eventually released into a feast of field mice fattened by corn or wheat or whatever crop was suffering from rodents.

As Carter got closer to the lakeshore, a rock rolled from his toe into the canyon and cracked apart on a flat, brown boulder, echoing in the darkness. This was exactly the kind of alone he needed to think things through. He looked out over the lake and spotted a trail leading around its perimeter. He clambered over the rocks until he joined it, looking across the brilliant blue water to the copper crags that surrounded the lake.

The coulee was so much more beautiful than the bare rock hills around the dam site. More lush and colorful, with more plant and animal life. A chipmunk scurried across the trail in front of him.

There was a bleakness to life around the dam he hadn't thought about before coming to work there, with its mud and dust, the competition for resources, the grift, the booze, all of it. Here though, everything felt wide and airy. He hiked around the lake for a few miles, looking over its wide expanse. A fish jumped, leaving a ripple on the otherwise smooth surface of the water. At last, the day started to heat up, and his knapsack left sweat marks on his back. He laid his knapsack on the ground and sat on a rock high above the water. From his perch, he sought out a flat piece of shaded rock closer to the water's edge where he could stretch out along its sandy surface. His skin felt tight with the sweat of the day, which cooled and dried.

He climbed down to the rock and dropped his pack in the shade. He stripped off his dusty, sweaty clothes and dropped them in a pile, standing naked in front of no one, the shelter of the coulee walls all around him. He dove deep into the lake, the cool glacial water enveloping him, washing all the sweat and dirt away, washing all the fretting from yesterday and the weeks before out of his mind, the blue of the lake even bluer when he opened his eyes underwater, nothing but rocks and more rocks below, and tiny fish darting away from him.

He popped to the surface and floated, letting the warmth of the sun and coolness of the water refresh him. He thought of the night he pulled the drunk man out of the river, how cold the water was and the series of events that led him to this moment—blasting with Joe and Reynolds, patrolling the river at night, their weeks on Camp Ferry and in the mines, his time in town selling to the workers. He thought about Starks and his philosophy in life, tearing down to build up, seeking opportunity even if it meant sacrifice. Carter squinted up at the afternoon sun, the cool lake water lapping at his shoulders, and wondered where to go from here.

He didn't know if he should go back and do another tour on Camp Ferry or head home and check on his family, settle things with Mae so they could both move on. He knew he didn't want to be like Starks. He understood and appreciated the idea of seizing opportunity, but not at all costs the way Starks operated. He didn't want to cling to the past either, like his father, or lose all hope that anything could turn around to such a degree as the man he and Joe found near Gifford.

He climbed out of lake and sat naked on the rock. His clothes were dusty and sweaty from walking, and he swished them in the water, watching the dirt break loose and swirl around the fabric, and then threw them over sagebrush to dry in the sun. He tossed his sleeping mat down in the shade and lay down, closing his eyes and letting the warm air dry his skin and hair.

Carter drifted to sleep naked, shaded by sagebrush from the afternoon sun, and woke to the splash of martins washing their paws in the lake. The rocks clattered and echoed across the water as they played, the sound amplified on its surface.

Carter watched the martins fish along the shore, brown fur and humped backs blending in with the rocks around them. They reminded him of the martins that pestered him during his nights sitting in the rowboat under the catwalk from B Street to Shack Town. There were three of them, one clearly bigger—the mother maybe—and they buried their paws among the rocks, digging for minnows in the shallow water and clucking to one another. The lake stretched dark and blue against the burnished red of the canyon. One of the martins dragged a wriggling fish out of the water, slick and gray green, the sun reflecting tiny rainbows off its wet scales like the edge of an oil puddle.

Carter could almost smell the metallic sweetness of lake trout, and his stomach rumbled. On the other side of the lake, where the martins fished, the coulee walls scooped down to the water, and he could climb down to the edge himself.

His clothes were mostly dry after a couple of hours in the arid heat. He put on his boxers and boots and threw his shirt on, leaving it unbuttoned. He grabbed his fishing pole and tackle bag and made his way over the rocks toward the martins, picking his footing carefully to keep from rolling on the precarious rocks into the lake. His boots, still dusty from the road, left russet prints on what smooth rock surfaces they found on the way down.

The martins must have heard him coming because they dragged their fish into the rocks, back into the crevices where at night they avoided the bobcats that prowled the lakeshore.

He cast his line in, the first meditative thing he'd done in so long. Something grabbed his line and pulled. Another creature struggling to hang on, and here he was pulling it out of the water, beating it over the head with the handle of his knife and gutting it for a meal. He circled stones to make a fire pit and gathered up sticks from the brush for a fire to cook it.

His father's attempt to make a scene at the dedication came as no surprise, but the revelation about Mrs. Powell puzzled Carter. He'd not thought of his father as interested in anyone besides their mother. It would have been more surprising if Mrs. Powell said yes, but still, it implied some hope was left in the old man yet.

After he ate, Carter pulled one of Joe's paperbacks from his knapsack and read by the shore until the sun started to set and it was hard to see the page. He would need to let Joe know his plans soon, but for now, he wanted to think it through.

He finished setting his camp spot up for the night. The rock cliffs didn't leave many places to sleep comfortably, but Carter had slept on enough hard dirt before. He sat on the rocks and watched the sunset, burning bright yellows, pinks, and eventually a deep red overhead, reflected in the lake, as though everything around him was temporarily on fire. Then it was gone behind the walls of the coulee, and the cool purple bowl of the sky filled with stars. The lake water was black in the moonlight, and he could hear it, popping and lapping against the phosphorescent canyon walls that made the steep shoreline. The algae on the rock cliffs around him shimmered yellow green, an eerie, fluttering light.

In the morning, Carter's shoulder blades felt bruised from sleeping on rock, and when he took a first breath, a pain shot through his ribs. It was still dark, but a glow on the eastern edge was breaking over the cliffs. As the sun came up, it turned into a beating heat.

Carter waited to hike out until late afternoon when the sun was less direct. He swam again and dried in the warm air, letting his mind rest. As he climbed back up the trail to the road, he eyed the rocks carefully for snakes this time, announcing his approach with a heavy footfall among the fallen stones. At the trailhead, he looked into the underbrush for the gopher snake he'd seen on his way down the day before, knowing it would no longer be there, but looking all the same. The bushes were still, nothing quickened but a tiny finch that shot across with a nervous trill to another bush.

When he got to the road, he could see a dark shadow a few yards down stretched across the gravel highway like a tree bough blown from its trunk. As he neared on the shoulder of the highway, Carter recognized the gopher snake flopping in the road, two tire tracks approaching, descending, departing, one in the pillowy dirt beyond the snake's tail, the other square across its abdomen. The snake's belly was split open, and its guts tangled on the gravel road as it struggled to release itself and slink away. There would be no safety for this mouse catcher now; Carter could see that.

All he had on him to relieve the snake of its predicament was his fish knife, which would only work if he could grab the snake, hold it still, and saw its head off. Carter looked around for a good size rock on the edge of the road and hucked one at the snake's head. It landed with a crumpling thud. The snake thwapped its tail. Carter threw another stone and another and another. The snake whipped furiously, finally relenting, its tail trailing from a monument of rocks.

Carter wiped his forehead of sweat and cloudy dirt. He felt sick to his stomach and sorry for the thing. He followed the tracks with his eyes as they led a swerving line off the road and into the brush. Could be anyone. Anyone careless enough not to swerve around a gopher snake trying to cross the road.

The tire tracks that crossed the snake veered into the grass and brush alongside the road. He followed them from the dusty shoulder into the brush to see who these people were. Who knew if they would be friendly or not. He decided to chance it and walked off the road once again, following the tire tracks through the dry terrain.

He could see the cinder of a dinner-time campfire in the distance, and as he approached, he smelled smoke and heard voices. He called out a tentative hello, but no one answered. They must not have been able to hear him from that distance. They kept talking as he approached.

At last, when he could see the glow of the fire through the brush, he pulled the bushes apart from around their circle, stepping into the light, and said hello again. He expected silence or hostility or fright as he invaded their ring like a prairie apparition, but the folks sitting around the fire looked up like they expected him.

There were four of them. A white man and woman who seemed to be husband and wife, another white man who wore an army hat and was missing half the fingers of his right hand, and a Native American fellow, probably Colville or Sanpoil.

"Well, pull up a seat, feller," the man with the wife said. "You been cracking sticks out there for a while. About time you showed up." The man laughed heartily at his own joke, nudging his snickering wife in the side, his craggy dark teeth lit up by the fire. He trailed off in a half laugh, half cough.

His wife was pretty with blondish curls and a darker complexion, and she stood and walked a few feet from the fire, her skirt swishing around her thick hips.

Carter stepped closer to the fire, feeling sheepish. He looked from one face to another and then sat cross-legged on the ground. The man with the wife continued grinning at Carter all the while as though waiting for Carter to give him the punchline to a joke. "Mabel, fetch our friend here something to drink."

The man in the army hat looked at Carter quizzically. "Say, you're that fella selling cigarettes at the dam. With the Indian fella."

Before Carter could answer him, the woman named Mabel handed him a metal cup. He was expecting moonshine or worse and was relieved to taste the warm, tinny flavor of canteen water.

"You're welcome to stay the night here," she said, looking at his knapsack and tackle bag carefully. "Why don't you throw down your things over there and then come sit by the fire with us?"

He threw down his bedroll in the spot she directed him to, a few yards into the underbrush away from the fire. His head swam without warning, and he felt woozy and tired. All the walking and sun and everything that happened lately must have worn him out. His eyes watered with sleepiness, and he looked over to the campfire where all four of them were watching him.

The sparks from the fire broke up to the sky through his swimming eyes, seeming to join the wash of stars already coming out on the horizon. He could see the couple by the fire huddled together on their makeshift seat and wondered what hurt the man's wife filled for him. How could Carter blame Mae for looking to another man when her own husband could never make her happy? And now she wanted to be married again to someone other than him, a thought as impossible to comprehend as the distance to the stars.

His head swam as he watched the couple lean on each other against the speckled blue sky wisped with scant clouds, the wife's hair glowing orange in the firelight, whispering in her husband's ear, his cackling laugh wafting lightly as they looked back at Carter.

He felt like he could fall asleep on his feet. He opened his mouth to tell them he was going to call it a night, but his tongue didn't cooperate, and the words wouldn't come out. His balance was off, and he stumbled, landing on his knees. They smiled at him but didn't move. He realized as he slumped on his own sleeping mat that they must have put something in the canteen water to knock him out. He didn't even want to fight it. The drug eased his tension and allowed a spring of sorrow to gurgle up in him. A few warm tears ran down his dry cheeks before he passed out cold on the ground.

When Carter woke up in the morning, his clothes were damp with dew, his face covered in dry dirt. His head pounded and his mouth was dry and still tasted of tinny canteen water. He sat up and looked around, expecting signs of the group. His boots were off, and as he scrambled up in his socks as best he could, the throbbing in his head reached a new crescendo. The car was nowhere to be seen, the fire was snuffed out, and nothing accounted for their presence the day before but a smoldering pile of wood.

He found Lloyd's knapsack overturned a few feet away, all the contents dumped on the ground. He should have known folks were capable of that kind of duplicity in this desperate world. His pockets had been gone through too, and as he collected himself, he saw that all his nonvaluable belongings were littered around the site.

He scoured the site, finding his boots, two bits, and his pocketknife but not much else. He sat on the log the man and his wife sat on the night before, lacing his boots back up. At least they'd been kind enough to leave them for him, but the rest wouldn't get him very far.

Defeat washed over him as he thought of all his earnings from the operation with Joe and from Camp Ferry now gone. He could head back to the dam and figure it out, or he could finally head home. It was unlikely his father would welcome him back, but his cousin would. The thought of a friendly face brought such relief that he gathered up what was left of his things in his knapsack and headed back onto the highway toward Lloyd's.

CHAPTER 12
August 1937

Carter stood in front of the white gate of Fort Spokane again. It was near dusk on his second day of walking home when he took the turnoff for the fort from the main highway. On his walk back to Lloyd's, he spent his first night sleeping in a grassy field alongside the highway, the cicadas loud, the stars bright. The next afternoon, when he made it to the gas station where he met the truck driver who drove him to the dam so many months before, he recalled his brief but memorable night at the fort. They'd put him up easily enough. Maybe he could find out what kind of scheme they were up to and stay for a while and figure out his next move.

Looking at the gate, he thought how much had happened since he spent the night here so long before. Many things had changed, and many had not.

The fort looked completely different without snow on the ground. The doors to the gate hung wide open on the flat, dusty road that led past the empty artillery and stables.

Carter walked up the main drive, lined with shiny, yellow grass, and looked around. Since he spent the night in the barracks his last time here, more of the buildings had been pulled away, but in the warm summer evening, the demolition looked much less bleak than it had in winter. He could hear music and laughter coming from the orchard.

In the open stable doors where he'd seen the young woman peering out at him, a hay bailer was parked as though ready for use. Carter cinched his knapsack tighter and looked around, his taste buds cringing at the memory of the drugged water from two nights before.

The parade grounds had been mown, bales of hay as tall as a man curled to dry in rows across the lawn. In the fenced pasture next to the stable, a handful of spotted Appaloosa horses and cows grazed quietly in the dusk. They looked up at him with interest as he passed. The people there were farming the abandoned fort.

He inhaled the smell of pine smoke that wafted across the flat, dim expanse. The back side of the property glowed with a few campfires. Apricot and peach trees lined the drive and rattled in the evening breeze, which swept campfire smoke through the orchard ahead of him and into the pine bluff above the highway, rustling his hair. Grasshoppers leapt out of his way each time he set a foot down in the pillowy dust.

At the big house he remembered from his first time there, men coming in and out, he recognized Charlie, the old, bearded man who had shown him where to sleep in the barracks, leaning against a porch column in the fading light. He was smoking a cigarette and cradling his rifle.

"So you're back," Charlie said, smiling down at Carter from the porch.

"You remember me?" Carter said, looking up and dropping his knapsack and what was left of its contents to the ground. "It's been a bit."

"Didn't find what you was looking for out there?"

"In a manner of speaking."

A man came through the screen door behind Charlie, paused to look at Carter, and then walked off behind the house.

"Think it might be here, then?" Charlie grinned at him, his perfectly straight teeth an odd slice behind his full whiskers.

"I don't mean to impose, but if you could spare me a campsite in your orchard, I'd be grateful." Carter ran his hands through his damp hair, his muscles twitching and sore from the walk.

Charlie chuckled and swung his rifle onto his shoulder, barrel down. "Traveling light. You picked a good time to show up. We're celebrating the Colonel's birthday." He nodded toward the orchard. "C'mon, I'll take you back."

Charlie led Carter through the trees, the grasshoppers leaping aside at their steps. The peach and apricot grove was illuminated in an ethereal light from the campfires, and it seemed like Carter had stepped into another world. Something about the paradise of it made him feel an expansion inside, as though entering a dense, earthly heaven. In the winter, the place had unnerved him, but now, even despite his experience with strangers only nights before, he was not so averse to its tenor. In the summer dusk, it was easier to see it for the hardscrabble Eden that it was.

He missed the main event, but the birthday celebration was still going. They had built a long, low table of roughhewn pine boards on stacked bricks in the grove, kerosene lamps in a row down its center, heaps of cooked vegetables on metal cafeteria trays, the remnants of rabbit and goose, fruit pies, and jugs of wine. They barely noticed when Carter walked to the edge of the scene with his guide.

Charlie pointed around the table. Carter thought about the caravan from a couple nights before, torn between caution and the welcoming of this place.

"Came in a week ago," Charlie said of two men across from them, one holding a mandolin, the other a guitar. They strummed together and sang softly under the din of conversation.

To the left, a man sat with his wife and two small children. The woman smiled at him, and Carter nodded back.

"Been here a few months now," Charlie said.

The ground around the family was speckled with ripe peaches. Each child had a peach in one hand, and they bit off huge mouthfuls of flesh, the juice gumming their lips and running down their forearms.

At the far right, framed by apricot trees, two women sat on a pile of blankets. Carter recognized the younger of the two instantly from the stables when he was here before and looked quickly away with embarrassment.

"Those two, Penelope and Faith, have been here a while. Nowhere else to go, I guess."

Behind the two women, the dark orchard spread out to the tree line.

"Help yourself to food and wine," Charlie said, and then gestured out to the yawning orchard beyond. "You can set up anywhere you like for the night."

Carter thanked him, his relief at having a feast available to him far outweighing any awkwardness for showing up at their table uninvited. He tried not to let his hunger override his table manners while he helped himself to the best meal he'd had since his Christmas at Lloyd's. He waited to taste the wine until he saw someone else drink from the same bottle, but despite his bad experience in the desert, he hoped his concerns about this place from his first visit were unfounded.

The young woman's companion nodded to him across the makeshift table.

"I'm Faith, and this one's Penelope, but she likes to be called Penn," she said, smiling warmly in the kerosene light.

"You been here long?" Carter asked Faith.

"I've been here many months, but this one a couple years," she said, nodding toward Penn, who looked distracted by the rest of the night picnic.

So they hadn't come together, he noted.

"You come from around here?" he asked Faith, not sure what else to say.

"I came from Idaho; she's from Spokane," Faith said, gesturing to Penn. "Found this spot and decided to rest a while."

He nodded, not wanting to pry but curious about their history. "It's a good spot," he said.

Penn looked at him and then quickly away, and he wondered if it was possible that she could remember him, the way she was burned in his memory.

"It's a safe spot for the time being," Faith said.

Certainly safer than camping with strangers in the brush along the highway.

"What about you?" Penn piped in now, looking his way, and he got the distinct feeling that she was changing the subject on purpose to keep her companion from continuing.

"Looking for work, like every man on God's earth," he said, a white lie, but the easiest explanation. Nervous, he couldn't help but smile at her.

Faith smiled too. "You've come to the right place then."

"Where'd you come from?" Penn asked.

"Up river," he said. "Originally."

A joyful uproar at the other end of the table distracted them all, and the musicians stood to play a song while another platter of food was added to the table, and the party erupted with clapping.

Carter couldn't help but stare at Penn while he ate. Her dark hair was cut in a long bob. Not as stylishly as Mae would have insisted. There was something more carefree about this woman. She didn't need to prove she was fashionable like Mae did. She had pale skin even in summer, freckled lightly, and the bright periwinkle eyes he remembered so well from when he first saw her were almost wolf-like in the lamp light, offset by her dark hair. There was a leanness, a litheness to her, and Carter could tell that despite her small size, she was strong and fast.

She stared back at him with a confidence that made his face

burn red even though no one could see it in the gold glow of kerosene, her top lip a smirk of two perfect points that made his heart pound.

After dinner, he excused himself from the celebration early, exhausted from everything that had happened the past few days. He set his pack down in the dark orchard between two gnarled apricot trees and a blossom of grasshoppers escaped it. The grasshoppers flew again as he lay down, using his knapsack as a pillow, and he wondered if they would be leaping and crawling on him through the night. The air smelled of campfire smoke. A coyote howled in the woods. He could hear the murmur of women's voices a few yards away and the strum of instruments deeper in the orchard. The women rustled and murmured again, but he could not see them. Penn and Faith must be settling in for the night while the party continued. He was relieved they were still here, that she was still here.

He stared up at the stars. The Milky Way streamed a thick spatter of tiny lights across the sky, like a highway to another world. In his camp bed, he fell into a restless sleep, all the events of the last many months swirling in his tired mind.

Here though, everything seemed different. None of his history was known to anyone here. Another fresh start. Be smart this time, he told himself, as he drifted into sleep.

By morning, any lingering uncertainty he had about the place dissipated, and in the dim sunrise, the orchard seemed like a normal grove, not the ethereal world of last night. The river rushed in the distance, and he was not, as he feared, covered with grasshoppers.

The camp rustled awake, and as Carter eased out of bed, Penn's companion, Faith, stepped from behind an apricot tree. She had a sturdy walk, not being small and lithe like her companion, her old-fashioned dress and pinafore paired with men's boots.

"We have coffee at our camp if you would like some," she said.

Even though the trees were not big, the orchard was dense, and he could barely see Penn's feet through the trees as she folded their bedding only a few yards away from him.

He nodded to Faith and limply smoothed his clothes, reminding himself of his decision to be smart the night before.

"Much obliged."

He watched Penn's feet through the trees, and his ears turned hot. Now that he had an invitation to talk with her, he didn't know what to do.

"Come by when you're ready," Faith said and disappeared back through the orchard.

Carter rubbed his hand over his stubbly chin, embarrassed by his shoddy appearance. There must be a washroom around here, but *where* was another matter.

At their camp, Faith sat on a log, while Penn rolled up their blankets, looking at him occasionally, his face flushed.

"Hope you slept well," Faith said, lifting a metal pot from the fire, pouring coffee into a tin cup and handing it to him. He nodded and sat on the log next to Faith, stealing glances at Penn.

"Thank you," he said.

Faith smiled and cradled her coffee cup against the fabric of her dress, stretched tight across her lap.

"You think you'll be staying or moving on?" she asked.

"Not sure," he started and trailed off.

Across the orchard, a movement from the big house caught Carter's eye. A man came out onto the porch, letting the screen door slam behind him, and lit a pipe. The man stood on the porch, near the rail, looking out at the buildings as if surveying their construction, a thin reed of smoke trailing from his pipe into the sky.

In the morning light, the buildings on that side of the fort were more visible, and Carter saw that they were missing whole sections, piles of lumber and brick stacked nearby.

The front door of the main house opened again, and two Native American men came out onto the porch. The three stood talking and gesturing toward the demolition.

Carter turned back to the fire before his attention to the men became impolite. It was hard to figure out where to look around here, and he wished he could go back to his campsite but couldn't think of a way to excuse himself.

"How's the coffee?" Faith asked, seeming to sense his awkwardness.

"Fine, thank you, ma'am," he smiled and tried to look reassuring. "Haven't had coffee in a few days now."

He drained the cup and handed it back. "I appreciate it. And I appreciate you all letting me stay here last night."

Carter rose to his feet as Faith tucked the cup next to her own in her lap, Penn watching as he tried to excuse himself.

"I'd like to pay my respects to Charlie," he said. "Could you point me in the right direction?"

Penn eyed him, her cat-like eyes sending him into a new fit of nerves, and then she pointed toward the stables.

"He stays in the quartermaster's lodging next to the stables," she said.

Carter had known that actually, but he couldn't think of another way on the spot to get away. He made his way toward the stables, knowing the two women watched his back as he went.

Charlie was setting a bucket of water in front of the stall of an Appaloosa horse when Carter walked into the stable.

"Sleep easy?" Charlie asked, running a brush down the mare's wincing, spotted neck.

"Easy enough," Carter answered.

"Orchard's not so bad in summer," Charlie said, lifting the mare's front foot to check for clods. "Barracks stay too hot in summer."

Carter wanted to ask about the demolition but wasn't sure how to bring it up. He thought hard for something to say to introduce the subject.

Standing upright, Charlie asked, "You'll be wanting to meet the Colonel, then?" His wrinkled face flushed with his motion, strings of his greasy white hair sticking to his face.

Carter hadn't expected it to be so easy. He followed Charlie out of the stables and across the parade grounds, where the original troops would have practiced their drills, to the big house that presided over the whole encampment.

As they passed the men on the porch with a hello and entered the main house of the fort, Carter was certain this was the fanciest home he'd ever been inside.

As they walked into the foyer, Charlie said, "Back in the day when this was still an operating fort, this was the head officer's house."

Many of the details were still intact. What was left of the furniture looked imported from Europe. The walls were papered with an old-fashioned print that looked like it once had velvet strips in it, the kind of wall covering Carter had seen in old hotels and photos in Mae's magazines.

A grand piano languished in a room adjacent to the foyer, and the windows were draped in rich dark fabric. Each room they passed through had some kind of chandelier or medallion in the ceiling.

Charlie led Carter into what was probably the house's parlor. The furniture was pushed to the edges of the room, and an enormous table, its legs curved and inlaid with gold carvings, sat square in its center. The Colonel—easily identified by the Great War military jacket he wore with blue jeans and cowboy boots—stood at the table over a mess of papers. He ran a hand through his longish, dirty-blond hair, slicking it back away from his forehead only for it to fall back around his eyes. The gesture reminded Carter of Joe Mainzer, but Joe did it nervously, where this man was preening.

A second man with a thick mustache wearing an army-green work shirt sat on an old settee against the wall. He smoked a cigarette and watched the Colonel silently. They both carried pistols in holsters on their hips, like outlaws who'd taken over a war room and didn't know how to use it.

As Charlie and Carter walked into the room, the two men looked up.

"Happy birthday," Carter said, lifting a hand in hopes of a peaceful gesture.

"You must be the new fella in camp," the Colonel said, walking around the table and shaking Carter's hand with surprising friendliness. "How long will you be staying with us then?"

"No real plans at the moment, sir. Thank you for the camp spot." Carter was surprised at his own deference to this colonel, clearly either never or no longer a real military man.

"Ah, it's nothing," the Colonel said, leaning against the table and crossing his arms casually in front of him. "What's the rush then? You got some lady waiting on ya?"

"No rush—," Carter started uncomfortably. A woman was indeed waiting on him to sign divorce papers for her, but he wasn't about to get into that. The Colonel interrupted him with a laugh and his companion snorted a smoky chuckle, the man's first reaction to any of the interaction so far.

"I'm kidding you, buddy," the Colonel said, and clapped Carter on the shoulder. His interest half lost, the Colonel walked back to the other side of the table and resumed his planning.

"This man's looking for work," Charlie said, and Carter looked at Charlie with surprise.

"That so?" the Colonel said, not looking up from his papers. "You and everyone else," he chuckled. The Colonel shuffled through the papers on his table, as though he was looking for something. "Know anything about trading?" The Colonel looked up at Carter then, watching to see how he would respond.

"More of a labor man, myself." Carter answered, his work on the mines, building his house, working for his father, and his time at the dam all more about physically moving resources from one place to another than about what they were worth.

"Heading to the dam then, are you?"

"Just came from there."

"That bad, eh?" the Colonel preened his long hair again. "You handy with a sledgehammer?"

Carter thought about his work on the overburden rocks at the dam and his time in the mines outside Colville and on the reservation, the hours of chipping and deeper descent into the hard rock of the hill.

"What do you have in mind?"

"See them falling-down buildings? No one from the government's been here in years. All this lumber, all those shingles, bricks, furnishings, rotting away out there. It's gonna fall down anyway, so we're taking it down."

"You planning to build something?" Carter regretted immediately that he pried into the Colonel's business, but the Colonel cracked a smile.

"Not me. Maybe someone else, though…No sense wasting history." The Colonel nodded toward his silent companion. "We could use more strong, skilled hands."

When Carter didn't answer right away, the Colonel dug in his jeans pocket and pulled out a few dollar coins.

"Tell you what," he held the coins out in Carter's direction. "I'll give you an advance on your cut of profits. You give it a week, see how it goes, earn your advance. Then decide."

Carter definitely could use the money after giving most of his cash to his sister at the dam and losing the rest in the desert.

"What's the cut?" Carter asked, reaching for the coins in the Colonel's hand.

"New man gets five percent."

"What's the expected take?"

The Colonel glanced at his number two man on the settee. "Hard to say as of yet."

Carter looked at Charlie, and Charlie shrugged.

"I'm in," Carter said quietly, looking down at the coins in this hand. There were plenty of men ready to take his place on Camp Ferry. Would Starks even know if he walked off the job? He shoved the coins deep in his pocket. It wasn't much, but it was enough to keep him going until he could head home, and he did not want to return empty handed.

"Good," the Colonel said, shifting his attention away from Carter and back to his papers as though dismissing him from a royal audience.

CHAPTER 13
September 1937

The Colonel put Carter to work knocking mortar off bricks with a sledgehammer and then stacking them for reuse. Days at the fort stretched to weeks, and Carter waited to get paid. He learned that members of the Palouse tribe—Joe Mainzer's tribe, he recalled—were the men who came in and out of the fort trading spotted Appaloosa horses for goods the Colonel bargained with. The Colonel's number two, also not an actual military man, was referred to as Sarge.

Carter thought with a pang how Joe would surely be curious of his whereabouts by now, but he had no desire to go back anytime soon to Electric City or the mine or Camp Ferry, not when this place had everything he needed until he was ready to head for home.

Around the fort, the men stacked parts of buildings, pieces of anything useful they found on the grounds, sorted into piles by their use. The women worked at sorting silverware and other small household items abandoned in the buildings.

Carter couldn't stop himself from watching Penn while she worked. He stole looks at her while she sorted, her dark hair falling in her face. Her expression was always mysterious, and the brightness of her eyes, which first struck him as so alive, had moments of aloofness.

One of Penn's many jobs was to help Charlie exercise the Appaloosa horses in the coral outside the stables. She rode bareback, clinging to the reins, her short dark hair winging in the wake of the horse's gallop—not an orderly, circular ride, but zigzagging across the dry, yellow grass like she was testing the horse and herself. There was such an oddness about her clothes and the way she wore her hair, with a bright but quiet independence and a fire behind her lavender eyes. She couldn't be more different from Mae, who dressed like a starlet to buy eggs and who depended on anyone who would let her, an implicit desperation for notice and approval that bordered on pathological. It had drawn him to Mae and repulsed him all at the same time.

Penn was nothing like any of the other woman he knew. She was self-reliant and not in need of his attention. Anytime their eyes met, it sent a prickle from his scalp down his spine and other places.

The buildings seemed even more dilapidated now that Carter was part of the scheme. Whole exterior walls were missing, and the insides gaped open like a gutted fish. It reminded him of his work on Camp Ferry, only more orderly and less wasteful. Chairs were stacked beyond the far north building, and crates of silverware were lined inside, sorted by knife, fork, and spoon. It was a low business, this tearing down and sorting of useful parts from the discarded whole. They would have to do something of the sort back home in Kettle Rapids before the water rose, and before they could move the buildings uphill. There would be a reckoning of materials, the kind of judgment that was never anticipated when the elements to construct all the buildings, businesses, and homes like his own were chosen for their use.

He wondered what people back home would do with their houses, if they would tear them down and rebuild them, leave them to be drowned by the river, or move them to new property. Someone would need to do that work. Ozzie would have to make a decision soon about what to do about his house. Who knew what his sister was dealing with back home with their father. Ozzie wouldn't have the strength to tear down his house on his own, move it, and rebuild it, and the amount the federal government offered him wasn't enough to pay someone else to do it or to buy something new.

Charlie told Carter about a trail behind the orchard that led to a fishing hole on the river, and Carter borrowed a fishing pole from the salvage pile. He walked into the tree line, following it until it broke outside the camp. A hill dropped behind it into a canyon and then to the riverbank. It was farther than he expected, but some extra walking would do him good despite how tired he was from working. He wished he had more money he could send home to help out. With fish and peaches, he wouldn't starve, and for at least the next few weeks, the occupation was a change he rather liked.

During the day, they destroyed to build, like Starks said. In the evening, everyone who was staying at the fort gathered in the orchard for communal dinners, members of one another, like President Roosevelt said. At night in his bed, stars blanketing the sky, Carter contemplated how both could be true and both could be a good thing. He wondered what Starks—or his father for that matter—would think about what they were doing at the fort.

Carter's payday finally came, and the Colonel summoned him to the main officer's house to get his cut. While the Colonel stood behind his impressive planning table, Sarge counted out a few coins into Carter's hand, enough to get him by and get him home.

"You gonna stay, right?" the Colonel asked, his military jacket popping open on his undershirt as he ran a hand through his long hair. "We got some big trades coming up."

"Thinking I might head home, see my family," Carter said, putting the coins in his pocket.

Sarge raised his eyebrows and looked at the Colonel.

"You too 'grand' for this work then since you been at the

dam and all?" the Colonel said, folding his arms and leaning back against the windowsill, his cowboy boots crossed in front of him as though in judgement.

Carter looked back and forth between the two men, weighing the situation.

"Maybe he's a snitch," Sarge said to the Colonel, and the Colonel cocked his head, pondering this suggestion.

"Could be. Could be."

Carter looked them over. Why would they be worried about snitches? He looked for where they had their weapons in case he needed to make a break for it.

Sarge sat alert on the settee, as though ready to make a move with any gesture from the Colonel.

Finally, the Colonel stood back up from the windowsill. "Tell you what, new guy," he said, looking Carter down from across his planning table. "I'll give you six percent, you stick around a few more weeks and help us out with a deal we're working on. Seven percent you give me your word you won't tell a soul we're here once you decide to hit the road."

Carter accepted, holding out his hand to shake on it, not feeling like he had much choice. A little more time, a little more money before heading home wouldn't be a bad thing. A little more time to spend with Penn was also enticing.

Late summer crept into fall, and the bowl of the sky tipped enough to soften the blaze of sun so that everything looked golden. Rotting peaches dotted the ground throughout the orchard, and grasshoppers covered them like ticks. Winter wasn't far away, but Carter didn't want to think about that, didn't want to think about the cold and dark, the orchard masked in a white blanket of snow, the chill of cold concrete inside the barracks he'd slept in the first time he came to the fort, the frozen and muddied tire tracks of Shack

Town, the dark dank of the mine, and an unsettling uncertainty about what he would do or where he would go next.

Carter made progress with Penn in small steps, much like how they all chipped away at tearing down the walls of the buildings inside the fort—a small gesture such as loading a box onto the truck for her, a kind word in the orchard, deference to her companion Faith, tokens of neighborliness like a handful of blackberries picked from the river shore. Or, leaning against the fence, watching her ride in the corral behind the stable. He hesitated to make an overture, knowing where it might go, not sure he could trust himself to handle the responsibility of falling in love again.

Still, he couldn't help but be aware of her throughout the fort, as when she stopped work, stood up and stared into the sky as a cluster of starlings flew over the buildings and into the tree line. Or when she disappeared into the stables for an hour some evenings: what was she doing in there? He tried to remember how he'd opened up conversation with Mae, but Mae hadn't been hard to crack, and they were kids then. Mae saw a sucker and opened up to him like a summer rose blossom, fragrant and thorny. All his rusty tricks were useless with Penn. She was sharp and self-reliant.

For now, he was content to watch her from a distance as she moved on horseback with bird-like twitters through this gilded world, her eyes bright, her black hair swinging around her shoulders while she rode, while she worked, her boots swishing through the yellowed grass.

When he saw her wrestling with a resistant box, he dropped his sledgehammer and broke it apart for her. She looked up at him, her perfect top lip motionless, and a mirth in her eyes dug into his own for a moment before she flung her hair aside and said, "Thanks," barely audible, taking his breath away.

In that moment, his face close to hers, he saw what he'd seen the first time he ever laid eyes on her, the working behind her eyes that she couldn't mask with her tough attitude or pretensions of indifference. She was thinking, and she was thinking about him. Maybe it was fleeting, but he'd made an impression.

He wanted so badly to touch her, even a small touch, like the brushing of hands or the leaning of shoulders, but he was afraid of what would happen next. She gave him a sly smile and then turned her back on him, resuming her work. He took that thought back with him to his sledgehammer and pounded with renewed vigor at his brick wall, feeling the full swing and crash with a new joy.

Carter was surprised to come across Penn alone at the beach, leaning against a log, a battered book propped open across her lap, her bare toes splayed wide on the rocks of the riverbank. Carter planned to sit and fish, but when he saw her, he stopped, panicked, and immediately thought to run off with his borrowed fishing pole. She had already seen him, though, so he froze, not knowing where to go, his lure bouncing ridiculously after the abrupt stop.

She looked up, waiting for him to do or say something, but he couldn't think what. This was his moment, and he was coming up short. She turned back to her book, and his heart sank in relief and regret at the same time. Maybe if he climbed down shore on the rocks, it wouldn't look so much like he was trying to avoid her and more that he was giving her space to read while he fished.

He started down the river away from her, trying to think what to do. She must have read his hesitation because she closed her book, got up, and dusted off her jeans.

"Don't give up your favorite fishing spot on my account," she said. "I can find someplace else to read."

"No," he said, reaching his hand out feebly.

She looked at him waiting for him to say more, but he was tongue-tied.

"It's really okay. I'll go up by the stables," she said.

She tucked her book under her arm and started toward the trail, her boots wobbling on the rocks. He stepped toward her, hoping he wouldn't seem threatening or scare her.

"Stay," he said. "Please don't go."

She was so close to him he could feel the heat from her body near his chest and see the faint hint of summer freckles fading from her forehead and cheeks. She stared straight into his face, her eyes keen. He should have known better than to think he might have frightened her. He looked at the spine of her book, trying to read the title to see what she was reading.

"Why not?" she said, smiling, and with a hot flush he realized that she knew, probably knew all along, that he was attracted to her. He was mortified, and yet she didn't seem to be discouraging him.

He smiled back and swallowed the lump in his throat and said, "If you leave, I can't enjoy your company."

She chuckled softly and looked back out over the river. It was running quietly today, discs of light cascading along its surface as the sun broke through the trees.

"If you insist," she said, smirking, "I'll stay."

Penn sat back against the log, her closed book propped on her knees, watching curiously as Carter sat next to her and cast his line into the water, trying not to look as awkward as he felt while the lure flew and landed with a plunk.

It had been such a long time since he'd tried to court someone, he couldn't quite remember what to do. He let his fishing line run loose and propped the base of his pole between the logs and the rocks of the shore. They both stared at the river, hypnotic with its glistening.

It wasn't like he'd never spoken to her before; they'd had plenty of idle chats around the fort. Here they were completely alone and unobserved for the first time. Carter's mind swirled with all the questions he wanted to ask. What brought her out here? Why was she alone? What did she do in the empty stables by herself?

Her top lip quivered like she might laugh.

"You like to read?" was all he could think to say, looking at the beat-up leather-bound copy she held of Lewis and Clark's journals. She must have found it in the former boarding school classrooms or the library of one of the officer's houses.

"I do." She smiled again, the apples of her cheeks brightening. "It feels good to know I'm not alone in the world," she said.

Their arms were almost touching, the whole lengths of their bodies, down their arms, legs, feet. Where they nearly touched was electric.

"You feel alone most of the time?"

"I guess. Don't most people?"

He thought about that for a moment. He certainly did. He wasn't sure he'd thought about everyone else feeling the same way.

"You have Faith."

"True. For right now, I do. Is one person you've recently met enough to feel not alone?"

He smiled at her. "Depends, I guess. If you'd been trapped by yourself in a cave, one person could seem like a welcome relief."

"Yeah, well, my life doesn't seem too full of options at the moment."

He stood and recast his line, thinking about that. He'd been so focused on his reasons for being there he hadn't thought that she might feel trapped and alone. He remembered Ona's face at the ceremony, how he'd wanted to help her, take back all the thoughtless things he'd ever said or done.

"You remind me of my sister," he said.

Penn looked up at him with surprise, and he realized how strange that must have sounded.

"I only mean, you seem like you're looking for your place."

She stared at him, not saying anything.

"I'm looking for mine too," he said, trying to recover the moment.

He stood looking out at the water, feeling stupid and not knowing what to say.

"What was the dam like?" Penn finally asked.

"Lots of men," he said.

She laughed. "Not unlike here, then."

He hadn't thought about that. Of course, she was outnumbered at the fort by all the Colonel's men and those who came and went. A protective impulse rose up in him. If he wasn't ready to make his move, at least he could help her feel safe.

They both watched as his lure bobbed in the river.

"Would you like me to read to you?" she asked.

He looked back at her, surprised. He wouldn't have thought of this on his own, and he didn't want to say it out loud, but he couldn't think of many things he wanted more right now in this moment than to listen to her read to him. More than hearing the familiarity of his father's distinctive voice ring out over the river, more than his fascination with how Starks described progress, more than the welcoming hum of Joe's recitations.

"Sure," he said, trying to sound more nonchalant than he actually felt, sitting back down on the beach and leaning against the log next to her.

She flipped the volume of Lewis and Clark's diary back open to a dog-eared page and began to read out loud.

"As we passed on, it seemed those scenes of visionary enchantment would never have an end...."

He closed his eyes and listened, resting his head against the log, his whole body relaxing for the first time in so long. Her voice was soft and fluid like the soothing run of a creek, and it paused to work out the pronunciation of old-fashioned words like water hitting a snag on its inevitable way downstream.

Carter forgot about his lure and everything else, letting the sun heat his face, wanting this moment with Penn to never end.

CHAPTER 14
October 1937

Summer faded into fall. In the dusk of the orchard one night, Carter wasn't entirely surprised to see Joe Mainzer show up at his campfire. Carter had mentioned the fort to his friend many times, probably as often as he'd mentioned home, in their hours working together. It wasn't much of a stretch for Joe to look for Carter here before heading farther upriver. Even still, Carter was embarrassed he told his friend he would be back soon and that Joe had come looking for him. He watched Joe kick clear a place to sit on the ground and waited for him to say something.

"Smells good in here," Joe said, looking around the dim orchard.

"It's the peach trees and ponderosa firewood."

"Yeah."

The campfire popped and collapsed down. Carter kneeled forward to poke at it, trying to think of something to say.

"How'd you get up here?"

"Drove Moses's truck. It's parked up on the highway. All your stuff is in it."

"Business good?"

"Yeah, it's pretty good."

"Sorry I didn't come back."

"I figured it out."

"What brought you up here?"

"See how you were getting along. Brought you this." Joe pulled a letter from his jacket pocket and tossed it on the ground next to Carter in the dark. It was a letter from Kettle Rapids. "It's been sitting at the Silver Dollar Club for a few weeks. Thought it might be important."

Carter recognized his father's handwriting on the envelope. He assumed it was some rant following the event with President Roosevelt. Wondering how long the Secret Service kept him, Carter tossed the letter aside to read another time.

The two of them were quiet for a while, and Carter jabbed at the fire.

Finally, Joe said, "The fellow from Indian Affairs has been hanging around."

Carter stopped what he was doing and stared at him. "At the mine?"

"No, in town."

"Nothing illegal about town."

"No…," Joe said and drew the word out. "Still, thought it might not be a bad idea to clear out for a bit, see what you're up to."

"And bring him with you?"

Joe looked up from the fire. "Why? What's going on here?"

Carter eyed his friend to see if he was kidding around. "Do you really think he followed you?"

"No."

"Should I be worried?" Carter asked.

"Not yet," Joe said.

Carter poked at the fire again, hoping his friend was right.

"It will blow over," Joe said. "Don't be worried."

"You bring any whiskey?" Carter asked him with a smile, even though his friend never drank, and the sound of Joe's chuckle was a mighty relief.

"What's wrong with the whiskey here?" Joe asked him.

"Don't have any."

"That's rough," Joe grinned at Carter. "What about women? You got ladies up in this place?"

Carter's mind raced to find an answer that didn't overstate his progress with Penn but also eliminated her as a possibility for his friend.

"I'm kidding you," Joe said, and pulled a pint from inside his jacket and held it out. "Brought you something."

Carter laughed, his face warm from the campfire and his happiness at seeing his friend again. The bellow of his laugh surprised even him, as it echoed against the ponderosas roping the orchard and ricocheted around the makeshift camp.

"You're a good man, Joe Mainzer." Carter took a swig from the bottle and cringed at the bite, the heat easing down his throat and pooling in his stomach.

"I figured it was only polite for a guest to show up bearing gifts," Joe said, opening a bottle of Coca Cola for himself.

"Gifts, huh. All right then. Tell me all the gossip about Shack Town."

"Better get yourself a pillow."

"Oh ho! That so?"

Maybe it was the whiskey or the weeks of being away from people he knew, but watching Joe by his campfire and knowing his friend had come not out of anger or a need to guilt him for leaving but because Joe wanted to make sure he got his letter from home gave Carter a new perspective on their friendship.

Joe rustled his legs in the dust from across the fire as Carter took another swig from the whiskey bottle. "What's with all these grasshoppers, anyway?" Joe asked.

In the morning, Carter had a shooting pain over his right eye, but, of course, Joe was as clear as a bell, even after spending the night on the ground next to their smoldering fire. Joe's hair, however, was fanning up in the back like a bird raising its hackles, so Carter wasn't surprised when his friend excused himself to walk back up to the highway where Moses's truck was parked.

As Carter built a fire, he puzzled out how to introduce Joe to the camp. He hadn't been there long enough to establish the credibility to enlist outsiders, and yet it was hardly a secretive operation from Carter when he arrived. Joe cut him into the mine operation after all and was instrumental in managing relationships with the tribes during their time on Camp Ferry. Carter knew the Colonel did business with the Palouse, Joe's own tribe, and that connection could prove to be of use here too.

While he was waiting for his friend, Carter remembered the letter from his father that Joe brought the night before and found it on the ground next to the fire. He tore it open, wanting to take the opportunity while his friend was gone to read whatever nonsense this was in private.

Dear Son—

The opening alone, simple as it was, in his father's handwriting was enough to put Carter on edge.

I am obliged against my wishes to write to inform you of the death of your wife, Mae Haufmann Price.

Carter flinched, not believing what he was reading.

I asked your sister Ona to write you, and she told me to do it myself, that on an occasion such as this, I should be able to overcome our differences and write to you as your father. Now you know that I am not much of an overcomer of differences, but seeing as how you are my son, and you would want to hear this news, I agreed with her and set down to write this letter.

It took me many tries to write it without getting into why I am angry with you. Your sister made me promise that I would not. Many times I had to tear up my letter and start again.

Carter tossed the first sheet on the ground, looking to the next.

I'm telling you this so you know why it has taken me more than a month since her passing to send this letter to you. She died shortly after I returned home from the unfortunate event at the dam, which I will not get into here for the reasons stated above.

It is of particular relevance I suppose that this letter should come from me as I am the one who found your wife and held her hand while she passed and so I am better equipped than any living person to tell you the circumstances surrounding her death.

I cannot say her passing was peaceful and though I think she may have become a better person in the moments of her death, in her regular life she lived like a woman who would not deserve a peaceful passing. You know I am a man who sees others get their justs, and though I know there was a time when you loved her and though I know there will be a time when I will get my justs as well, I can say of her that she was not a woman who I'd expect would see some mercy from the Almighty.

Carter sank to the ground, grasshoppers leaping around him in the dust.

Her new fellow wasn't with her, and I thought you might find some comfort in that fact. Your sister tells me you had not finalized your paperwork, so if it is any solace, you were still married when she passed.

In the moments before she passed, she seemed subdued, more than any other time I saw her when she spent a regular day. Not that I would expect you would wish her to be alone—she was with me, by accident of course, and I suppose if there's one thing to be thankful for in all this it's that before she died she had a reminder of you because she could see me there and doubtless her last thoughts were of you. Maybe she was even sorry about the way things happened between you two. She looked sorry, but in a moment like that, it's hard to tell what someone is thinking.

Carter threw another page in the dust. It was over for good.

There would be no back and forth now. No divorce.

You know that I am forthright, and so I will say, even though if your mother were still with us she would tell me it's wrong or bad luck to speak ill of the dead, that I never thought Mae was a good choice for you. I know people in town say I never deserved your mother, and they're right. I didn't. Not one day did I ever do anything worthy of having her. But that's how a good wife should be, son. She stays a good wife even if she's married to someone like me. Or you.

No one ever thought it was your fault Mae wanted to end things. I know maybe you did with everything that happened. And maybe she did too. But nothing you could have ever done made her right to kick you out. If your mother could put up with me, then Mae could put up with worse. She liked to think she was so tough, coming around the tavern and staying out late dancing. She was a fun gal; I will say that of her. But she had a bewilderment in her eyes that did not bode well. Why you thought to marry her instead of go around with her, I never understood.

Tears welled in his eyes at the indignity that his father could presume to know what he should value in a marriage.

She reminded me of a buck I once found in the woods up by Myers Falls back before you were born. I was marking trees for the mill one afternoon and came upon a buck standing in the woods. It was a big son of a bitch, and as I came up the trail, it didn't seem to notice me even though it was looking right at me. It seemed almost like it was daring me to come up to it, like it didn't give a damn that I was getting closer. Then I must have kicked a rock or something because all of a sudden, it took off like a shot with no particular direction and plowed right into a tree stump. Its own force knocked it back on its haunches and it looked around with that same bewildered look I would sometimes see in Mae. I figured out then that the buck was blind, and I ran back to my buggy and grabbed a rope. When I got back, it was still there where I'd seen it and since it couldn't see what

I was doing, I was able to loop a lasso around its head. That thing kicked like the devil, and I was afraid to get too close to it in case it gored me with its antlers, so I tied it up out there and went all the way home to get my rifle. It was almost dark by the time I got back, and the buck must have tired itself out while I was gone because it was lying down in the grass like a fawn, staring out into space.

I almost didn't have the heart to shoot it. Its eyes were so blank and almost digging into the darkness, trying to find something to see. I didn't have the heart to let it run loose like that either, so I did it. I shot it. It was the loudest shot I can remember hearing. The buck slumped over with a thump, real peaceful.

That buck could have fed a family for a year, but when I cut it open, the insides were all covered with something white, almost like it had been stuffed with cotton. And the meat was full of tumors. Whatever was making that animal blind was killing it slowly from inside. What I'm trying to say, son, is that sometimes a creature wanders confused because it's not well on the inside. And in my opinion, that's how it was with your Mae.

A burble of anger rose up in Carter reading his father's judgement of his relationship with Mae, even in her dying and his own grief at losing her.

There isn't much to say about the accident, really. It happened before I got to her, and there didn't seem to be anyone else involved. It was late and the roads were slick with a fresh rain after many months of dry heat, so she must have skidded going around the turn and flipped over. When I got there, your car was upside down by the side of the road and the doors were crushed so as not to open. The windshield was gone, but when I tried to pull her through, she cried out and I realized her neck must be broken and I couldn't move her. Her face was so full of blood I didn't recognize her at first, but she started whispering and even though I couldn't understand what she was saying, something about the way she moved her lips made me realize who she was. Then I saw she was wearing the fur collar you gave her when you first got married.

I told her I was going for help, and she seemed to understand, but when I tried to leave she cried out again. It didn't look good for her, so I sat with her, holding her hand through the empty windshield, waiting for a car to come by. She was gone by the time help arrived.

I hope you will not take this news too hard. You were as good to her as you knew how to be, and you should have no regrets in regards to Mae. As for the other matters between us, those you should have regrets for, but that is another letter, and I'm too close to the end of this one to rewrite it again.

Your father.

Carter put his head in his hands, relief and grief racking through him with the same intensity it had the night he'd been drugged in the desert. The tears mingled with the dust on his hands. She was gone, this time for good. There was no uncertainty anymore.

When Joe came back from the truck, Carter stuffed the letter into his back pants pocket and hastily wiped his face with his hands.

"Bad news?" Joe asked.

"Can we go fishing?" Carter asked, and his friend nodded, putting a hand on his shoulder not pressing for more.

Joe Mainzer stayed on at the fort for several more days. Having Joe at his campsite with him reminded him of their time at the mines, sitting with each other at the fire, talking about the people they sold to in Electric City. Carter introduced Joe to Charlie, who insisted Joe meet the Colonel and Sarge. It turned out Joe knew some of the Palouse who came from the Colville reservation, and the Colonel liked that Mainzer could put them at ease. Joe likewise was excited to see the growing herd of Appaloosas they had in the corral outside the stable. He was curious about how they moved goods and suggested they might be another mechanism for moving artifacts back to the tribes on the other side of the river.

Once Carter found Joe in the fort's cemetery. "Colville kids," Joe said, squatting in front of the gravestones. Carter remembered his father telling him about the fort's history as a forced boarding school for children from the reservation and thought of when he and Joe accidentally lit dynamite in a burial site during their time on Camp Ferry.

Carter didn't say anything to his friend or the others at the fort about Mae's death, but he could tell his recent somberness puzzled them. He steered clear of Penn, feeling like it was the right thing to do out of respect to Mae and to himself, so he could mourn the finality of their marriage without burdening anyone else. The leaves started to fall from the trees in the orchard, and he knew he needed to put his pensive mood behind him soon and go home.

One morning at their campsite in the orchard, Joe woke him, looking nervous enough to scatter all sleep from Carter's mind.

"There's an Indian Affairs truck parked up on the road," Joe said, looking panicked.

"Are you sure?"

Joe didn't answer him but pulled his pistol from the back of his waistband and checked the bullets in the chamber. Carter tried to think of what to do. Faith was building a fire at her nearby camp. Joe must have gone up to Moses's truck, so she would have seen Joe walk back from the road. Carter didn't have the heart to point out they must have followed Joe to the fort. Surely Joe knew or at least suspected that. There was no chance of sneaking him out unnoticed.

"It has the logo on the doors."

Carter needed time to think. There wasn't any evidence the agent could pin on them that he knew of unless Joe had artifacts in the truck. The Colonel certainly wouldn't appreciate scrutiny from a federal officer though.

"Let's go fishing," he said to Joe.

"Fishing?"

Faith was looking over curiously from her breakfast fire, like she might invite them over. "We'll clear out for a bit," Carter said. "See if he does the same."

Carter walked Joe Mainzer down the long switchbacks to the shore. Carter dropped his lure in, while Joe sat on a log closer to the tree line and rolled a cigarette.

Carter wasn't even paying attention to what was going on at the end of his line, so when he felt a tug, it shocked him back into the frivolous action for a split second before the line snapped and went slack. He looked at Joe, who didn't say anything. They'd been through so much together. The blast. The tension at camp and on B Street. Everything they'd seen and done on Camp Ferry. Their time in the mine. Their successful business in town.

It was unnerving to see his friend, whom he thought of as so confident, looking scared. Carter was the one who couldn't decide or defend himself, who lurched about for an opportunity or explanation, who showed up at his cousin's house hoping for redemption. Not Joe. Joe had provided his stability for over a year now. Yet, when he looked at his friend, cigarette smoke curling around Joe's black hair fraying miserably around his handsome face, his mouth a hard line instead of the smile that first charmed Carter, he felt only compassion and kindness and wanted to be strong for Joe.

They sat this way through the cooling fall afternoon, not saying much. Carter watched the light dim and brighten as clouds passed overhead.

The Colonel and his men were not going to take kindly to the extra attention, but they were resourceful, enterprising, perhaps even criminal minds. Carter had no idea what he'd really fallen in with. His and Joe's only recourse now would be to ask for help. No use avoiding it.

"What if we take the direct approach?" Carter asked Joe.

"What does that mean?"

"We go up to the Colonel's house and tell them what we want them to know," Carter said.

"You think that will work?" Joe asked.

"I think it's worth a try. Any other ideas?"

Joe shook his head no.

On the walk back up the damp trail, the underbrush still thick, the conifers overhead a deep autumn evergreen speckled with the turning reds and golds of intermittent maples, Carter had a momentary second thought to tell his friend to make himself scarce. By now, the Indian Affairs man either lost interest or upset the Colonel, so Carter would need to go all the way with it or it was already a moot point.

They threw their fishing gear down at Carter's campsite, the blackened wood from last night's fire coated with papery ashes.

Carter looked toward the Colonel's house. Nothing seemed out of the ordinary.

Joe Mainzer followed a few steps behind Carter as though uncertain this was a good move.

When they got to the porch, Carter turned and told his friend, "Wait here."

Carter walked to the door of the Colonel's war room and paused. He could see the Indian Affairs man seated on the Colonel's settee, his hat still on, pistol holstered on his hip. Sarge stood behind the Colonel, their guns on the desk, looking suspiciously at Carter.

"Price, come in here a minute," the Colonel called out.

"Yessir?" Carter responded stepping into the doorway.

"You know anything about a Palouse fella from the Colville reservation come by here?"

Carter tried to read the situation. Of course, the Colonel and Sarge already knew Joe, but people who fit the Colonel's description came by all the time, so he said so, hoping he was following the Colonel's plan of defense.

"Oh sure, Colville fellas come in and out of here all the time," Carter said, and Sarge smiled at him.

"Seems a particular one is in possession of some valuable government property, and this gentleman would like it returned. Says he'll ignore the machinery of our operation if we help him out. You have any idea how to facilitate this exchange?"

Carter had left Joe on the front porch like a fish in a barrel. It hadn't occurred to him that it could go this direction. He needed to buy some time.

"Don't know anything about any property, but I can ask around," Carter said and watched the men exchange looks. "I have a Colville friend, maybe he'll know something."

"Why don't we go out to the orchard and ask him right now," the Colonel said, and he and Sarge retrieved their guns.

There had to be a way to sort this out; maybe if Carter stayed calm, they could come to an understanding. He wasn't sure what the Colonel's game was, but he would try to play things to his and Joe's advantage. He walked in front of the three men down the hall and toward the door, his heart burning for his friend waiting patiently for this ambush, but when he swung open the front door to the porch, Joe was not there.

Carter headed toward the orchard, scanning as discretely as he could to see where Joe could have gone, the Colonel, Sarge, and the man from Indian Affairs trailing behind. Before Carter could get far into the parade grounds, he spotted Joe lying on his belly in the bushes, his pistol pointed at them.

Carter heard the pop of Joe's pistol and the glass of a kerosene lantern explode behind them, then the pizzing of gunfire as the Colonel, Sarge, and the man from Indian affairs opened fire, a whirring of flames shooting behind them up to the sky.

Joe took off through the woods toward Moses's truck, and Carter ran toward the main gate of the fort, crashing into the stables away from the bullets. Carter peered cautiously out the stable window, his face covered in sweat. The Colonel ran inside the house, shooting as he went. Sarge took cover behind a tree in the parade grounds. The man from Indian Affairs fired from where he lay on the ground, a dark stain growing on his pant leg. The drapes inside the house licked with fire. Joe Mainzer was nowhere in sight.

A splash behind him made Carter duck and scurry under the window. In front of him, Penn stood naked, her eyes wide and frightened, ankle deep in a bucket of soapy water, one arm covering her breasts, the other hand holding a washrag over her dark, plumed muff. It was a sight he very much wanted to see for some time.

"We have to get out of here," he whispered to her, even though there was no one else around to possibly hear him. Light from the fire outside glowed through the window.

She splashed out of the metal washtub, reached for her clothes on hooks nailed to the wall of the barn. Carter tried not to look but could not help but see her body as she dressed, her pale freckled skin, her pink nipples, her dark pubic hair. She met his eyes, unfazed, buttoning her shirt.

He motioned her toward the door, but she grabbed a bridle from a nail on the wall and quickly slid it over the face of her favorite horse. She stepped on the rails of the horse's stall, slung her legs over the horse's back, and nudged it out into the open stable.

"Open the door and get on," she said. Carter flung open the door to the stable, and Penn reached down for him, lending him her arm to hoist him up behind her. With Penn holding the reins and Carter's arms around her waist, they bolted out the stable doors, galloping toward the road, while the Colonel's house blazed behind them like an untamed candle.

It was the dark of night when Carter and Penn got to Lloyd's barn and put the horse in an empty stall by the cows. They'd made it close to forty miles from the fort through the night, the horse spent and panting. They rode for hours, Penn in front, directing the horse, Carter holding on to her hips. They rode in near silence as though they were afraid of being heard in the night, Carter leaning into her ear to tell her where to turn along the way, and she followed him without hesitation. There was something about her confidence and trust in him that made him feel warm and strong.

Inside the barn smelled of sweet-and-sour fermented hay that had been rolled wet and left damp in the sun for too long. The cows rustled in their stalls, unnerved by the late-night activity. Carter lit the lantern and sat down on a bench by the wine barrels with a tired, relieved sigh.

Penn looked all around the barn, not seeming to be worn out. Carter smiled to himself as he watched her, her bright eyes peering into dark corners, the rafters, the shelves, the stalls. She wandered to the cows, gently touching their velvet noses. She leaned in close to them, her dark hair swinging around her face, curious and confident. It dawned on Carter then that he loved her, but in a much different way than the reckless insecurity he had felt with Mae.

Penn walked back toward the wine barrels and perched on one of the benches. A deck of playing cards was strewn on the table in the middle of the chairs, and she turned a few cards over to see what they were.

"You going to tell me what happened back there?" she asked finally.

He pulled his legs underneath him and sat upright to face her. "I'm not sure I know. I wanted to get the hell away from there before it got worse."

"What about your friend?"

"He knows how to take care of himself. What about your friend?"

"She knows how to take care of herself. And me?"

Carter's face turned red, and he stared down at the floor of the barn, scratching at the dirt floor with the heel of his boot. He hated these moments where he knew he had the opening to say how he felt about something, but it would probably come out awkward and he didn't know how it would be received.

"That's different," he started.

The barn door flew open, banging against the inside wall. The barrel of a rifle was pointed at them, but it lowered as soon as Lloyd saw Carter next to the stove.

"Jesus, Carter, you scared the piss out of me."

Carter stood up, embarrassed in front of Penn. "I tried not to wake you."

"Not me, the dog. She's been whining and scratching." Then Lloyd saw Penn on the other side of Carter. "Well, hello."

Penn smiled but didn't say anything.

"Right," Lloyd said, looking like he didn't know how to react. "So, we'll talk about this in the morning then." He turned to go, the rifle slung over his shoulder. Then he turned back. "You have blankets? I guess it's warm enough. Okay, then."

He backed his way out of the barn door and closed it gently behind him.

Penn let out a whispered laugh in the dark, and Carter couldn't help but join her. He had some explaining to do in the morning, but for now he wanted to enjoy this moment alone in the dark with her. His muscles twitched from the ride, and his eyes begged to close, but he didn't want to miss any chance to be awake with her.

"Where are we going to sleep?" she whispered, as though they could be heard from the house.

"The loft is probably best," he whispered back. He got up and went over to where Lloyd found him a blanket when he first left town. Almost nothing remained of the gear he took with him, and yet he felt confident now that he could get by anywhere. He pulled a couple of blankets from the shelf. "It's warm enough, and you can put these down for padding."

She came over and pulled a few out too and followed him up the ladder to the loft.

The slope of the eaves was close to his head, and he crouched while she threw her blankets down. It looked like a nest when she had them laid out on the wisps of hay.

She stood back, hands on her hips, and admired her work. The lantern light cast long shadows up to where they were standing in the dark eaves of the barn, the cows shuffling in their disturbed sleep below.

"Will it do?" he whispered.

She looked directly at him then, her light eyes black in the shadows, her smile only inches away, her fair skin and black hair almost blue in the darkness. His brain was a hot cloud, and he reached out and touched the coolness of her hair, lifting a lock of it and letting it run through his fingers. Lloyd took his moment away, but he had it here again.

"You have beautiful hands," she said, touching his fingers with hers as her hair fell from them. He looked at his hands, never having thought of it, only the work and demolition they'd done, and wanted them to do more good things that she could be proud of.

She leaned in and kissed him, and he folded around her with surprising ease. After so long of being afraid to approach her, it was effortless, natural.

He took a lock of her hair again and raised it to his face, smelling it, an intoxicating mix of rosemary, campfire smoke, and the musky oil of human skin prickling a forgotten feral place inside him.

"The reason I wanted you to come with me is because I didn't want to risk not finding you again," he said, and she took his hands in hers and pulled him down into her nest of blankets in the hay.

In the morning, Lloyd and Marie didn't ask too many questions, but Marie did insist on Penn sleeping in the house and Carter sleeping alone in the barn the next few nights.

PART 5
RECLAMATION

Fall 1937
Charlotte Creek, Washington

A light-grey, two-story house with white trim teetered down the highway on a long, narrow trailer towed behind a work truck, the house's outer walls hanging out past the width of the truck and trailer, a precarious vision moving slowly up the dirt road. Not far behind it, a wide, brown, three-story, with a man standing on the eves, rolled along, its windows reflecting the grass—still brown and matted from summer—along the highway. The high school and the municipal buildings were planned next.

The Bureau of Reclamation's deadline for residents to move before the waters rose loomed and then passed for Kettle Rapids and the many other towns scattered along the banks of the Columbia, and they ran out of time to relocate their structures. More than a thousand families, payout letter in hand or not, needed to move or abandon their homes in search of a new location.

The local papers printed a photo of Mr. Banks from the Bureau felling the last tree in what would become the reservoir behind the Grand Coulee Dam. Overall, the land-based crews and Camp Ferry cleared more than 180,000 acres that would soon be flooded along the Columbia's shoreline.

Bureau crews worked with Colville tribal leaders to move what graves they could from their traditional burial grounds. Reports of grave lootings and theft of Native American artifacts circulated in the community, while negotiations for land payments and power profits to the tribes stalled out, and no clear commitments were made.

The falls that once made the river unnavigable here, the kettles the area was famous for, and the salmon runs would all soon vanish under the water of the massive Lake Roosevelt.

CHAPTER 15
October 1937

After a few days, Lloyd drove Carter and Penn from his dairy farm to Kettle Rapids in his pickup. Penn sat in the middle of the cab between them, her black bob shining, her mouth a perfect smirk, her feet propped on the hump of the transmission, her shoulder, hip, and knee bumping against Carter's as they drove the highway, a conspiracy of bodies. His every cell where they touched tingled, and he took pains to hide his giddy butterflies from her and from Lloyd, but he couldn't fool himself.

Lloyd glanced at them occasionally, a soft, quiet smile revealing his awkward appreciation for their newfound whatever it was. He'd agreed to let them leave their horse in the barn with his dairy cows for the time being.

Carter felt like a teenager again, the thrilling excitement of potential romance, of finding someone after so long of feeling like not enough, of all the possibility and wonder, the curiosity and imagination, the breathlessness—like a universe of stars was exploding in his eyes and she was looking at them in awe with him too.

There was a familiarity from loves past but also the freshness of a new beginning, of lessons learned, along with something different. No guile. No games. Only acceptance and a shared sense of discovered treasure.

They no more than kissed in Lloyd's barn, and Carter wanted to keep it that way until it was time. To savor her, this, and whatever their paths brought next.

Along the highway, they passed familiar places—Jackson's gas station, the turn off to Mrs. Powell's—and Carter recalled what his father revealed at the dedication ceremony. The house Carter built with his father for Mae was a few yards ahead.

As they approached, Lloyd asked, "You want me to stop?"

Carter nodded silently, and Lloyd pulled his truck into the driveway. He'd told Penn enough about his history during their days at Lloyd's that she knew where they were.

The place looked so different to him now, the house shabbier than he remembered, the garage dusty and unused. One of the rails from the fence had fallen out again; the nail he had pounded in had worked loose from the post. There was no point in putting it back together now.

Lloyd and Penn waited in the truck while Carter peered inside the kitchen window, the room nearly empty. He tried the doorknob, and it opened easily, unlocked. Inside a note from Mae's father lay folded on the kitchen counter. Mae's family had collected her things. How strange it must have been for them to pack up the evidence of her life.

Only a few items of furniture remained. The twin bed in the second bedroom he'd added for their future children, the kitchen table and chairs. The sofa she loved so much was gone, the dressing table she inherited from her grandmother, all her clothes and jewelry, her toiletries from the bathroom, all gone.

He wandered through, remembering how empty it was when he and his father first finished building it, before he and Mae moved in and made it their home. He thought of it as Mae's house for so long, it was strange to think of it as his again now. That would need reckoning later. For now, he needed to see his father and put their differences to rest.

It was no surprise that Ozzie and Ona were waiting for them on the porch when they drove up in Lloyd's truck. The drive from the road to the house was long and dusty. The cloud of dust from Lloyd's truck was visible from a ways off. Carter hoped having Lloyd and Penn with him would encourage good behavior from his father. Lloyd parked his truck under the ponderosa in the front yard, and the three of them got out.

"Oh ho! Would you look what the cat dragged in?" Ozzie boomed off the porch in his noteworthy voice. "You got some Grand Coulee dust on you, Benedict Arnold?"

Ona looked curiously at Penn, and Carter realized this was the first time he'd seen his sister since Ona would have learned of Mae's death and would surely be grieving the loss of her friend and confidante.

Lloyd raised his eyebrows at Carter, looking for a sign on how to proceed. His cousin knew Ozzie well enough to expect outbursts, but was only related to him through his aunt, Carter's mother, so Lloyd was not used to dealing with Ozzie on a regular basis.

"I didn't come to fight with you, Pops," Carter said. "I'm here to get my things is all. Take them back to the house."

"You think you can waltz back here after letting those goons grab me at the dam?"

"I'd say you did that to yourself, Pops."

"He was home the next day," Ona said. "Who's this then?" she asked, smiling at Penn.

"This here is Penn," Carter said. Penn smiled feebly and said hello with a wave, friendly in spite of the tension of the moment. "Could use a place for her to stay until we can get settled."

"We don't put up traitors or friends of traitors," Ozzie said, waving a dismissive hand at Carter, and Lloyd chuckled. "You think that's funny, do you?"

Lloyd raised peaceful hands in front of him and shook his head.

Carter thought about the strength of rhetoric he'd seen in Starks, the magnificence of delivery he'd watched in Joe's recitations, the power in his own small victories working at the dam, and his own goddamn determination not to be humiliated in front of Penn, not now, not when he was so close to something new and real.

"Don't talk to me like that and don't be rude to them," Carter said. "I'm not a traitor. I went away to find something to save myself and to help you. And I found it. It's not money. And it's not government contracts, and it's not a piece of paper with empty promises or a perfect safety record."

"Bah," Ozzie said, waving a hand again. "You're full of fancy talk now?"

Carter looked at Lloyd and Penn standing in the yard; his sister watched, her hands gripping the rail of the front porch.

"You know what I found?" Carter continued, ignoring his father. "It's something I should have known all along. It's resilience. It's the belief that you cannot fail because you will always get back up. That no matter what comes at you, you will not quit. Even when all seems lost, you never give up. You keep trying, you keep going, you persevere, and you don't let anyone else around you quit either. You help them get back up and persevere too. You know who taught me that, Pops? You. You did."

Ozzie didn't have anything to say to this, and there was a lingering silence.

After an awkward pause, his sister cleared her throat. "I'll get your things," she said to Carter and disappeared inside the house.

Everyone else stood silently, Lloyd, Penn, and Carter on the front lawn, Ozzie still leaning his bulk against the railing of his porch, staring out toward the road.

When Ona came back out, she handed Carter a cotton flour sack full of clothes. He hadn't left much but needed what there was.

"I bet Mrs. Powell would put your friend up," Ona said. Her father shot her a sharp look. "What? She's my friend, and she has lots of space for her seasonal workers."

Ona looked back to Carter. "If Lloyd can take us back to Mae's—your place—I can walk over there with you and ask her. I'm sure she won't mind."

"Much obliged," Penn said, softly, nodding a thank you to Ona.

Lloyd drove them back, the two women sitting up front and Carter in the bed of the truck with his flour sack full of belongings, which was pretty much everything he had left in the world. Somehow, he didn't mind, though. The house was his to cash out or move. He was free of his relationship woes with Mae. Penn was here in his new world with him. They had only possibility ahead.

When they got to the house, Ona pulled Carter aside in the driveway. She dug inside her handbag and pulled out a wad of cash and coins.

"Here," she said, holding it balled in her fist out to Carter. "I want you to have this back."

"What is this?" he asked, letting her drop it in his hand.

"It's the money you gave me at the dam," she said. "I don't need it."

Carter stared at her. "What do you mean?"

"Mrs. Powell and I are working together," she said. "We're selling pieces of her orchard to people who need a place to move their house. You keep this. Use it to move this place or buy something else."

Carter was impressed by this new enterprising Ona. "Thanks, Sis," he said, shoving the cash in his pocket. He was flush when he gave it to her, but lost most of what he had since.

The money she gave him plus what little he had left over from the fort would be enough to get him and Penn started. He would have to rely on his creativity to turn it into something more. Ona mentioned people moving houses. He thought of his time working with Joe, the many things they moved, the enterprising way Joe channeled one cash flow into another. Someone would need to move the houses. Maybe Carter could start a business moving families out of the flood zone onto Mrs. Powell's property.

Lloyd approached them. "You need a ride back home?" he asked Ona.

Ona shook her head, no. "Mrs. Powell can take me back when she goes into town," she said.

Lloyd turned to Carter. "You sure you know what you're doing?"

"No," Carter said, and they both laughed. "But I'll figure it out."

"You will indeed," Lloyd said, gripping Carter on the shoulder. "You take care. Come see us again when you can."

As Lloyd's truck turned south onto the highway toward his farm, Ona led Carter and Penn up the hill toward Charlotte Powell's house.

Mrs. Powell was, of course, amenable to providing hospitality for Penn. "Glad to have some company besides the dog around here," she said with a wide smile, her thumbs looped through the straps of her overalls as the dog yelped and followed them, ushering Penn into the farmhouse, the orchard extending into the distance, the apple trees loaded with small, growing fruit.

Carter walked back down the hill alone, leaving Penn in the care of his sister and his…almost stepmother? He smiled imagining how that conversation between Mrs. Powell and his father must have played out.

Everything was so different now, as though the earth had shifted slightly on its axis, and he was okay with it. Back at the house, the fence rail was still lying on the ground, fallen out of the post. He thought of the many times Mae drove angrily in and out of this driveway in their car. The many fights they'd had in the front drive over the years. And now she was gone. He was tired of putting these fence rails back up. For what? For who?

He ripped the rail out and tossed it in the front yard, watching it land with a powdery thud in the grass. What was the point anymore? He pulled out the rail underneath and tossed it on top. All this time, nearly two years, tearing everything down, blasting rock, clearing the river basin, mining on the reservation. If he'd learned anything, it was that nothing lasted. Everything was temporary, and that was okay. That was necessary. That was nothing to be afraid of. That was progress, if you asked Starks. It was not wasting history, if you asked the Colonel.

Mae was gone. Their life together was gone for good. Nothing would ever be the same. And he would be okay. He would keep moving forward.

He ripped the entire front fence apart stacking the lumber in a pile in the front yard. He would never tack one of those rails back into place again.

Once the fence was completely demolished, Carter stood back, breathless, in the dusk, looking at his handiwork. He looked at the garage, serviceable but nothing special. He'd built it with his father's help, but it was not worth moving to higher ground.

He looked over the house, simple, its best moments long gone, when its meaning had less to do with the sum of its parts, and everything to do with love and hope. He wanted something more this time, for himself, for Penn, and if he had to admit it, for Mae. Something more for her legacy, from their time together.

He stood in the driveway, his hands on his hips, sweat running from his scalp to his forehead, as the light faded. All this work, all this pain, embodied in this place. He didn't want to move this house, but he didn't want to destroy it either. He wanted to tear it down and rebuild it. He wanted to sort it into its useful parts, the inventory of a former life stacked neatly on the lawn like the contents of Fort Spokane, like Mae's family gathering her belongings—boards, bricks, shingles, plumbing—and put it back together again, better this time, a tribute to what came before and what could be. A flood of relief swirled through him, and he couldn't wait to hear what Penn thought about his idea.

When Carter told Penn his plans for the house the next morning, she looked at him quietly for a while, and he panicked a little.

"You don't think it's a good idea?"

She looked down at the ground, and he really started to worry.

"Are you telling me this because you see me living in it someday?" she asked, turning her bright lavender eyes back up at him, catching his breath.

He hadn't realized it before, but indeed he pictured her there, assumed she would be there, like a dream of some far-off wish. He took her hands in his, rested his forehead against hers.

"I hope so," he said.

Days rolled into weeks, and fall took its time getting earnest, the deciduous leaves changing to yellow then orange then a deep red in defiance of the persistent green conifers that surrounded them. Carter and Penn had not heard anything about Joe Mainzer or Penn's companion Faith from Fort Spokane, although they could hardly expect to.

Carter set up a home base at his and Mae's former house, consolidating his living area to the core part of the structure while he and Penn worked on dismantling the house together, board by board, brick by brick. Penn stayed at Mrs. Powell's and helped with chores and whatever else "Miss Charlotte," as Penn liked to call her, needed around the place.

During the day, Carter and Penn worked together like they had at Fort Spokane, first dismantling the garage. Stacking and sorting its parts in the yard. Then they started on the less necessary parts of the house. Breaking down, sorting, stacking. What seemed a low business at the fort felt purposeful now.

At the end of the day, Carter would walk Penn back up the hill to Mrs. Powell's, all tender smiles and chatter between them, and Charlotte would insist on making them dinner, the old dog waiting patiently for any dropped scraps, accidental or not.

Penn and Charlotte quickly discovered their mutual love of books. Penn pawed through Charlotte's library, finding title after title that fascinated her, but Charlotte was committed to the *Tarzan* books.

They would sit in the warm fall evening, watching the stars overhead, smelling the deep ripening of apples throughout the orchard, and Penn would read aloud to them. The nightly ritual was a pleasure for everyone, and Charlotte and Penn jokingly argued over what Penn should read. Sometimes Ona would drive Ozzie's Ford over and spend the evening with them.

One night, a meteor shower blessed them with its show. A spirited streak of stars shot across the sky while they watched. Carter looked at Penn as she gazed up at the shooting stars, her eyes bright, her perfect mouth curled in joy.

"You have to read from this," Charlotte said, coming back out of the house and handing Penn a battered copy of *Tarzan of the Apes.* She pointed to an underlined passage. "Your voice is so beautiful."

Penn scanned the page, her brow furrowing, looking at Carter, embarrassed.

"You have to read it," Charlotte said again, looking up at the meteor show above.

So Penn read:

"I am Tarzan of the Apes. I want you. I am yours. You are mine. We live here together always in my house."

Penn paused and looked at Carter. He smiled at her, now understanding her embarrassment, and gestured jokingly for her to go on. She glared at him, smiling too, but continued to read.

"I will bring you the best of fruits, the tenderest deer, the finest meats that roam the jungle."

Carter and Penn chuckled, but Charlotte was insistent.

"It gets better," she said, circling a finger in the air for Penn to keep going.

"I will hunt for you. I am the greatest of the jungle fighters. I will fight for you. I am the mightiest of the jungle fighters. When you see this you will know that Tarzan of the Apes loves you."

Charlotte leaned back, nodding, her hands on her knees, looking satisfied.

Penn looked sheepishly at Carter, and he met her gaze with confidence, hoping she could see his resolve, his love for her.

After they finished dinner, Carter walked home alone down the hill to what was left of his house, what would soon be a pile of supplies, feeling apish, wishing he could fold Penn in his arms, in his bed, letting the stars shoot over their heads every night, providing her with *the best fruits, the finest meats.* He wanted to know everything about her. Where she came from. What hurts she ran from. What she thought about when she didn't say anything. The workings of her sharp mind, her bright eyes. How to fight for her, how to fight alongside her.

Back home, he lay down on the creaking twin mattress, his mind a swirl of meteors, his thoughts thick, other parts of him thicker.

CHAPTER 16
November 1937

Carter agreed to go with Ona to look at an empty office space in downtown Kettle Rapids. He'd used the money she returned to him to buy an old car from Jackson's service shop, not in much better shape than his father's beat up Ford, and he pulled up the long driveway to pick his sister up from their father's house and drive her into town to look through the place.

As his sister described it, they could combine his moving business idea with her real estate enterprise and help each other out. He would be the proprietor, of course, since she was still underage, and he would pay her a wage until she was eighteen. Then they would share the profits. Members of one another, he thought with a smile, having never anticipated this outcome.

He didn't disagree with his sister's ideas, and frankly was impressed by her Starksian approach to the situation. She beamed as she showed him the offices, pointing to where she wanted to put what, her face bright, her lips brighter with red lipstick.

He would need to hire workers, something he'd never had to do before. He wished Soop was here to advise him on what to ask, what to look for.

"What do you think?" Ona asked finally, gesturing around the space, her face animated.

"Seems good to me," he said, looking around the place, and he meant it. At some point, they would have to relocate out of the flood zone, but for now this was an inexpensive place to get started. Plus, he trusted this new Ona and the enterprise they were about to undertake. This time he knew he could start fresh again, that he would be fine, that he had the skills and support to make it work.

"Are you sure?" she asked, seeming surprised at how easily he agreed.

"I am," he said, and his sister grabbed his shoulders, laughing excitedly as she hugged him.

"We should shake on it," she said, reaching her hand out, and the two grasped hands and shook an exaggerated rubber-armed handshake only siblings can pull off, Ona's handbag bobbing on her elbow.

Charlotte agreed to keep Penn on at the orchard in exchange for help around the place. Truth be told, she wanted the company more than she needed the help, and it was nice to have some vibrancy and youth around the place with the Price kids coming over regularly these days.

She and Ona negotiated the transfer of one thousand acres of her land, nearly half her property, to use to form the new Charlotte Creek community in exchange for the amount Ona negotiated from the Starks Company.

Charlotte hadn't told Ona yet, but she took the check Ona gave her and put it in a trust that Ona could cash out when she turned eighteen. Lord knew Charlotte didn't need the money. It would be a good lesson for Ona, learning to make her own way. Who knew if Charlotte would even still be around in a few years. Better for Ona to come into the money she'd negotiated from one of the most profitable developers in the country, a woman soon, ready to take on the great big world.

Carter and Ona set up their makeshift offices in downtown Kettle Rapids, hanging a sign, which after much debate read, "Price Salvage and Relocation Services." Carter was surprised how many people from town were interested in resettling in nearby Charlotte Creek, though some were moving as far away as Colville and Spokane. The Bureau of Reclamation's deadline for all buildings to be off the land was long passed, and movers from the nearest city centers didn't want to make the trek all the way out to Kettle Rapids. Business prospects were looking good if Carter could line up the laborers as fast as his sister could talk people into parcels in Charlotte Creek.

He hired a few workers from the land-based clearing camp, even though there were rumors his father had unleashed a pack of coyotes on them.

"Bah," was Ozzie's response to this claim.

Never having hired a crew before, Carter invested in a clipboard and started writing down names of men he knew were reliable and skilled to help with the work.

One evening, he picked Penn and Ona up and drove them all out to see Lloyd and Marie for the first time since Carter arrived back in town. After hellos, Penn went straight for the barn to check on her horse, and Carter followed.

"We'll have a place of our own for her soon," Carter told Penn, tucking a lock of her dark hair behind her ear. She smiled up at him and turned back to the horse.

"I know," she said. She stroked the horse's long muzzle, muttered soothing words to her.

At dinner, Carter asked Lloyd about hiring.

"You interested?" Carter asked, knowing the answer.

Lloyd smiled and shook his head. "I have my hands full here, but did you ever think of asking your father about what it's like to run a business? Or hire skilled labor?"

His cousin had a point, but the prospect of having that conversation with his father filled Carter with dread.

"Mrs. Powell will know people," Ona chimed in. "She's been

hiring workers around here for years."

Carter hadn't thought of that.

The next day, they approached Charlotte about finding skilled labor, and she volunteered her services to hiring on their behalf.

"I'll help," Penn offered, and the two of them joined Ona and Carter at their downtown offices every day, contacting laborers who'd worked at Charlotte's orchard, interviewing and screening them for work.

The activity downtown started to attract attention, and Sheriff Bill stopped in, asking for Carter. Carter felt sheepish having to face the sheriff after all this time, even though he knew he had nothing legally to be concerned about anymore.

"I'm sorry about everything, Bill," Carter offered, extending a hand.

"You and I are square," the sheriff said, taking Carter's hand in a cordial shake. "No need to worry about the past. I came by to wish you well in your endeavors, is all."

"I just…I feel bad about how I left things," Carter said.

"No need to dwell on that. I believe in redemption," the sheriff said. "Wouldn't have got into law enforcement if I didn't think people deserved a second chance."

In a few weeks, Ona had enough buyers and Charlotte and Penn had enough workers that it was time for Carter to lead the crew in starting the moves. He pinned a huge piece of butcher paper up on the wall of the offices, scratching notes on it, staying late into the evening, willing knowledge from Soop and Starks and the Colonel to come forth and help him like messages from the gods.

Quite like a message from the gods, one morning after letting Penn and Ona take his car back to Mrs. Powell's and spending the night on a cot in the office puzzling over his plans, he saw the familiar shape and color of a truck like the one he and Joe borrowed from Moses pass through town. He peered through the blinds as the pickup drove by, turned around, and circled back, stopping out front.

Joe Mainzer sat in the front seat, looking at their sign, with Reynolds from their crew at the dam in the passenger seat next to him as the truck idled.

Carter burst out the front door of the office onto the wooden sidewalk, waving to his friends, making sure they didn't keep driving. Joe hopped out, grasping Carter in a hug, and Reynolds walked over with a big smile.

"You're okay!" Carter said, and Joe smiled. Carter hadn't heard anything about his friends since his last night at Fort Spokane many weeks ago and thought of him often with concern.

"Of course I am."

"You too?" Carter asked, Reynolds.

"Good as new," Reynolds told him, rotating his shoulder. "Been helping Joe out in the mines since you've been gone." Ah, well that made some sense, Carter thought. He'd left his friend without much choice.

"What brings you here?"

"Looking for you," Joe said, glancing up at the sign on the front of the office with Carter's last name on it. "Things are winding down in town."

"B Street is pretty much gone now," Reynolds said.

"No more pretty ladies?" Carter asked, smiling.

"Pretty ladies all moved on," Joe chuckled.

"We're heading to California soon," Reynolds elaborated. "Soop needs guys down on the Friant Dam project. Thought you might want to come with us."

Carter put his hands on his hips and looked around downtown.

"Oh, I don't know. I've got a good thing going here now. When do you leave?"

"We head to Seattle to board the train in six weeks," Joe told him.

It was sad to think of his friends heading so far south. Who knew when they would all see one another again, if ever. He had come too far now to leave again, that much he knew for sure.

"Come over to my place for dinner tonight. We can catch up on everything," Carter said. "Come inside, and I'll write directions for you."

They followed him in, looking around the offices with curiosity. Carter grabbed a pen and notepad and sketched out a rough map to his house.

It had been so long since Carter played host, he enlisted help from Ona, Penn, and Charlotte to plan the food. Even though the night air was cool, Charlotte helped Carter set up an outdoor dinner, a nearby bonfire prepared to throw heat to the table. The scene reminded him of the night picnic his first night back at Fort Spokane but with a chill in the air, like his Christmas drink in Lloyd's barn before he left town.

When his friends arrived, they all sat around the bonfire, excited to see one another again. It seemed like so long since their time at the dam, so much had happened, so many things had changed, but really only a few months had gone by. Ona said she was going inside to get wine, and Reynolds, maybe too enthusiastically for Carter's taste, offered to help.

"What happened back there?" Carter asked Joe, referring to the last night at Fort Spokane.

"I shot out the porchlight to distract them. Then Sarge started shooting, and I'm not sure about every detail. I did see the Indian Affairs guy go down. Looked like he took a bullet in the thigh. I took off, like you. Came back the next day to see what happened.

Watched from the trees by the road. The Colonel's house burned almost to the ground, and all his men cleared out. Orchard too."

Ona and Reynolds came back out of the house, handing around mismatched jelly jars Ona found in the pantry and filled with wine for them to drink while they waited for chickens to finish roasting in the oven for dinner.

Penn held her glass tightly and looked up at Joe.

"I didn't see your friend," Joe told her. "Would she think to look for you here?"

Penn shook her head no, looking down into her glass. "I didn't know her before the Fort," she said. "I'm sure she moved on to the next place."

"Charlie was still there," Joe went on. "Said a couple of the horses were missing and that everyone else cleared out during the night. I didn't see any sign of the Indian Affairs guy or his truck. Charlie didn't seem to know anything about it."

"Wouldn't take much to hide any sign of him in the river," Carter said, and Joe nodded, looking into the fire.

"And you're headed to California soon?" Carter asked.

"You sure you don't want to come?" Reynolds asked. "We drove a hundred miles to convince you."

Penn looked at Carter with concern, and he smiled at her across the fire. The best fruits, the finest meats.

"Nah," Carter said, keeping Penn's eyes locked in his. "I want to get things going here, see how it goes."

She smiled back shyly across the fire, then looked at her glass.

"What about when everyone here is moved?" Joe asked.

"Cross that bridge when I come to it," Carter said, smiling. "Find the next thing."

He'd come a long way since he started out, running off from this very house, not sure where to go or what to do or if he had what it took to start over.

"I could use your help getting this going while you're waiting," he told them. "I know it's not much, but you can stay at my place for free while you're here and what I can pay will be a decent wage if you don't have living expenses."

"We were hoping you'd ask," Joe said, laughing. "Do we have to call you, 'boss'?"

Carter laughed. "Of course not."

"Speaking of bosses, did you hear about Mr. Starks?" Reynolds asked.

Carter shook his head no. "What happened?"

"Massive heart attack right as he was boarding the train in Seattle to go back to Minneapolis. Died right there on the platform."

So that was how the great M.J. Starks met his end. Whether Starks knew it or not, he'd given Carter the confidence to start over. Carter wished Starks could see what he was building here now, how he'd come home and figured out how to turn their situation into an opportunity—make him proud.

"To Starks," Carter said, raising his jelly jar of wine.

Joe and Reynolds stayed on in Kettle Rapids, helping Carter and his crew get the moving business going. They moved houses and stores, schools and municipal buildings. With Charlotte's help, they hired more laborers from the surrounding towns.

Ozzie resisted at first, but Ona convinced him to move his house to Charlotte Creek, telling him Charlotte gave them the land as a gift, Carter could do the moving, and Joe could trade the ferry cables, spools, and pieces of the landing for the trucks and platforms they needed.

"In exchange for helping me rebuild my house like we did before," Carter told his father, Ozzie pursing his lips. They were all three huddled on Ozzie's front porch.

"I suppose I don't have much choice," Ozzie said, looking from Carter to Ona.

"This way, you can keep the house and live off the payouts for the land here and at the ferry crossing. You don't have to start over," Ona told him.

Eventually, even Ozzie agreed to help manage the books for them and spent most of his days in the office with Ona, Penn, and Charlotte while they booked the jobs and hired the workers.

On his mother's birthday, Carter and Ozzie made the trip to the cemetery together. The leaves on the trees all around them were speckled golden orange and a deep, rich red, interspersed with pine trees. The cemetery would be under snow soon enough. Ozzie brought a bouquet of white carnations, his wife's favorite, and laid them on her grave, squatting level with her headstone. Carter stood behind him and looked out over the markers to the river beyond. He wondered whether a clearing crew would come take the stones away before the water filled in. A clean stone with brown decaying flowers caught his eye. A hard lump formed in his throat, and he didn't need to go over to the grave to know whose it was.

His father stood and saw where Carter was looking. He put a hand on Carter's shoulder and kept silent. They walked over to Mae's headstone together.

"I would have thought they'd bury her someplace else, considering," Carter said.

Ozzie nodded and squeezed his son's shoulder.

Mae would be forever preserved under the water of the reservoir, drowned in the back up of the biggest dam in the state.

When Carter got home, Penn looked up from the yard. She wore her usual coveralls with a man's work shirt and welder's gloves and had a hammer in one hand.

Carter pulled her close, kissed her on the forehead.

"Everything okay?" she asked.

He nodded and looked at the work she'd done.

Most of the siding was gone from the house and stacked neatly in a pile next to the garage at the end of the driveway. Joe would be there soon with a flatbed truck to load what they'd dismantled and drive it to Charlotte's orchard to rebuild.

The Colonel was right about not wasting history, turning it into something new. Carter knew that now. It would never have worked to move the house the way it was to another spot. He didn't want to live in its haunted corners anymore, but that didn't mean there was nothing to salvage in its walls.

Ozzie paced in Charlotte's orchard watching the roof of his house appear behind the hill that sloped down from Charlotte's upper property to the highway below. Around him, a small community of homes assembled. His house rested precariously on the back of a long flatbed truck, and he huffed and snorted watching it wiggle up the hill, more and more of it visible as Carter drove it up the road, as though it was rising out of the ground. Carter's crew would put it next to the spot where he and Carter planned to reassemble Carter's house in its new and improved form. For now, there was a pile of rubble, waiting to be rebuilt. Ozzie watched his son negotiating with new customers, reminding Ozzie of his younger self when he was a starting entrepreneur, trying to make his way in the world and support his family.

Six weeks went by quickly, and frost already tinged the air by the time they moved most of what was left of Kettle Rapids up to high ground at Charlotte Creek.

The first thing he and his father built was a small barn and corral for Penn's horse, and Carter and Penn went to Lloyd's to get her, smiling at each other in the barn, remembering their time there. Penn trotted the horse up the highway to her new home, Carter following slowly behind in the car, making sure they made it safely.

At last, it was time for Joe and Reynolds to head to Seattle to catch their train south. Charlotte offered to make everyone an early Christmas dinner. Ozzie was surprisingly compliant about this and even shot a wild turkey for them to eat. They sat around Charlotte's dining room table together, the turkey in the oven, one last meal before Joe and Reynolds headed out. Carter wondered if he would ever see either of his friends again.

Charlotte and Ona brought the turkey to the table, with all the sides their mother used to make and new traditions scattering the surrounding counters. Kerosene lamps lit the faces of the people Carter held closest. So much had changed, so much of it good.

The moment overtook him, and he stood, raising his glass.

"We are members of one another," he started off, faltering a bit. Joe looked surprised, then nodded in support to go on. Carter tried to conjure Starks, his ability to command a room, to say the right thing.

"Our world looks different. Our circumstances have changed."

"Here, here," the table said, raising their drinks higher, their laughter and the chinking of glasses urging Carter on.

"We adapted," Carter said, raising his glass with them. "And here we are together."

He met eyes with Joe, who held a bottle of Coca Cola aloft, and thought of the few times he'd been part of Joe's recitation endeavors and everything they'd been through together. He looked at Penn, her eyes proud and warm, seeing him and not shrinking away. His sister smiled at him. Never in his wildest dreams did he imagine they'd be business partners.

"We adapted and transformed our circumstances in our favor.

We saw the opportunity and the value of what lies ahead."

The people he loved most murmured in agreement with him.

"To us," Carter said, raising his glass higher.

"To us!" they hollered back at him, laughing as they clanked their glasses around the table.

After dinner, in a moment alone, Ozzie put his hand on Carter's shoulder.

"Not bad," Ozzie said.

EPILOGUE
June 1940

The Price family made their final visit to the cemetery together. Spring was brightening into summer and the hillside was flush with wildflowers, the sun warm, the sky cloudless. The town would gather that day to watch the famous falls, kettles, and rapids be lost to the river. The cemetery was expected to flood shortly after.

Charlotte joined them to say her final respects to her son and her husband, her last look at the river from this memorable spot she'd been visiting for so long.

Ozzie brought white carnations for his wife, and Ona brought pink roses for Mae. Carter watched as his father and sister placed the flowers in front of the two gravestones, his arm looped around Penn's waist, the other holding a picnic blanket they would take down to the river later. They'd been married for nearly two years now, the feeling still fresh and new.

Charlotte stood in front of the two headstones, folding her hands in front of her.

"Let's pick flowers for Charlotte to leave," Ona said to Penn, and the two of them wandered toward a patch of wild lupine and poppies that grew along the hill down to the shore.

Carter watched Penn and his sister as they wandered toward the river, then looked out across its broad expanse. Already the water line was noticeably higher and would rise even more today to cover the falls for good.

Life was so different now. Business was still good, but soon they would move everyone who wanted to. He and Ona relocated their operations to what used to be his garage, now rebuilt as an office next to his house in Charlotte Creek. His check for the property from the federal government came, and though not much, he reinvested the money in their business.

The war in Europe was escalating. Germany invaded Poland, and Britain, France, and Canada entered the war. It seemed like only a matter of time before President Roosevelt would have no choice but to enter as well. Carter wondered who of their friends would enlist.

"I've had another letter from Reynolds," Ona told Penn under her breath as they gathered flowers from the hillside. Ona was nineteen now. Once Charlotte told her about the trust on her eighteenth birthday, the world became full of opportunity.

"What does he say?" Penn smiled and fashioned two small bouquets of lupine and poppies for Charlotte to put on the graves. Ona tucked one of the poppies over her ear.

"He finished his engineering degree," Ona said, looking out over the graves to make sure her father couldn't hear her. "He says I would like California."

They made a wrist corsage out of lupine for Penn and one for Charlotte and walked over to where Charlotte stood quietly contemplating the river.

Penn handed Charlotte the corsage, but she waved her off, saying, "Oh, I'm too old for all that." They placed the bouquets on the two headstones.

Across the Columbia, a huge piece of riverbank fell with a rumbling crash into the water, startling them all.

In town, a crowd of several thousand people gathered on the shrinking shore to hear their senator commemorate the moment the falls would disappear under the reservoir filling in behind the Grand Coulee Dam. The local tribes planned three days of ceremonies and events throughout the town to memorialize the occasion. Carter spotted Lloyd and Marie with their boys in the crowd of many familiar faces and led the rest of their group over to his cousin to stake out a spot to watch the ceremony.

As they made their way through the crowd, Ozzie told Penn, "I once saw a steamboat shoot these falls. Back when the falls were at their full height." Everyone else had either heard this story a hundred times already or seen the event with their own eyes.

"The captain backed his boat up the river, hit the throttle, and shot the thing straight out past the falls," Ozzie said, pointing out to what was now a short drop spanning the Columbia.

"The steamboat hung there in midair long enough for the captain to blast the whistle three times, but you couldn't even hear it over the water. Then they fell straight down into the river. Broke off part of the front deck even. Of course, the falls aren't so loud anymore."

The water now was bloated and subdued, its color murky and muddy. Debris floated in the river—lumber, tree limbs—and Carter thought of his time on Camp Ferry years before, clearing whatever he and Joe could find. He got a postcard from Joe every once in a while, as his friend traveled around the country, blasting the way for new dams on more and more rivers.

Already, Carter heard stories that salmon appeared at the base of the Grand Coulee Dam, trying to swim upriver to spawn. There was no way for them to get to the falls now, this once great fishing spot for the tribes completely gone.

The senator took the stage, and Carter couldn't help but think of the day they'd all gone to see President Roosevelt speak at the dam. How long ago that seemed now. He glanced at his father, but Ozzie watched calmly next to Penn, no outburst seeming imminent.

After obligatory introductions, the senator brought up the lack of salmon.

He said the local tribes fished here for thousands of years, that this spot was sacred because it was a source of food and beauty. The crowd clapped unenthusiastically.

He continued by promising that future generations of local tribes would see benefits from electricity sales.

The senator went on to talk about how the power from the Grand Coulee Dam would help the war effort, that it would allow the United States to build more airplanes and tanks and to train more pilots faster than any other nation.

After the senator finished his remarks, Carter and his group took their picnic blanket to the edge of the new shoreline and sat in the afternoon sun for the several hours it took for the reservoir to fill enough to completely cover the falls and rapids. Carter spotted the boulder he sat on the day of the town hall meeting when they first learned about what would happen to their town. That day was the first time he ever saw M.J. Starks speak, the moment when Starks sent Carter down a new path in life. Carter only got to know Starks for a couple of short years of his life, but what an impression he made. Carter watched the water rise around the boulder, eventually covering the top until only a ripple on the surface remained.

Harold Burnes made his final trip to Kettle Rapids for his last assignment with the *Colville Scintilla*. His stories about the Grand Coulee Dam earned him regional recognition, and after this last piece, he was heading home to Oregon to accept an offer from a bigger paper in the bigger town of Bend.

Kettle Rapids was hosting a three-day commemoration, the "Ceremony of Tears," as the waters finally took over the falls, the rapids, the tribal fishing grounds, and much of the town. Tents and teepees dotted the remaining shoreline, and from what he could tell, tribal representation extended from all over the region.

Harold wandered through the makeshift village. Despite the solemnness of the gathering, the attendees found ways to enjoy being together and honor their traditions. In between the tents and teepees, salmon caught from downriver below the dam and brought for the occasion were wind dried or hanging on frames to smoke over smoldering fires. The people gathered played games and advertised a boxing competition. There was a carnival and a dance planned for the final night.

The next morning, Harold set his pages on his editor's desk. All his belonging were in his car parked out front of the newspaper office. It would take him about eight hours to drive from Colville to Bend to start his new job. He looked around the office one last time, at the bank of typewriters, the pencil sharpener bolted to the counter. He laid his key to the office next to his pages and left, gently locking the door behind him.

VICTIMS OF PROGRESS

Earlier this week, the Confederated Tribes of the Colville Reservation hosted a multi-day "Ceremony of Tears" in honor of the disappearance of the falls at Kettle Rapids under Lake Roosevelt as it backs up behind the Grand Coulee Dam. The June date is significant as June is traditionally the start of the Chinook runs here, although salmon can no longer traverse the river this far north. Before the construction of dams along the lower Columbia cut off 1,100 miles of salmon spawning grounds, nearly one million fish per year were caught in this area, in what was thought to be the greatest salmon run in the world. In years past, tribes from around the region would gather in June to celebrate the start of the season. The Salmon Chief would stand below the falls in the Columbia River, or the "Swah net ka" as it is known to the local tribe, and spear the first salmon of the year, thereby blessing the months of fishing season ahead. Now there are no more salmon.

The local senator addressed the crowd, paying some attention to the impact on the local tribes, and hinting at the intended use of hydropower to build airplanes and tanks to support the United States joining the war in Europe. Then the crowd watched as this important regional landmark vanished under Lake Roosevelt.

In anticipation of the rising water, the local tribes worked with the Office of Indian Affairs and the Bureau of Reclamation to move their gravesites, historical sites and artifacts out of the flood zone. Since last fall, nearly 3,000 human remains were relocated, but time eventually ran out to move any more, and the waters ascended.

It is not yet known what kind of compensation the local tribes can expect for their loss of traditional sites or for the economic impact from the loss of one million fish per year.

At their ceremony, chiefs from the Sanpoil and Colville tribes spoke of their sadness at losing the falls that provided food for so many.

Despite the loss of land for the tribes and the community of Kettle Rapids, the construction of the dam provided thousands of jobs during the Great Depression. Hundreds of small businesses formed around the construction site to support the workers. The massive reservoir behind the dam will provide widespread reliable irrigation to farmers for miles around the Columbia Plateau. The electricity will power industrial growth throughout the state.

In the end, we all have to look within and ask ourselves, was it worth it?

ACKNOWLEDGEMENTS

First and foremost, I want to thank my editor, Michael Daley, for taking a chance on this project and shepherding this story. Deepest thanks to my fellow Empty Bowl author, Finn Wilcox, for believing this book would find a press and not letting me give up. To my publicist Mary Bisbee Beek, for telling me, "pencils down!" To designer, Lauren Grosskopf, who turned this book into a piece of visual art. And to my sensitivity reader, Renee Roman Nose, for her honesty and asking me to listen openly.

Many Native American people lost their homes and traditions in this area long before the Grand Coulee Dam was built, and I am grateful for help from the Confederated Tribes of the Colville Reservation, both for the historical resources on their website and the advice of their staff. Much gratitude also to the many people who offered their networks to help me find a sensitivity reader.

My family has history in this area, and I want to thank them too. My mom, Sandy Anderson, who taught me to be resilient and kind. My grandparents, Cal and Freda, who Carter and Penn are based on. My cousin Steve Botts, who helped with research and is one of my favorite people I happen to be related to.

Also thanks to Dane Fitzgerald, my steady rock and dedicated re-reader. And Pat Fitzgerald for her early reads. We will toast this book together someday somewhere.

Huge thanks to my developmental readers: Chris Arkills, DeMisty Bellinger, Steve Botts, Dave Brewer, Dane Fitzgerald, Jane Hodges, and Finn Wilcox. Also to the writers who were willing to put their names behind my manuscript with a blurb.

I relied on several historical resources: *Grand Coulee: Harnessing a Dream* by Paul C. Pitzer; *B Street: The Notorious Playground of Coulee Dam* by Lsxawney L. Reycs; *A Brief History of Kettle*

Falls: The First 50 Years, written and compiled by Lewis and Joan Nullet; *Images of America: Grand Coulee Dam* by Ray Bottenberg; *Confederated Tribes of the Colville Reservation: A Brief History,* created by The History and Archaeology Program, and many other online resources.

Excerpts from Franklin D. Roosevelt's "Remarks at the Site of the Grand Coulee Dam, Washington," were sourced online from Gerhard Peters and John T. Woolley of The American Presidency Project, and his informal remarks in Spokane from the Franklin D. Roosevelt Presidential Library and Museum.

Literary works in the public domain are quoted: *Tarzan of the Apes,* by Edgar Rice Burroughs, *The Waste Land* by T.S. Eliot, and *The Essential Lewis and Clark,* by William Clark and Meriwether Lewis.

I also want to thank those who contributed to the development of the cover illustration, transforming the photo I took at the original Kettle Falls site to look more like a historic national park poster: Dorian Kensok, Katya Marritz, Let's Go Travel and Thomas Cunningham. And to Rachel Mae for my author photos.

So many fellow writers, instructors, classmates, friends, and colleagues have provided inspiration, feedback, advice and support for my writing over the years through NYU's Creative Writing Program, Bread Loaf Writers Conference, Port Townsend Writers Conference, Hugo House's novel workshop, as a board member for Mineral School and other literary endeavors. There are too many to list, but know that I honor you and hold gratitude for you in my heart.

REBEKAH ANDERSON

is a Seattle-based writer and third generation Washington native whose family came to the Pacific Northwest as a result of the Homesteading Act. She earned an MFA in Fiction from New York University, where she worked under the mentorship of E.L. Doctorow. Loosely based on her family history, *The Grand Promise* is her first novel. Visit her at RebekahLAnderson.com.